PALACE OF THORNS

AN ELA OF SALISBURY MEDIEVAL MYSTERY

J. G. LEWIS

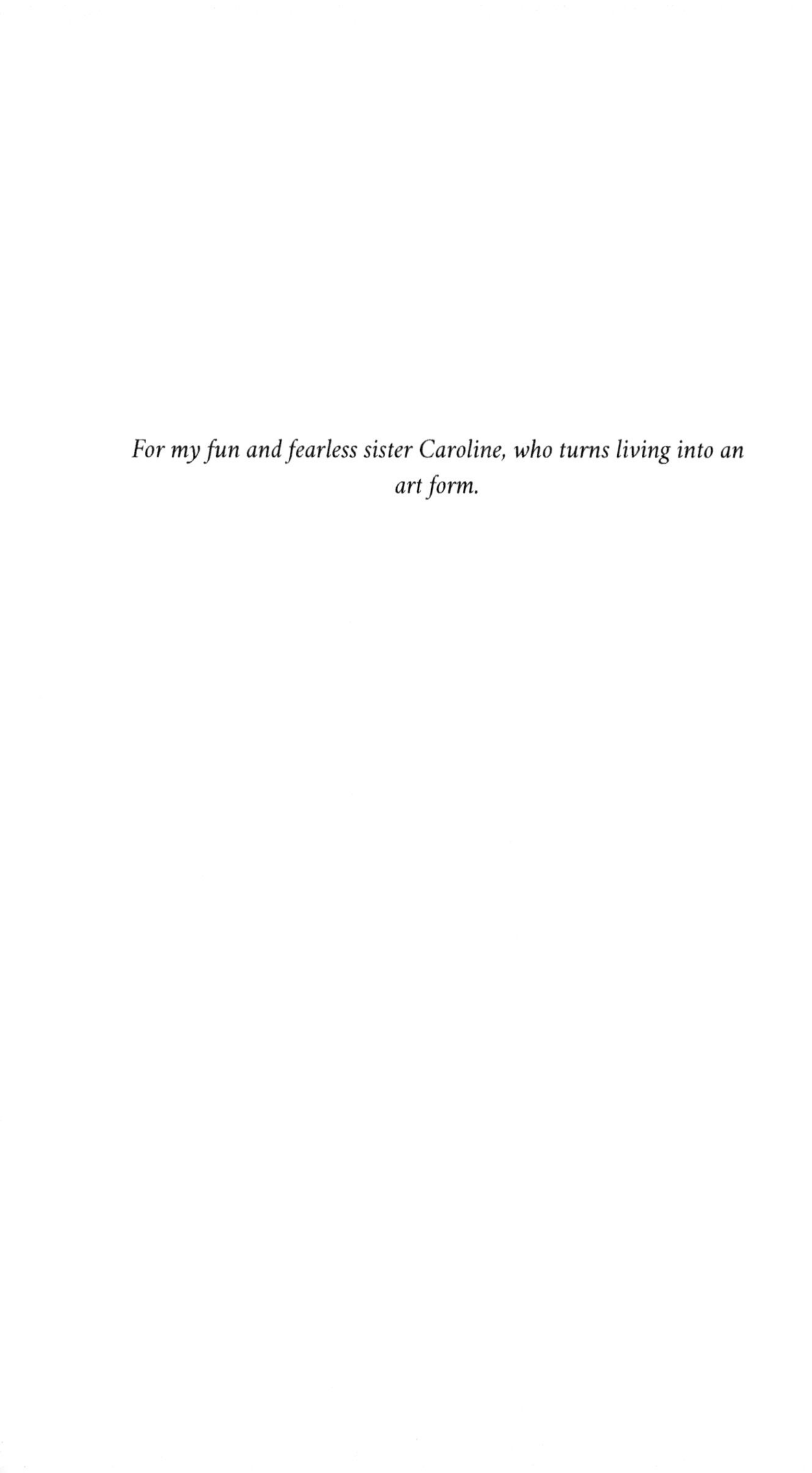

For my fun and fearless sister Caroline, who turns living into an art form.

ACKNOWLEDGMENTS

Many thanks, once again, to Rebecca Hazell, Betsy van der Hoek, and Judith Tilden for their careful readings and excellent suggestions. And my enduring gratitude to the dauntless Lynn Messina. All remaining errors are mine.

CHAPTER 1

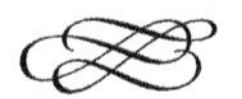

S*alisbury, November 1227*

"Marriage is like a tournament." Alice de Gilbert's pretty pink mouth pouted for a moment. She and Ela had put on their cloaks to take a stroll around inside the castle walls despite the cold winter air. "That's what my mother once told me. She said there are contests to face and accolades to win and times when you'll be broken and sobbing."

"Goodness." Ela barely remembered Alice's mother, a friend of her mother's whom she'd last met more than fifteen years ago. She'd known her as a small quiet woman, rather faded in every aspect, from her pale blue eyes to her white-blonde hair.

"She said the important thing was to get back on your horse and keep fighting." Alice took after her father, tall and well built, with dark chestnut hair and sparkling dark eyes. "But I'm starting to realize that in my marriage, I'm the horse."

Ela laughed, then realized that Alice wasn't laughing with her. She wiped the smile from her face. "Marriage—life—can definitely be a test of strength. No one knows that better than I."

Alice had come to visit on her way back to her home in western Wiltshire, following her father's funeral near Marlborough. They walked through a small apple orchard protected from the wind by the castle's outer walls. The leaves were long gone and the gnarled branches cast shadows against the stone walls.

"You're triumphant in your tournament," said Alice. "Look at you! Castellan and sheriff and mistress of all you survey, and no husband to crush you under his heel."

Ela rankled at the implied characterization of her late husband. "William was a kind husband who encouraged me to—"

"Oh, I didn't mean to imply anything bad about him. And naturally I'm very sorry for your cruel loss. It's always the good husbands that die, isn't it?"

There was some truth to this. Ela's loving father had left her mother widowed at a young age, and it often seemed like the most loved husbands of her friends were the first to be lost in battle or to a passing sickness. But Ela couldn't keep ignoring her friend's hints. "Are you unhappy in your marriage?" She asked it quietly, so that no one could overhear.

"Never been unhappier, and that's saying something," said Alice with a sigh. "Thirteen years! And each one seems longer and drearier than the last. I find myself wishing for widowhood, but my husband is only fifty-four and could live for many more years." Thankfully Alice had enough discretion to keep her voice down, but Ela couldn't help but be shocked by her blunt words.

"Thirteen years? Is it that long? And it must be that long since we saw each other. I think your wedding was the last time I laid eyes on you. You don't look a day older." Alice's hair was still thick and wavy and her figure trim and shapely, though her cheeks did lack color and her eyes lacked some of the sparkle Ela remembered.

"No need to flatter me. I know my misery has carved lines around my eyes and mouth. I swear I could bear anything if I had children to love and care for. That's all I ever wanted, really, but we tried for years and nothing came of it. Not even a miscarriage."

"He has children from an earlier marriage, doesn't he?" Ela could dimly recall two sons, barely younger than Alice at that time, who'd been at her friend's wedding.

"Yes, which of course points to me as a barren acre where no seed grows. They're both grown and in their majority, so it's just the two of us and the servants rattling around his drafty old ancestral castle in the middle of nowhere. It feels like centuries in purgatory."

Ela didn't know what to say. This avalanche of confidences shocked her, especially since she hadn't seen Alice for so long and didn't even know her all that well back then. Alice was a young and rather silly girl of eighteen, sent to Alianore's for the summer because her mother had taken ill. Ela was a young mother leaning on her own mother's wisdom and experience while her husband was away traveling—yet again—with his half-brother King John. They'd spent an enjoyable summer in each other's company, and Alice had made a great fuss of her babies, but they'd only exchanged the occasional letter since.

"The Lord may still bless you with children."

"I'm thirty-three! And it would have to be the immaculate conception as Humphrey can't even make a rod to stoke my fire these days. He blames it on me, of course."

"Perhaps you could find joy in doing good works for the people of your manors? I find considerable solace in helping those in need."

"Dear me, no. Humphrey would frown hard on such profligate expenditure. It's all I can do to bargain a few pennies to buy embroidery thread to keep my fingers busy. He'd rather melt his money in his own fire than give it to the poor. He thinks everyone other than him is an idle wastrel. I wouldn't dare to suggest that the time he spends translating books from one dead language into another is a waste of time and energy. At least it keeps him shut away in his book room most of the time and not snapping at the servants or berating me for every trivial failing."

Ela inhaled. "Marriages do have their seasons. That's what my mother told me." Her mother's marital seasons had all been fairly short as Alianore was currently on her fourth husband. "Let's hope a better season is coming."

"It's always winter in my marriage. Sometimes I heartily wish there was an untraceable poison so I could send him to the distant and eternal paradise all his tedious ancient texts wax on about."

"Alice!" Ela stopped and took her hand. "Don't talk so. I'm the High Sheriff of Wiltshire, in case you've forgotten."

"So you should know all the good poisons!"

Ela was relieved to see a twinkle of mischief in her friend's eyes.

"I do, I'm afraid. You'd be shocked by how common poisoning is." She didn't continue that her own dear husband had likely been poisoned—by the king's justiciar. She couldn't prove it and had resolved not to risk her life and those of her children by making the accusation. "But the coroner has ways of telling when poison was used and can often tell which one."

"How unfortunate. I would smother him, but the old goat is stronger than he looks." Alice shot Ela a sly smile.

"I'm going to pray for your marriage and your soul," said Ela, quite seriously. "But there must be a way to introduce joy into your life within the confines of your marriage. Marriage is a sacred bond and it's your duty to—" *To stick it out, no matter what.* She couldn't come up with a delicate way to put it.

"To sacrifice myself at the altar of duty?"

"I hardly think that's necessary. Does he beat you?" Ela wondered just how bad this marriage was.

"No. He's never laid a hand on me."

"Does he berate you?"

"Constantly, but not in a loud public way. It's more an unending stream of minor gripes that eat away at my spirit."

"Perhaps you could take a pet? My sweet dogs bring me so much joy that—"

Alice suddenly let out a whimper and burst into sobbing. "My little Harry died last spring. You remember him? I had him since I was a girl. He was eighteen years old." Ela dimly remembered a small brown and white terrier who used to lick her friend's face. "Since he died I'm bereft and he won't let me get another because he says they smell and deposit hair on my clothing. He says he'd been waiting for Harry to die and only wants animals outside the house now. I'm sure he just doesn't want me to have any creature in my life that can give me joy." Alice's wail of distress was loud enough to draw the attention of a garden boy sweeping dead leaves nearby and of a young maid carrying a basket of washing to the laundry.

"Come now, let's go into my solar, where you can rest a while." Ela didn't want her friend making a spectacle of herself in the garden. "When is your husband expecting you home?"

"He told me to hurry straight home after the funeral, but I begged and pleaded to spend a day or two in my old childhood home. I didn't tell him when I was leaving, so he may not expect me back for a day or two. I swear he wouldn't have let me leave for anything other than my father's funeral. He's deathly afraid that I'll enjoy myself." Another burst of sobbing racked her. "He must hate me so, that he wants me to be so miserable."

"I'm sure the loss of your dear father has set all your emotions churning." Ela hurried Alice back inside the castle and headed toward the stairs up to her solar. "Death makes you reflect on your life, and small and large dissatisfactions can bubble to the surface and overwhelm you."

They climbed the stairs, Alice still racked with sobs, and Ela wondering how to calm her down and bring her back to her senses. Inside Ela's solar, her maid Elsie was spreading fresh linens on the bed. "Elsie, dear, please have a nearby chamber made up for Alice de Gilbert. She'll be staying the night."

"May I really?" Alice's face brightened. "Anything to delay my return to that tomb of a castle at Mere. Your home is so bright and bustling with life. And you're lucky to live in a busy and exciting part of the country, with so much going on and the glorious new cathedral. Even that spooky circle of ancient stones is rather intriguing."

"We are blessed, here in Salisbury." Ela wasn't immune to pride in her home. "We have the best of old and new."

She helped settle Alice into a chair by the fire, which Elsie had just banked, and gave her a fresh handkerchief to dry her tears.

"I'm so sorry to hear of the loss of your father. Was he ill for long?"

"He'd been ailing for more than a year. My brother wrote to me to say his skin had turned quite yellow before last Christmas. But Humphrey didn't want me to travel the distance to see him."

"Are you close to your brothers?"

"Sadly, no. They're both older than me and by a different

mother. I was the product of my father's second marriage, and on the whole they'd prefer to forget I exist. Now I'm all alone in the world." She dabbed at her eyes. "Or at least I wish I was, and not chained to the dreary and penny-pinching Humphrey de Gilbert."

"Are his manors not profitable?" Ela knew it was a rather forward question, but she'd discovered a gift for finding profit in even the most remote and unpromising manors she owned.

"They're profitable enough. He has some of the finest sheep and cows in all of Wiltshire if his son's warm words about them are to be believed. But he's afflicted with miserliness. I see it as a disease of his shriveled soul. Unfortunately, he sees the ailment as one of his most shining qualities." Alice blew her nose into the handkerchief, causing the delicate embroidery of daisies to flutter. "If only you lived closer and could talk some sense into him."

"It's not my place to tell a nobleman how to conduct his affairs." Though sometimes the temptation was great.

"But it is! You're the sheriff."

"I'm afraid counseling men on their private financial matters falls well outside my purview. Unfortunately I can only counsel you to bear your fate bravely. Think of your immortal soul."

"My immortal soul will be all withered up like cheap parchment by the time it stands at the gates of Heaven."

"I shall pray for you, and you must pray for your husband. Perhaps there's still hope you could bear a child that could bring joy and life into your home."

Fresh tears sprang to Alice's eyes. "If that were to happen I could bear almost anything."

THE NEXT DAY, Ela took Alice on a ride around the old stone henge. Breathless and glowing after a short gallop, Alice swore that she hadn't had so much fun in years because her husband didn't believe in riding for pure pleasure.

That night after dinner, Alice enjoyed showing the younger children some games she remembered from her youth, and Ela could see she was almost tearful with emotion after enjoying the childhood amusements again after so long.

"Do you think your husband would object to your staying for a week or two?" asked Ela when Alice sat down after a rousing game of charades that had even the older children in stitches.

"Probably," replied Alice, glumly.

"What if I write to him and say that I need your womanly counsel and company and that I beseeched you to stay with me?"

Alice stared at her doubtfully.

Ela took a fresh cup of spiced wine from a serving boy and sipped it. "What would he approve of?"

"Perhaps you could say you needed my help on some sheriff's business?" said Alice, with sudden excitement. "He could hardly argue with that, could he?"

It was now Ela's turn to look doubtful.

"Not that I'd be helping you to arrest people, of course," continued Alice. "But you could say you need help distributing alms to the poor or something like that."

"Better yet, we could actually do it. I'm in the process of restoring the cottages and spirits of a group of downtrodden villagers not far from here. You could come help me inspire the women to whitewash their walls and scrub their floors. If nothing else it will make you appreciate your clean and quiet hall at home."

Alice's eyes sparkled. "Will you write to him at once?"

"Tonight. I have parchment and ink in my solar."

Alice clapped her hands. "He can hardly refuse a request from the Countess of Salisbury and High Sheriff of Wiltshire. And I promise to be as useful as I can. And it will only be for a week or two—or three..."

Ela smiled. "Everyone needs a change of scenery sometimes. I always gripe that I detest the smoke and grime of London, but I admit that I do enjoy visiting my mother there and admiring the bustle and industry of the city."

"I've never been to London," said Alice. "I'm sure it must be most exciting."

"It's not for the faint of heart. You can hardly imagine the strange characters you see there, just walking the streets. Seamen from Venice and princes from the Rhinelands, fishwives and peddlers and beggars and wastrels and all manner of extraordinary folk."

Alice sighed. "Perhaps one day I'll have the opportunity to visit. I don't suppose you need to go in the next week or so, do you?"

"No." Ela smiled. "It's a long journey and quite the opposite direction from your home."

"Perhaps that's one of the attractions," said Alice wistfully.

"I suspect that after a few days in the busy atmosphere of my hall, you'll be craving the quiet of Mere."

"You're very kind to let me stay."

"I'm delighted to enjoy your company."

Ela's brief missive to Humphrey de Gilbert was duly stamped with her official seal and dispatched by messenger. Ela proceeded to show Alice the wonders of Salisbury cathedral and the smaller joys of the nearby shops and market stalls. They visited a shop that sold baskets and bottles, where Ela's former maid Sibel now lived and worked with her new husband.

When Ela saw Sibel, her eyes took in an uncharacteristic thickening at the waistline of her plain blue gown. "Sibel, my dear. This is one of my oldest friends, Alice de Gilbert, visiting from her home in western Wiltshire. You look so well, I can see married life must be agreeing with you."

"God be praised, my lady, it is indeed! I've been meaning to come visit you these last few weeks to share our exciting news." Sibel's face glowed, and Ela became increasingly certain what her news would be. "We didn't think it could happen, with both of us being on in years, but it seems the stork will be visiting our shop in the coming months."

Ela exclaimed with joy and clapped her hands together. "I'm so happy for you, my dear Sibel. I know that you and Piers will be wonderful parents." She glanced at Alice—whose face suddenly looked white and pinched, like she was trying not to cry.

Oh, poor Alice, thought Ela. To see another's joy must throw her own sorrow into sharper relief. "Alice, will you help me find some new bottles for my herbal tonics?" She hoped to distract her.

"Yes," said Alice blankly.

Ela exclaimed a bit more over Sibel's exciting news, then chose and paid for some bottles and a basket to carry them in. Her guards carried their purchases out of the store and followed them back to the castle mound as she and Alice rode ahead.

"Sibel is certainly older than you, dear Alice, which shows you that God can still bless you with children."

"Only if he plans to send the angel Gabriel to sow one inside me," said Alice quietly. "As my husband will no longer entertain me in his bedroom."

"I suspect he can be persuaded. We shall put our heads

together and come up with a plan. There are herbs and tinctures to stimulate his appetites. We can make a tonic for him to put in our new bottles."

Alice didn't look terribly excited by this. "He probably won't drink it. He has to drink a nasty tonic two times a day for his gout already, and he's awfully fussy. He won't stand for any spices or pepper in his food."

"We shall make it taste like sweet rosewater, you'll see. He won't be able to resist it or you."

HUMPHREY rather grudgingly assented for Alice to enjoy a brief stay at Salisbury in the few lines he sent back by messenger.

"Are you sure you don't mind having me under your roof for a while longer?"

"I love having you here to share things with. Sir William Talbot is my oldest and dearest friend, but one can hardly expect him to become excited about which quilted blanket should be gifted to an elderly widow, or which flavor of jam she might enjoy with her daily bread."

Alice laughed. "I see your dilemma."

"My two oldest daughters, Ida and Isabella, used to enjoy fussing over such feminine problems, but dear Petronella finds such questions frivolous and insists that they should be grateful for whatever they're given, like the nuns in the cloister she craves."

"You must miss your oldest daughters terribly!"

"It was sheer agony sending them away into their own households. See? That's the kind of thing I can't really talk about with anyone else. My mother is so businesslike about marriage and tells me I should be glad to see them well settled, but my heart aches for their company."

"You're so lucky to still have younger children to enjoy."

"I know! Little Ellie and Nicky will be with me for years to come, God willing."

She and Alice rode out to the surrounding villages, bringing alms of both a practical and somewhat frivolous nature, taking pleasure in bringing a smile to people's lips as well as sustenance to their bellies.

They visited the village of Biddesden, where Ela had recently deposited two of Elsie's orphaned siblings to live with a man who'd been crippled with melancholy following the loss of his wife and children. They brought with them a wagonload of wood, which would give the newly formed family more time to rest by the fire during these winter months, instead of spending their days out gleaning sticks from the nearby forest. She also brought a sack of flour and a basket of apples to augment their meagre supplies. She and Alice were cheered to find their humble cottage clean and tidy, and all in good spirits.

After two weeks, Ela wrote a second letter to Humphrey de Gilbert, asking if he would mind if his wife stayed for a longer visit—perhaps until after Christmas.

His answer was unexpected.

CHAPTER 2

"It's my turn to go first!" cried Stephen, as he set up the chessboard for a game with his older brother Richard. "You went first last time." They all sat around the long table closest to the fire that roared at one end of the great hall.

"No, I didn't. I let you go first." Richard straightened up his defensive line of pawns.

"Don't fuss now, boys," said Ela. "We're about to dine, and your game can wait until after we've eaten."

"Cook said it won't be ready for a while yet," replied Stephen. "I just asked her. And he went first last time."

"Why don't we toss a coin to see who will go first?" chimed in Sir William Talbot, always the peacemaker. He pulled a silver penny from the purse at his waist. "Who calls heads?"

"Me!" replied both boys in the same instant.

Ela looked at Alice and shook her head. Alice giggled.

They all turned as the tall doors at the far end of the great hall were opened by two guards, and Albert the porter shuffled in. "Sir Humphrey de Gilbert."

Alice seemed to turn to stone. All color drained from her face, and she almost dropped the cup of wine she'd been sipping. "My husband," she whispered.

Ela realized she was frowning and governed her face into a more welcoming expression. "How unexpected," she muttered under her breath. "I suppose he missed you."

Servants took the new arrival's dark wool cape. He and Ela walked toward each other from opposite ends of the hall. Alice hung back. "What an unexpected pleasure," managed Ela with her best attempt at a smile.

"I believe my wife is under your roof." Humphrey de Gilbert had gained a good deal of weight since Ela had last seen him. With that plus the addition of many silver strands to his dark brown hair, she likely wouldn't have recognized him at all had he not been announced. He'd been a fairly good-looking man in his youth, but his square jaw had softened into multiple chins and his eyes seemed to have shrunk back into his head like raisins into a scone. "And I've come to take her home. I'm sure you've enjoyed quite enough of her unrivaled wit and wisdom these last weeks."

"She's been a most helpful and encouraging companion in my almsgiving. I shall miss her terribly, so I quite understand that you must feel the same way in her absence."

Ela turned to see where Alice had got to. She'd risen from her chair but still hovered near the table like a ghost—or like a dog that expected a whipping.

"Alice, my dear. You're presuming too long on your generous hostess." He strode toward her. Ela could tell that Alice would have shrunk backward away from him if she could, but the solid wood table blocked her way.

"How kind of you to come fetch me," she said tonelessly. "Must we leave at once?"

"You can't possibly leave in the dark," said Ela firmly. "Sir Humphrey must join us for dinner and we shall make up a comfortable bed for him." She fully intended that he and Alice should sleep in the same room. Perhaps this could be the night that Alice might conceive a child which would transform the bitter emptiness of her life into companionship and joy.

Servants rushed up to Humphrey de Gilbert with a bowl of water and cloths for him to refresh his hands and face after the journey. He was plied with wine and settled into a chair and, while supper was served, Ela drew from him what details she could about his journey across Wiltshire.

"My condolences on the loss of your father-in-law," she said. "I'm so grateful that Alice was able to spend some time with me here on her journey home. It's been wonderful to reminisce over old times when we were both young and foolish."

"Dear Alice may not be young any longer, but she's still lamentably foolish, as you've no doubt discovered." Humphrey de Gilbert had started sliding into his cups during the soup this shocking rudeness must be the result.

Ela rankled at his cruel characterization of his wife—and in front of her family and everyone else within earshot! "Alice is blessed with an exuberance and enthusiasm that I greatly admire. She's brought tremendous joy to my household during her short stay here."

When Humphrey left the hall to use the garderobe, Alice cast a desperate glance at Ela.

"I see what you mean," muttered Ela under her breath. Humphrey's small group of attendants dined on the far side of the hall, at a table usually frequented by the garrison soldiers.

"He hates me." Alice bit her lip to stop it quivering. "How am I to spend the rest of my life with a man who despises me?" She spoke low, but Ela knew her children might hear and found the whole situation mortifying.

"He came to fetch you. He must miss your company." Ela tried to be reassuring. "Men aren't raised to be demonstrative in their affections, but it's clear he wants you back at home with him."

Alice looked down at the table.

"I've arranged for you to share a bedchamber tonight," said Ela quietly. "Perhaps if you were to give him one of the bottles of tonic we made?"

"He'll never try it," said Alice glumly.

"Run and get one! We shall try it out on him and see."

Alice looked doubtful.

"You want a child, don't you?" asked Ela. One had to be practical about such things.

"I do." Alice inhaled slowly. "Do you really think it will work?"

"There's only one way to find out. Hurry and get the bottle before he comes back! Have Elsie pour some into a cup for him and garnish it with fresh mint leaves."

HUMPHREY RETURNED to the table before Alice and demanded to know where his wife was. "I sent her to fetch something for me," said Ela as sweetly as she could. "You have no idea what a pleasure it's been for me to spend precious time with my old childhood friend. I'm so grateful that you were able to spare her for at least a couple of weeks."

"I hardly had a choice, did I?" Humphrey's face had taken on a florid hue as he drank. "The servants are quite incompetent at scraping my corns. Between that and the pain from my gout I'm half crippled in her absence."

Ela shuddered at the thought of poor Alice having to bend over his gnarled and crusty feet. "You're blessed to have such a kind and caring wife. May God grant you the blessing of children soon."

"I've had all the children I want and need, especially with bubble-headed Alice wafting around the castle like a butterfly. The last thing I need is a squalling babe."

Alice arrived in time to catch his last few words, and she looked right at Ela. Whose heart squeezed with mortification and sorrow for her poor friend. "I brought the herbal tincture we made," she said calmly. "Humphrey, dearest, Ela tells me this blend of herbs will do wonders for your gout."

Gout? They'd made the tonic to stimulate his libido. For gout they should have added sour cherry or apple cider vinegar to the tincture. Still, she didn't mind Alice using wiles if it would achieve her goal. "Alice and I have spent time preparing a delicious and refreshing drink. Do try it."

The potion had been decanted into a lovely tooled silver cup and garnished with a sprig of mint and a pinch of rose petals.

"No, thank you." Humphrey looked at the drink, and then his wife, with distaste.

"At least have a sip," said Ela. "It's my own recipe that I've used myself for years."

"You have gout?" asked Humphrey curiously.

"Mercifully, no," said Ela. "And I'm sure this potion is half the reason why." Would a small white lie in her friend's favor condemn her soul to decades in purgatory? Possibly, but it might be worth it. "Just try a sip!"

Humphrey de Gilbert wrinkled his long nose and sniffed at the potion. Then he raised the cup to his lips and took a sip. He swallowed. Everyone watched in an almost eerie silence. "It's not as bad as I expected."

Ela smiled. "Drink up and you'll feel marvelous in the morning." She glanced at Alice, who looked very nervous. As well she might. Ela wouldn't relish the prospect of spending a night in the same bed with Humphrey de Gilbert, either. She half wished she'd prepared separate rooms for them. But then there would be no chance of her friend's fondest dream coming true.

~

THEY STAYED UP, playing board games and chatting. Eventually the children were sent to bed and the adults sat around talking about inconsequential things and eating sweetmeats. Ela turned the conversation to the benefit of providing alms to the people of her manors. How the recipients of both money and advice became more productive and profitable tenants and increased God's bounty on earth.

"My tenants' role is to provide me with income, not the other way around," growled Humphrey, even deeper into his cups. "Lazy and idle, they are. If I could whip them to work harder I wouldn't hesitate to do it."

Ela glanced at Alice, whose eyes met hers with a flash of *I told you so.*

She steered the conversation to practical matters, such as which wines might last the longest in a cellar or which breeds of sheep produced the best fleeces. Her goal was to show Humphrey that women could hold thoughts about matters of business. But her efforts seemed fruitless. Humphrey became increasingly silent the more he drank, and Bill Talbot was eventually pressed into service to help Humphrey's long-suffering manservant remove him to the chamber that he'd share with Alice.

Alice gave the green bottle with the remains of the tonic to her husband's manservant, then hung back in the great hall after Humphrey had been escorted upstairs. Her face looked drawn, and her fingers worked into the fabric of her gown. Ela suspected that she needed support and encouragement. "Would you like to join me in my solar for a quick prayer?"

Alice nodded. Ela led the way up to her bedchamber and told Elsie that she'd call for her if she needed her but that she could go to bed, then she led Alice inside and closed the door.

They looked at each other. Ela suspected her friend would rather slit her own throat than have sex with her unloving and unlovable husband. She tried to rally herself to encourage Alice. Truthfully, her own womb recoiled from the prospect of the evening of baby-making that she'd planned and schemed for her friend.

"I can't do it," said Alice. "I just can't."

"I understand." Ela took her hands and squeezed them.

"I try my best to be a dutiful wife, I really do." Alice inhaled and heaved a long sigh. "But my life would be so much easier if the herbs we gave him were to kill him rather than arouse him."

"You really mustn't allow such thoughts into your head, let alone utter them aloud," scolded Ela. "Murder is a mortal sin, and your soul would suffer extreme torment in the flames of hell for all eternity if you were to be tempted down that path."

"You're right, of course." Tears hovered in Alice's big brown eyes. "It's just that every day seems so long sometimes I wonder if I'm in hell right now." She looked at Ela suddenly. "Not here with you. Just when I'm shut away with him in that mausoleum of a castle. How many more nights of lonely privation must I endure in this sham of a marriage?"

Ela's heart ached for her friend. "Those of us who find love and happiness within marriage are blessed indeed. Nothing is promised here in this life. That which we don't enjoy we must endure bravely and with dignity."

A fat tear rolled down Alice's cheek. "To crave widowhood seems so sinful, but I know I'm not alone in my longing."

"Indeed you're not, but you must pray for fortitude, not deliverance, for to wish for your husband's death is a sin indeed."

"I know you would bear it more bravely than I. I shall endeavor to be more like you, Ela."

"Don't think I'm so perfect. I'm cursed with ambition that draws me away from my family and into the public eye." She wasn't sure she'd ever confessed this aloud before. "My children wish I spent my days embroidering before the fire. They hate the fact that I'm sheriff and put myself in danger by meddling in what most consider to be the affairs of men."

"Do you wish you found full satisfaction in the simpler and smaller affairs of womanhood?"

"Sometimes I do. But then I realize that the Lord would not have called me to seek the office of sheriff if he didn't want me to serve in it. I pray daily for the humility to conduct myself according to his wishes."

"I wish I knew what the Lord wanted me to do. I have a heart filled with love that no one wants or needs. My life seems like such a waste. But perhaps that's just a different kind of ambition that I need to mortify."

They said a decade of the rosary together—though the prayer was punctuated a few times by sobs and sniffles from Alice—then Ela ushered Alice to the door of the room. "May God be with you. Most likely he's drunk too much wine to be fit for anything more than sleeping through the night."

Alice nodded, and went silently into her chamber.

Ela said a fervent prayer for her friend. While she wished Alice could be blessed with a child, she didn't wish for her to suffer through any unwelcome acts of intercourse to achieve her goal. She prayed that the de Gilberts would pass a peaceful night and that her friend would find solace in prayer to guide her through the rather empty husk of her life.

Ela awoke from her sleep suddenly and looked around her bed, wondering what had roused her in the middle of the night. Then she heard it again—a knocking on her bedroom door.

She pushed back her bed curtains and moved to the edge of her bed. "Who's there?"

"It's Alice," came the reply.

Frowning, Ela slid off the bed until her feet hit the cool wood floor, then she walked across the room. The fire had died down to a red glow. What time was it? A glance at the high window gave no answer as the sky outside was pitch-dark.

Ela unlocked her door and opened it to see Alice holding a candle, which flickered in the rush of air from the doorway. She peered outside to see where the guards were and noticed one of them stir slightly at the end of the hall.

"Is anything amiss, my lady," he asked in a low whisper. "Since I know she's your guest I didn't stop her from approaching your door."

"You did right. All is well." She ushered Alice into the room. "What's going on?"

The flame guttered as Alice's hand shook. Ela noticed that her eyes were wide and staring and her jaw tense almost as if she was about to yell.

"Alice, are you well?"

"He's dead." Alice's whisper almost blew out the candle flame, and her hand shook so hard that Ela took the candle from her before she could set the bed curtains alight with it.

"What do you mean?"

"My husband," said Alice, eyes wide and staring. "He's not breathing."

"He's probably just deeply asleep." Had her friend's fantasy grown so vivid that she now believed it?

"I don't think so." Alice stood in the middle of the room, eyes fixed straight ahead as if she were a sleepwalker. Maybe she was sleepwalking? Ela walked up to her and waved a hand in front of her eyes.

Alice blinked. "What are you doing?"

She certainly seemed to be awake. "Let me come see him." Ela put the candle down long enough to don her robe, then picked it up again and led Alice out of the room and down the hallway.

The door to the bedchamber where Alice and Humphrey de Gilbert slept was right outside where the sentry stood at the end of the hall. Alice had closed the door behind her and Ela hesitated outside it, then knocked.

"He won't answer," whispered Alice.

Ela knocked again, then opened the door gingerly. It creaked slightly as it slid across the floor. Ela stepped into the room, holding the candle ahead of her. The bed curtains were closed so she couldn't see Humphrey where he lay on the bed. "Close the door behind us." She didn't want the guard overhearing anything that might cause gossip in the morning.

He couldn't be dead, though...could he? He'd been hale and hearty with a tremendous appetite—especially for wine—at dinner. He couldn't have sickened to death in just a few hours.

Ela put the candle down on a small table near the fireplace. The fire had burned down to embers and provided little light or heat. She pulled back the bed curtains and could just make out the fairly substantial form of Humphrey de Gilbert humped under the bed covers.

"Sir Humphrey," she whispered. He didn't stir, or appear to move a muscle.

"He's dead!" whispered Alice, with some urgency. "I told you."

Ela leaned into the bed and touched him. He didn't feel especially dead, though he didn't react to her touch. She shook him. Rather than resisting and arousing, he only slumped further into the mattress, his face falling into his pillow.

Concern now flared in Ela's chest. She climbed onto the bed and put her ear to his ribcage.

"You won't hear a heartbeat," whispered Alice.

"Shhh." Ela strained to hear something, anything, that suggested the movement of blood or air through his rather fleshy body. But she didn't.

She pressed two fingertips to his wrist. That was usually the easiest place to feel a pulse, but once again, she felt nothing.

He really is dead.

Ela glanced up at Alice, who now stood, calmly, at the bedside, holding the curtains apart so she could see in. As Ela looked up, she blinked rapidly. "He is dead, isn't he?"

"I do believe he is."

"Can it really be true? Am I really free?"

"What?" Cool shock dropped through Ela. "Don't say such a thing."

"But you saw how he was with me last night. He probably only came here to make sure I couldn't possibly enjoy myself for another moment. And now I'm a widow."

Despite the darkness, Ela saw her friend's eyes light up.

"Alice! You mustn't show even the tiniest hint of pleasure at your husband's death."

"But why?"

Was she really this dense? "Because people will think you killed him."

"What people? They don't matter. You're the sheriff, and you know I didn't kill him."

"I am the sheriff, and therefore I will have to conduct the investigation into his death. If I think you killed him then I am duty bound to prosecute you to the fullest extent of the law."

"What?" The joy fled Alice's face and her mouth hung open. "You don't think I killed him, do you?"

Ela hesitated. "I…I don't know what to think. Of course you're my friend so I do think you're innocent, but the coroner will have to be called at once to avoid any appearance of impropriety."

CHAPTER 3

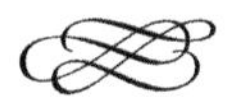

Alice stared at her, wide eyed. "The coroner? What will he do?"

"He'll examine the body for signs of foul play."

"Like what?"

Ela eased herself off the bed and back to a standing position. She held the candle high, wanting to get a good look at Alice's face. "To see if he shows signs of being smothered or strangled or poisoned."

A whimper escaped Alice's mouth. "How can he tell?"

"He's very experienced. He knows the signs." Ela peered at her friend's face. "Why do you look so worried?" Fear now clawed at her gut that her friend really had killed him. It probably wouldn't have been so hard to hold a pillow over his face until he stopped breathing, since he was so drunk.

"What if they think I did one of those things? I didn't! I swear it." Alice started to shake again. "Will they hang me?"

Ela drew in a steadying breath. "One thing at a time. I must call for the coroner, and he will examine the body, and I will tell him that you are my dear friend, and we shall see what he says and take it from there."

"I must sit down." Alice swayed as if she was about to faint, and Ela hurried her to a chair near the fire.

"Stay there. I'll try to keep matters as discreet as I can."

Ela summoned the guard and asked him to fetch Giles Haughton from his house inside the castle's outer walls, and to bring him back here personally with as little noise and fanfare as possible. She didn't want to alarm other members of the household and she had no wish to call for a jury at this unholy hour.

Once back in the room she told Alice to get dressed. She helped her to find a gown and to comb and pin up Alice's hair so that she didn't look like a madwoman. She didn't want to wake Alice's maid, who slept with the other servants. Alice kept sneaking horrified glances at the bed—with its closed curtains—as if the body of Humphrey de Gilbert might rise and climb out.

Ela needed to dress herself, but she didn't want to leave Alice alone with the body of her dead husband. If nothing else she might panic and do something that would make her look even more guilty.

Ela eventually took Alice back to her room with her, where she dressed and did her best to arrange her own hair without her maid Elsie's help. She didn't want to wake the girl, who—still young and impressionable—might shriek with terror at the idea of a dead body so close at hand. Since the household still slept, Ela waited in her chamber with Alice. If they went downstairs they'd have to wake people to start a fire and that would cause more commotion and interest than she wanted right now. Alice had fallen into a sort of stunned silence, and together they mumbled some prayers for the safe passage of Humphrey de Gilbert's soul.

In less than half an hour the guard returned with Giles Haughton and knocked on Ela's door to announce him.

Ela ushered him into her solar. "I'm sorry to rouse you

before dawn," said Ela. "But I'm afraid one of my guests has died. This is his wife, Alice de Gilbert."

Haughton bowed his head. "My deepest sympathies, my lady."

"Thank you," whispered Alice. Haughton looked at her expectantly, as if she might tell him what happened, but Alice just looked at Ela.

"Let's go see the body, and you can examine it." She led him back down the hall to the room Alice had shared with her husband. Ela could hear predawn stirrings in the castle, the servants rising and setting fires in the bedrooms, and pots starting to clatter down in the kitchens off the great hall.

Her candle guttered as they passed through the doorway. "He's on the bed. He seems to have died during his sleep." She crossed the room and pulled the bed curtains aside for Haughton to look.

At that moment Elsie poked her head in the door. "My lady, I didn't know you were up already. Can I get you anything?"

"You could fetch ties to pull back these curtains, Elsie, and then bring more candles. The coroner is here to attend a death." She couldn't shelter the girl from the situation for any longer.

Elsie's eyes widened, but she kept her composure. "I shall, my lady."

Giles Haughton leaned over the corpse. It was hard to see by the light of a flickering candle, but Humphrey de Gilbert still looked more asleep than dead. "Rigor mortis is starting to set in," said Haughton, feeling his hands and arms. "Which means he's been dead about two hours. When did you discover him?" He looked at Alice.

"I awoke in the night, and he was there next to me. Something about him seemed strange, so I listened for his breathing and didn't hear it. Then I touched him and he didn't move."

"Most likely his heart stopped in his sleep. How old was he?"

"Fifty-four."

Haughton looked surprised. "That's not so old." Humphrey de Gilbert's sedentary lifestyle had festooned his body with sagging pouches of skin that made him look older than his years. "But I see no obvious signs of violence or even a struggle suggesting pain. All indications are that he died peacefully. I won't be able to look closely until daylight, when I can examine him in the mortuary."

"You think he just died of natural causes?" said Alice softly.

"It certainly seems that way. I'm sorry for your loss."

"I thank you." Alice glanced at Ela, who felt considerable relief at Haughton's latest pronouncement. Hopefully Alice could bury her husband without undue attention and then start a new life as a widow. Perhaps it was indeed for the best.

Haughton closed the bed curtains. "I'll send my men up here to retrieve the body." Then he looked at Ela. "May I speak to you downstairs for a moment?"

Surprised, Ela agreed. "Will you be all right to stay here for a short while, Alice?" Since her friend wasn't exactly prostrate with grief, Ela thought she could manage it.

Alice nodded.

Ela accompanied Haughton down the stairs and along the columned passage that led to the great hall. Servants hurried past them carrying jugs of water and baskets of eggs and armfuls of kindling. "What is it?" Ela wondered what was so urgent that she must abandon her friend with the dead body of her husband.

"My lady." He hesitated for a moment and turned to look at her. "I'm wondering why you called me."

"Because a man is dead in my castle," said Ela, perplexed.

"I'm usually summoned with urgency in the dead of night if someone is bleeding from a stab wound or found strangled in your moat. Not when they're found quietly dead in their own bed having passed during the night."

"Oh. Well, I suppose not many of us are blessed to pass so peacefully, are we? I can't even think of another instance where a member of the household has simply passed without an illness or injury of some kind. I suppose I just wanted to follow the usual procedure."

"Indeed." Haughton looked skeptical. "Usually when I'm called in to witness such a death, it's because there's reason to suspect foul play. A poisoning or suffocation or some such. Is that the case here?"

"Oh, goodness, no. I do hope not. Alice is my dear friend." Ela swallowed. Had she made a miscalculation in calling for the coroner? "It's just that as the sheriff as well as the head of this household I do want to make sure that all proper protocol is followed so there can be no...cause for concern or accusation later."

"I see." He looked thoroughly confused. "I shall be sure to examine the body with that in mind."

"Would you like to stay to break your fast? The kitchen is astir as I can smell the first loaves baking."

"Thank you, but no. My wife asked me to pick up a fresh loaf for her on my way home. I'll be back when it's light to examine the body and will share my findings."

"I appreciate your help, and again I'm sorry to rouse you from your bed, especially if it seems so unnecessary."

"Don't ever hesitate to call for me. Even the most uneventful deaths may hold surprises. It's better to be safe than sorry."

"Indeed it is." She wished he would leave so she could go back to Alice. "I'll attend you at the mortuary when you return."

Ela hurried back upstairs. Alice, seated in a chair at the fire, turned when she entered the room. Elsie had tied back the bed curtains and lit three candles which illuminated the room almost as well as the daylight starting to peek through the single window.

"How are you doing, Alice?"

"I don't entirely know," said Alice. "What did the coroner have to say?"

"Oh, nothing much. He thinks it's just a natural death, but he'll have a good look at the body in daylight."

"I must break the news to his sons in a letter."

"I suppose that the eldest will claim the castle as his home?"

"No doubt, and I'm sure he won't want me in it."

"You said you have a manor that you expect as part of your inheritance?" Widowhood could put women in a tricky situation unless their portion was dictated by either their marriage documents or their husband's will. The Magna Carta had recently outlined the right of widows to enjoy a full third of their husband's estate, but enforcing this entitlement could prove difficult and expensive.

"I brought this particular manor into the marriage and it was in the contract that I should keep it, and a respectable income, on his death." Alice's marriage happened before the Magna Carta was finalized, and thus wouldn't have outlined all the rights endowed in that document. Still, there was no need to trouble poor Alice with the legal intricacies right now.

"Widowhood is a tremendous shock, as I know all too well," Ela said softly. "But I've gained much experience running my manors and would be glad to offer advice on the management of the lands and animals if you'd like it."

"I hope I'll find a new husband soon enough to have children before I grow too old. He or his steward can manage my manor. I don't have a head for such details." Alice had a strange look in her eye. Maybe she was already peering into a promising future filled with children's laughter.

Ela couldn't blame her.

"How did you come to marry Humphrey?" Truth be told, she'd been surprised at the wedding by how much older Alice's husband was than she.

"When my mother died, my father didn't know what to do with me. I'd already stayed with my older female relatives while she was ill, and he wanted me safely settled. He arranged the entire marriage and made all the negotiations without asking my opinion."

"I suppose that's not so unusual."

"He was pleased that the de Gilbert family was an ancient one that came here with the Conqueror and that my husband had a castle and several manors."

"And were you happy with the match?"

"At first I was. I didn't find my husband overly handsome, but I was glad to be mistress of my own home and I hoped to have children of my own. My happiness didn't last long, though."

"Were his sons kind to you?"

"I barely knew them. They'd already moved away to nearby manors even though they were barely in their majority. I suppose that tells you how much affection they had for their father." She frowned. "Or perhaps he sent them away to better enjoy his solitude in their absence. But I must write to them at once and tell them of his passing."

"I have ink and vellum in my solar."

Alice wrote the two letters, then they sealed them with

Ela's own seal and delivered them to a messenger to take at once.

"I suppose I must make arrangements to move my clothes and effects—such as they are—to my own manor. I haven't ever actually seen it. It was one my father owned but didn't visit often. I hope the house is still habitable."

"We must view it and see if repairs are needed. Where is it?"

"Not so far from here. It's up past Amesbury."

"Then we shall live close enough to see each other often!" Ela felt a burst of pleasure. Not that she had much time on her hands for socializing, but it would be better than seeing each other once every ten years.

"I do hope so." Alice looked at her shyly. "Perhaps you can help me find a new husband."

Ela blinked. "Yes, perhaps I can make some introductions. After a decent mourning period has been observed, of course."

Alice bit her lip. "But I'm already so old. I really should marry right away."

"You're not old at all!" Ela tried to reassure her. "Look at dear Sibel, newly pregnant. She must be nearly my age and I have a good six years on you."

"I do hope there's still time for me to be blessed with children." Alice knitted her hands together.

"I'm sure there will be. Don't fret over it. That never helps with anything."

ELA ATTENDED Haughton in the mortuary when he returned to examine Humphrey de Gilbert's body in daylight. She knocked, and Haughton invited her to enter. She braced herself for the unpleasant sight of the man's nakedness.

Humphrey de Gilbert's flaccid corpse lay sprawled along the length of the scarred wooden table. "I'm sorry. I should have covered him decently since he's a friend of yours."

"He's no friend of mine," said Ela quickly. She immediately realized that she should have kept her mouth shut. "I mean, I only met him at his wedding some years ago and then again last night."

"He's your good friend's husband?"

"Yes. He was quite a bit older than her, as you can see."

"Yes, but not so old. A few years younger than me." Haughton looked at her with humor.

"I believe he's fifty-four. A man can drop dead from heart failure or a brain seizure at that age, can he not?"

"Either of those misfortunes can befall us at any age, but they're certainly more common at a later age than this one."

"There aren't any signs of foul play, are there?" She really wanted to wrap this up and have the body sent back to his castle for burial.

Haughton lifted his lids and peered into his eyes. Ela held her breath for a second, knowing that dilated pupils were a sign of belladonna poisoning. Had Alice poisoned her husband?

Haughton closed the lids and opened de Gilbert's mouth. He fished out his tongue and peered at it. "The lips and tongue are swollen."

"What does that mean?"

"I'm not entirely sure. What did he ingest in the evening before his death?"

"Well, we all had some soup—made with turnips and leeks, then a roasted fish—turbot, I think—served with parsnips in an almond sauce. That was followed with some pastries made with raisins and nutmeats…." Should she tell him about the tonics? She'd supervised the making of them herself, so she knew they were harmless, but would they raise suspicion?

On the other hand, not mentioning them was a sin of omission. "And we served a drink with rose petals." There, she'd said it.

"Did you all drink it?"

Ela hesitated. Was a little white lie under these circumstances really so wrong?

It would be if Alice really did kill her husband. Even if he deserved it.

"No, just Sir Humphrey. To be quite frank it was intended to stimulate his…appetites of a non-digestive nature. Dear Alice was so hoping to conceive a child." She hoped this introduced the idea that Alice looked forward to many more happy years of married life.

"Might I see this tonic?"

"Um, yes, of course." Ela opened the door to the mortuary and asked the guard standing outside to fetch Elsie. "Hopefully the rest of it wasn't thrown away after dinner. It was in a bottle that we bought at the shop Sibel now keeps with her husband."

"Did the potion contain any part of the fly agaric mushroom?"

"It did not. I find myself quite skittish around mushrooms because sometimes the poisonous ones look just like the edible ones."

"Fly agaric is red with white spots," said Haughton, palpating Humphrey de Gilbert's gray-white belly. "And it's a potent aphrodisiac as well as a deadly poison."

"I'm familiar with it, and it certainly wasn't in the potion." *At least not that I know of.* Could Alice have added a poisonous substance to the tonic after they'd made it? Or could she have added the mushroom hoping to increase the tonic's potency, without knowing that it was deadly?

Ela's breathing grew shallower as she contemplated the awful possibilities. A knock on the door made her jump. "Come in," she said quickly.

Elsie poked her head around the door. "They said you needed me, my lady."

"Yes. Please find the green glass bottle of tonic that we served to Sir Humphrey at dinner last night. It might have been put back in the pantry, or I suppose his servant might have taken it up to the bedchamber. I don't quite remember. It was a tall narrow bottle with a clay stopper."

"I'll find it and bring it right here, my lady."

"If we're not here when you come back, you can bring it directly to my house," said Haughton. "And I can examine it there."

"Was it poisoned?" asked Elsie, eyes wide.

"Of course not!" said Ela much too fast. "I made it myself. Or at least I watched Alice make it."

HAUGHTON CONTINUED his examination of the body and satisfied himself that he'd discovered any useful details. He'd just pulled the linen sheet up over the corpse when Elsie flew back in, brandishing the green bottle. "I found it!"

She entered the room and handed it triumphantly to Ela.

"Where was it?" asked Ela quietly.

"In Alice's room," said Elsie. "And it was almost empty. Someone must have drunk it all up."

Or poured it out the window. Ela hated the way suspicions now crept into her mind. Could she blame Alice for wanting to be rid of such an odious man? Perhaps that was why she now suspected her friend of killing him.

Ela handed the bottle to Haughton, who sniffed it. "It

smells quite pleasant. I shall take it back to my home and test the last few drops."

"Test them? How?"

"We coroners have a few methods of discovering poison in food or drink." He smiled mysteriously. "Though in this case I suspect that I will find it to be quite harmless."

"Oh, good," said Ela in a rush. Again she realized she'd said the wrong thing and sounded like she was encouraging him to come to a particular conclusion.

This situation had her quite stumbling over herself. The sheriff in her wanted to prosecute all wrongs and suffer all sinners to be punished. The wife and mother and friend in her wanted Alice to flee the painful trap she'd been stuck in for what might have otherwise been the best years of her life.

"If we're done here I shall return to the hall, as I suspect the morning's petitioners are filling it by now."

"I'll let you know what I discover, my lady."

CHAPTER 4

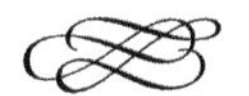

Arrangements were made to return Humphrey de Gilbert's body to his castle at Mere for the funeral and burial.

Alice seemed quite agitated. "It's raining, so I suppose his body will have to travel in our carriage. Since I don't want to travel with my husband's corpse, I shall have to stay here for a few days until the carriage can be sent back or else I'll have to ride in the rain." She said it all very fast, while pacing in Ela's solar.

"Stay here? But surely you'll attend your husband's funeral."

Alice hesitated. "Do you really think I must?"

Ela stared at her friend in disbelief. "Of course. What would his sons think if you didn't?"

"I don't think either of them wants to lay eyes on me. Even the one who lived nearby was always quite curt with me. I suspect they were worried their father would break off some of their inheritance and give it to me. Though such concern shows a total lack of understanding of their father, who would gnaw off his own arm before he'd use it to hand me his wealth or property."

"Alice! You're speaking ill of the dead."

She had the decency to look somewhat chastened. "I know I really shouldn't. But the thought of rattling around that chilly castle in the middle of nowhere, with his oldest scowling at me as he takes up residence there with his own family. It makes my gut churn."

"It will be a difficult few days, but you'll manage and then you can come back for another visit." She held out this dangling bait in the hope that she could get Alice to attend the funeral. It would look very odd if she didn't. And Ela wanted her out of Salisbury castle at least until any worries about the contents of the tonic were resolved. "You can take my carriage and return in it once the burial is completed."

"That's very generous of you." She didn't look entirely thrilled by Ela's offer. "Can I really come back?" Her worried gaze touched Ela's heart.

"Of course. I'll help you arrange the move to your own manor and will visit it to help you plan the best management of your land and livestock." Perhaps she could get Alice focused on the future that awaited once she managed to attend the funeral of her despised husband.

But Alice's face fell. "I suspect it's a remote manor with no near neighbors. I shall rot away there like my husband's body moldering in its coffin."

Ela felt a twinge of alarm. "You don't intend to move there?"

"I shall if I have no choice, but I'd far rather remarry."

"And I'm sure you shall, but you do understand that a decent interval of mourning for your late husband must be observed." Did Alice think she could ride straight from the funeral to an assignation with a prospective husband?

"How long is that?" Alice looked at her, dark eyes wide.

Ela inhaled, knowing Alice wouldn't like what she had to say. "I think a year is considered adequate."

"A year!" She half wailed it. "I shall be as old as Sarah in the Bible before I can even try for a child."

"Then perhaps you, too, shall be a mother of nations," said Ela coolly. Alice's behavior made her uncomfortable. How could she think that she could avoid her husband's funeral and immediately go in search of a replacement for him? If anyone wondered if she might have murdered him, this would almost confirm their suspicions.

"Another year older. More bloom gone from my cheeks. Perhaps I shall even have silver in my hair by then," said Alice sadly. "I suppose it's my fate to be alone and childless, though I don't know what I've done to deserve it."

"I'm sure you haven't done anything at all, but for now you must call on your sense of duty and propriety. If people gossip and speculate about you it will harm your marriage prospects." She hoped she could shock some sense into Alice. "You don't want people thinking you poisoned him to clear the way for a new husband."

Alice's eyes widened. "Surely no one will think that. Will they?"

"If you don't even attempt to play the grieving widow but immediately launch in to your new life as a merry one, they might."

Alice frowned. "I suppose you're right. Oh, dear. I do hate all this fakery. Pretending to feel things I don't feel and all the while I'm dying inside."

"You're restoring your strength and calming your mind, so you'll be ready to tackle this next phase of your life, whatever it brings."

"But I really can come back and visit you again after the funeral?"

Ela half wished she could say no. "Of course! And there's

no rush. If you'd like to settle into your manor and spend some time arranging your household you have an open invitation to return whenever you're ready."

"I shall return in your carriage as soon as my husband's body is in the ground." She looked quite excited at the prospect. "And I do welcome your advice about my manor, though I warn you it may well be damp and neglected. My husband was loath to spend money on his property, even to maintain it."

"Then I relish the prospect of lighting the hearths and breathing new life into it with you."

Alice insisted on leaving some of her belongings behind, perhaps to ensure that she'd soon be back to use them under Ela's roof again. Ela indulged her and promised they'd go for long rides together and that they could at least discuss her future and imagine potential marriage prospects, even if she couldn't decently act on her hopes yet.

Ela heaved a sigh of relief when her carriage rolled away, with Alice safely aboard, traveling just behind her own smaller and meaner carriage bearing the body of the late and not-much-lamented Humphrey de Gilbert.

SHORTLY AFTER ALICE'S DEPARTURE, Giles Haughton arrived and asked for a private audience with Ela. Alarm prickled the tips of her fingers. Surely if there were nothing suspicious about Humphrey de Gilbert's death, he could announce his findings in the great hall in front of all and sundry.

Ela led him into the armory, where swords and halberds shimmered in patterns on the stone walls. "Alice has returned to the de Gilbert castle for her husband's funeral," she announced. "I miss her already." She hoped he wasn't about to say anything to make her regret her friendship with Alice.

Haughton looked around at the gleaming weapons before clearing his throat. Ela felt her pulse quicken. "Yes?"

"There was enough of the liquid left at the bottom of the bottle for me to test it, and I'm afraid that I did find traces of poison in the tonic."

"How did you test it?"

"I gave it to a mouse. Their anatomy and general physiology are strikingly similar to ours."

"Oh." What an odd idea. And also that he would deliberately poison the poor creature to test the tonic. "And it died?"

"Yes and no. The first mouse I gave the tonic to died quickly. I then gave a drop of the tonic to a second mouse and quickly administered an equal amount of an antidote made from the belladonna plant. The second mouse rallied and recovered."

"Belladonna?" Ela looked at him in confusion. "That's a deadly poison."

"It is a deadly poison that excites and overstimulates the heart, which can cause death. It is, however, an effective antidote for another kind of poison." He hesitated for a moment. "Could you tell me what plants were included in the tonic that Alice prepared for her husband?"

Ela's head spun with confused thoughts. "Let me see. We made it honey, ginger, celery seed and ground pine nuts. It was quite smooth and sweet and we garnished it with rose petals. Definitely no fly agaric mushroom or anything poisonous."

"Did you include comfrey?"

"No." Ela peered at him. "Comfrey is soothing in a poultice, but it's not to be taken internally."

"Comfrey is not poisonous, but it closely resembles another very poisonous plant."

Ela searched her brain for another plant that might be mistaken for the fleshy rosette of leaves and the bell-like purple or blue flowers of comfrey. She froze as one occurred to her. "Foxglove? The flowers are quite different but the rosette of leaves in the first year of the plant's growth does look similar." The plant was a biennial, needing a full year of growth before it produced its distinctive flowers in its second spring.

"Exactly." Haughton drew in a breath. "Foxglove slows the heart and thus reverses the quickening effect of the belladonna."

Ela had never heard this before, and it rather astonished her. "We picked all the herbs for the tonics from the castle herb gardens directly outside the kitchen. I don't grow foxglove in my herb garden, so it wouldn't be possible to pick it by mistake here."

"But the woods are full of it."

"Yes, it's a prolific weed, but everyone knows it's poisonous and not to pick and eat it."

"Unless they intended to use it as poison."

Ela drew in a steadying breath. "Alice and I made the tonic together. It had no foxglove in it, nor comfrey either."

"Did she have custody of the bottle at any point after it was strained and corked?"

"Well, it did go up to their chamber after dinner..." She heard her voice trail off.

"Was your friend very fond of her husband?" Haughton looked steadily at her.

Ela felt her knees buckle slightly. Could she lie to her most trusted and helpful ally in the pursuit of justice in Salisbury?

No. She couldn't and she wouldn't, not even to protect a dear friend.

"I'm afraid their marriage wasn't the happiest. Her

husband was a good deal older than she and they were not blessed with children. He was a rather unpleasant man, judging from the brief time I spent in his company. Alice admitted to me that she wasn't happy in her marriage and that she longed for children, which is why we concocted the tonic to tempt him into making her pregnant."

Haughton winced very slightly.

"Perhaps it sounds conniving to you, but women are often forced to make the best of a bad lot in life."

"And I suppose the effort suggests that she intended for the marriage to be fruitful and to continue."

"Exactly." Ela was glad he could see sense.

"Unless she decided that widowhood would be preferable to enduring intercourse and bearing a child for a man she dislikes."

Ela swallowed. "I can't believe dear Alice would do such a thing. And when would she have had time to gather foxglove? She wasn't exactly wandering around the woods by herself."

"Did you walk or ride in the woods with her?"

"Of course, but I would have noticed if she'd stopped to pluck foxglove on the way."

"Was there ever a time when you might have, say, stopped to speak with a villager and left her unattended for a moment?"

She frowned. "I suppose so, but we always had at least two guards in attendance so someone would have seen her."

"Would the guards remark on someone stopping to pluck leaves and place them in her pouch?"

Ela tried to imagine this scenario. "Perhaps they wouldn't. And perhaps she thought she was picking wild comfrey, if indeed she did pick anything at all. Are you accusing Alice de Gilbert of poisoning her husband?"

His jaw twitched slightly. "I am saying that he was likely

killed by a poison made from the strained leaves or flowers of the foxglove plant. This would have slowed his heart and made him perhaps confused and lethargic, as if drunk."

"He was drinking wine. I just assumed..." Ela recalled the way he'd swayed and had to be helped upstairs. "He seemed tipsy, that's all."

"And he went to sleep, perhaps feeling tired and a little inebriated, but during the night his heart gave out and he died."

"His wife woke me in the middle of the night in a great state of distress. I didn't believe her when she said he was dead. Surely she wouldn't have done that if she'd killed him herself?"

"Perhaps she felt the need to feign shock and grief in order to allay suspicion?"

Ela blew out a slow breath. "I admit that she didn't feign grief. She did seem truly shocked, though."

"As coroner I feel duty bound to suggest that Alice de Gilbert is a suspect in her husband's murder."

Ela swallowed. "I'm afraid she's returned home for her husband's funeral. Do you expect me to send guards to arrest her?" She realized she sounded a little indignant.

"You are the sheriff, my lady, and you must pursue the course of action that you see fit."

She stiffened. He had—quite sensibly—laid the entire matter at her feet. "I admit that I can't imagine my dear friend committing such a vile act of murder. And I also can't bring myself to create a spectacle and a sensation by sending armed men out to arrest her as she rides behind her husband's coffin." She paused and sighed. "But I did promise that she could return to extend her visit after the funeral, so I expect her back here within a few days. She shall be questioned then and arrested if necessary." Her voice quavered a little. “So belladonna—a deadly poison—is an antidote for foxglove, another deadly poison?”

“Yes. And vice versa. One quickens the pace of the heart, and one slows it.”

“How extraordinary. How did you know about this?”

“Poisons have been studied and written about since Greek and Roman times. Unfortunately, the poisoner’s art is an ancient one.”

CHAPTER 5

Ela spent the evening reading through books of medical treatises from her library, looking for anything she could find about poisons. It appalled her that the means for murder grew all around them in the woods and fields and that—in the absence of a suspicious coroner—the crime could easily be passed off as a natural illness.

The next morning she was still poring over a tome as the children came down to breakfast. "Are you still reading books about poisons?" asked Petronella. "Wouldn't it be better for your soul if you were to fill your mind with prayer?"

Ela blinked, the picture of mandrake that she'd been staring at swimming in her mind. "I dare say it would, but then the crimes of Wiltshire might go unpunished."

"You speak as if there weren't perfectly capable men all around you to handle such matters. It would be far more seemly if you were to take the veil."

"And one day I shall, but not yet. Your younger siblings need me as their mother more than Christ needs me as his bride."

Petronella blew out a breath. "When am I to finally enjoy the peace of the cloister? I'm almost of age."

"I promise you that you shall take your vows at the new convent I am founding. The site is chosen—it's a field called Snails Mead near the village of Lacock—and the plans are well underway. All that remains is for us to build it."

"But that could take a lifetime!" whined Petronella. "Meanwhile I'm stuck here in the castle with all these uncouth soldiers and the hustle and bustle of this hall when I crave the quiet of a cell. Can I not take my vows with the sisters of Wilton?"

"Your earthly trials will prepare you all the better for life as a nun. It's important to know the world so that you can better pray for it."

"I don't understand why I can't just join a different order that already exists. What about Amesbury Abbey?"

"Such a wish seems petulant and selfish," scolded Ela. "Do you realize it will require a great deal of money for you to enjoy the contemplative life? Would you have our family give a great endowment to the Sisters of Amesbury or Wilton as well as pouring money into the creation of the new convent at Lacock?"

Petronella blinked. "How does it cost money? I shall barely eat a thing, and I promise to wear the oldest clothes they give me without complaining. I shan't require servants or any special luxuries."

"A lifetime of food and raiment and the repair of the roof over your head is a great expense even if you are frugal as a mouse! A cloistered life is a luxury that only girls from wealthy families can afford. Surely you can find the patience to wait for the monastery that I'm already pouring money into."

"But what if it takes years?"

"It will take years. But rest assured, as I live and breathe it shall be built and we shall both go there at last."

Ela's mother, on her way to London from her Wiltshire manor, arrived while they were talking. Elsie took her cloak, and she came to join them at the table.

"Grandmamma," said Petronella. "Do tell Mama to make haste with the plans for the new convent at Lacock. I live for the day when all three of us will walk the cloisters there together."

Alianore crossed herself. "Heaven forbid."

"What do you mean, Grandmamma?"

"I could hardly take the veil while I'm still married to my dear husband Jean, could I?"

"Well, no, but—"

"But what? You're hoping he'll fall from his horse and snap his neck? Or perhaps contract the pox? Or drown in a millrace?" Alianore helped herself to a hot bread roll fresh from the cook's oven.

"Well, no, but he will die eventually, won't he?"

"Not if I can help it." Alianore winked at Ela. "I've already buried three husbands and I intend to keep this one alive—and myself out of a nunnery—for as long as I can."

"Why don't you want to be a nun?"

"Do you know they wear the same clothing for months on end? That when the seasons change, their dismal colorless vestments are all packed up in a trunk and the old clothes from last year just handed out to everyone, with no care for who wore them before and got stains on them?"

"I'm sure they wash them in between wearers, Grandmamma."

"I don't care if they boil them overnight. I'd rather wear my own clothes than a rough woolen garment that someone else sweated into all last summer." Alianore feigned a shudder. "No, I'd rather die in the comfort of my London house, where all my friends can come visit me and where I can tell the cook what to make me for supper rather than accept a wooden bowl of whatever tasteless pottage the abbess orders."

Ela hid her smile behind her hand. Her mother so loved luxuries, company and entertainments that it was impossible to imagine her entering a cloister except under extreme duress.

"Mama wants to become a nun," said Petronella, with a pointed look at Ela as if she now doubted her intentions.

"Your mother is made of far sterner tuff than I am," said Alianore, taking a cup of hot spiced wine from the serving girl. "She's lasted far longer than I did in this drafty castle, for one thing. Of course she *will* want to be the abbess…"

"Why do you say that?" asked Ela, somewhat taken aback.

"Because you absolutely must be in charge of everything." Alianore helped herself to some apricot compote. "You can't help yourself."

"That's not true!" protested Ela.

"It most certainly is true, and the marvelous part is that you're very good at it," said Alianore. "I'm sure you'll make an excellent abbess."

"Perhaps Petronella will want to be abbess?" suggested Ela, looking at her daughter.

"Oh, no, that would feed my pride. I must constantly mortify my pride in order to secure my place at God's right hand. I'd much prefer to be a humble sister."

Ela felt chastened. Her pride could probably use a lot of mortification, but she certainly didn't crave it. Truth be told, she probably would want to be the abbess.

CONSIDERABLE TREPIDATION STALKED Ela once she received word that Alice was on her way back. For one thing, she hadn't told her mother that Alice was a suspect in her husband's death and wanted for questioning by the coroner. For another, she hadn't told Alice that, either.

She'd contemplated writing to Alice to alert her to Haughton's findings and tell her she was now under suspicion. But what would happen if Alice took this as a warning and either refused to come back or removed herself to some remote location where she might never be found?

Part of Ela wished for just such an outcome, but she was sheriff and as such was morally obliged to pursue the quest for justice, even when it was inconvenient or personally painful. She tried to focus on the best-case scenario, in which Alice had a perfectly good explanation for why there was foxglove in her husband's tonic and would be speedily exonerated of the crime—preferably without having to go before a jury.

Alice arrived back at Salisbury castle late in the afternoon, after a full day of travel.

"Oh, poor dear Alice," said Alianore when her arrival was announced.

"Why do you say that?" said Ela, alarm shooting through her. Did her mother somehow know of the accusations against her?

"Losing her husband so suddenly! It's a terrible blow, which—as you know—I've suffered more than once myself."

"Yes, of course." Ela hoped that Alice would at least pretend to be a little bit forlorn.

Instead Alice entered the hall with a brisk stride and a cheerful smile on her face. "Ela darling! Thank you so much for having me back again. I'd be at such a loose end by myself right now." Elsie hurried forward to take her traveling cloak.

Alianore rose. "My deepest condolences," she said in a sonorous voice. "My heart weeps with yours."

Alice paused, looking a bit stunned.

"You remember my mother, Alianore?" asked Ela.

"Of course I do," said Alice, taking Alianore's offered hand and pressing her lips to it. "Though it's been so many years since I had the pleasure of dwelling under your roof."

"And back then it was because your poor dear mother lay at death's door. I'm sorry that we meet again under such tragic circumstances, but perhaps I can help lift your heart as I've been widowed three times myself. I lost Ela's father when I was about your age. What a blow that was! I thought I'd never recover. At least I had Ela to dote on or I'd have quite lost my mind."

"I've not been blessed with children," said Alice quietly. For the first time since her arrival she did look like a grieving widow. "And I'd only just lost my dear father so I am a bit at sea." Elsie returned with a jug of spiced wine and some cups.

"We must cheer her up, mustn't we, Ela," said Alianore, with some enthusiasm.

Ela suspected that now was not the right time to bring up any accusations of poisoning. "Yes, of course."

"Sometimes a diversion is just what one needs. A visit to London for some amusements, for example," said Alianore.

Ela reflected that was the last thing she would have wanted in the wake of William's death. On the other hand, she had thrown herself into pursuit of the role of sheriff, and that had been diversion enough.

"I've never been to London," said Alice softly. "I've always wanted to, but my family and then my husband preferred a quiet life in the country."

"She's never been to London!" said Alianore to Ela, eyes wide. She turned to Alice. "Well, my dear, we must rectify that at once. I have the most charming house there, and I shall put it quite at your disposal. I have many friends in the city, and we shall dine among them and perhaps even find you a new husband."

"Mother! Her husband is only just buried. She's hardly ready for a new one yet."

Elsie arrived with a large platter of nutmeat tarts and a pile of linen napkins.

Alice glanced at Ela, then back at Alianore. "I'd like to find a new husband while I still might have a child."

"Quite! And while my Ela has a fiercely independent spirit, most of us women feel quite lost without a husband at our sides to steady and guide us."

Ela wanted to roll her eyes. Alianore ruled her good-natured husband with an iron fist and made nearly every decision in their household.

Alice nodded enthusiastically. "I don't want to do anything...improper, of course, but I would welcome the chance to meet a suitable husband."

Still not a good time to bring up the poisoning accusation.

"I've only just arrived here myself," said Alianore. "I was planning a visit of two weeks or more, but I see no reason not to head immediately to London if the prospect appeals to you. We can enjoy the quieter entertainments before the excessive festivities and drunken revelry of the Christmas season."

"I'd be delighted to accompany you."

"Ela can stay here and work, and leave you quite in my hands."

Alarm rippled through Ela at the thought of Alice melting away into the crowds of London and never facing and refuting the charges against her. "What makes you think I don't wish to come as well?"

"You're always so busy chasing after thieves and murderers." She looked at Alice. "She barely has time to breathe."

The only currently accused murderer in Wiltshire is seated at my table with us. "My co-sheriff, John Dacus, can take over the responsibilities of the office in my absence. I shall take advantage of the opportunity to do some shopping."

"Will you buy us presents for Christmas?" asked little Ellie, her face brightening.

"I might," said Ela. A trip to London now would provide a perfect opportunity to buy elegant gifts for her older married children as well as some trinkets for the younger ones. "But only if you are as good as gold in my absence."

"I promise I will be," said Ellie. "Won't I?" She implored her brother Nicky to agree with her. He nodded enthusiastically.

Ela was grateful that her children didn't mind her going away without them. She didn't like to bring them to London, where travel by carriage was difficult and even walking held a risk of being trampled or lost in the crush of the busy streets.

"Excellent. We shall leave tomorrow morning and stay at my favorite inn on the way," said Alianore.

"Not too early, though, please," said Ela. "I must meet with Giles Haughton before I leave, and I'd like Alice to be there too." She glanced at Alice.

"Whatever for?" asked Alianore, looking astonished.

"He has some questions...about Sir Humphrey's death."

"What kind of questions?" probed Alianore. "Surely he can't mean to torment a freshly bereaved widow?"

Ela glanced at Alice, who—busy tasting a nutmeat—didn't look very concerned. "I'm not really sure. Hopefully it won't take long."

She liked the idea that Haughton knew her carriage was waiting at the gates. It might make his inquisition of Alice more perfunctory. Of course if he pressed her to call a jury or even to arrest Alice she'd have to postpone the journey to London...

But hopefully that wouldn't happen.

THE NEXT MORNING Alice was alive with excitement about the journey to London. "How many days does it take to travel there?"

"We usually manage it with two days of travel and an overnight stay at an inn. Luckily there are several safe and comfortable establishments on the way. If the roads are difficult it can take longer, but at this time of year they should be reasonably good."

"Will we share a room?"

"Oh, no, the inns I frequent are very large and have plenty of chambers. You'll share with Minnie, your maidservant. I know I couldn't rest my head alone in a building full of strangers."

"I've never stayed in a large inn before," said Alice. "I'm sure there will be all sorts of fascinating characters. Will we take meals in the public rooms?"

"I usually take my meals in my room in order to avoid meeting fascinating characters," admitted Ela with a smile. "But we can eat in the public rooms if you like. Though my mother may not have the stomach to join us."

"Giles Haughton is here!" called Albert, the porter.

"Oh, good," said Ela, trying her best to conceal her trepidation. She'd sent a messenger for him with the news that Alice was here for him to interview. "Send him to the armory."

She didn't want the discussion to take place in the great hall, filled as it was with prying ears and eyes. The armory had thick walls and a solid door and was thus an excellent place for a private conversation. Ela led Alice out of the hall and across the hallway to the armory.

"Goodness me, you're ready to fight a war!" exclaimed Alice, when she saw the rows of shining blades arranged in on the walls.

"We must always be ready to defend the castle from a siege," said Ela, trying not to laugh at her friend's surprise. "God willing we'll never need to, but this castle houses the king's garrison and we have weapons for an army should the need arise."

Haughton entered and bowed slightly to both of them.

"God be with you, Sir Giles," said Ela.

"And with you." He nodded to both of them. "I presume you've informed your friend of my findings?"

"I've said nothing at all," said Ela. "You may tell her yourself."

Alice looked perplexed and glanced from Ela to Haughton. "What findings?"

"I tested the tonic that was found in your husband's chamber and discovered that it contained extract of digitalis."

Alice frowned. "What does that mean?"

"Digitalis is the foxglove plant," said Ela.

"But we didn't put any foxglove in the tonic," said Alice. "It's poisonous, isn't it?"

"It is indeed," said Haughton. "But is also readily mistaken for comfrey at the rosette stage, when no flowers are apparent. Is it possible that you included leaves that you thought were comfrey?"

"I don't think so," said Alice. "I believe all the herbs came from the gardens here at the castle, and I don't imagine they contain poisonous weeds."

"That's what I said," added Ela with some relief.

"Then how do you suppose that the tonic your husband

drank contained a deadly amount of digitalis?" Haughton peered at Alice.

"I can't imagine," said Alice. She looked remarkably unconcerned, which was good because it made her seen more innocent than if she'd looked nervous and fidgety.

"Did anyone else have access to the tonic he drank that night?"

"My husband's manservant, Clovis, would have helped get him ready for bed. And my maid Minnie likely entered the room to stoke the fire and arrange my washing water. Neither of them slept in the chamber, though. They both slept downstairs near the kitchens."

"The manservant helped Sir Humphrey upstairs, with assistance from Bill Talbot, then came down very soon afterward, according to my staff," said Ela. "He didn't go upstairs again until dawn."

"Is this normal?" asked Haughton of Alice.

Alice glanced at Ela. "At home my husband and I slept in separate bedrooms and his manservant did usually sleep in there with him. I had asked both servants to sleep downstairs that particular night...."

"To give her and her husband some privacy," added Ela, hoping that Haughton would remember why.

"I see. So you were all alone with your husband that night?"

"Yes." Alice was starting to look a little nervous. Her eyelashes flickered, and Ela could see her breath rising and falling more rapidly. "He was dead asleep and didn't rouse even when I tried to wake him." She glanced at Ela.

"I told Sir Giles that you were hoping for an opportunity to get with child that night and that the tonic was intended to stimulate him."

Alice's face flushed slightly. "It sounds terrible now that he's dead, doesn't it?"

"Not at all," said Ela.

"A tonic with digitalis in it would do the opposite of stimulate him, I'm afraid. It slows bodily functions to the point of extinguishing them in high enough doses."

"As I've explained, it certainly didn't end up in his tonic on purpose," said Ela.

"Which begs the question, how did it get in there?"

"There was another bottle in the room that night," said Alice. "A brown glass one that he brought with him. I remember seeing it on the floor next to his small traveling chest."

Haughton looked at Ela. "This is certainly new information. What do you know of this second bottle?"

"Nothing. I've never heard of it before. I don't remember seeing it in the room."

"Could it still be there?"

"Very unlikely. The room would have been stripped and cleaned, perhaps by Elsie. Sir Humphrey's chest was packed and sent home with him. I presume that his manservant, Clovis, packed his possessions."

"I'd like to talk to whoever was in the room and saw this second bottle."

"The brown bottle was a tonic he brought with him," said Alice. "He suffered from gout and took it every night before bed."

"Why didn't you mention it before?" asked Ela, truly perplexed.

"I didn't know it was important. You didn't say there was anything wrong with the tonic until now."

"Alice did leave to return home for the funeral before you discovered that the tonic was poisoned," said Ela. "Perhaps the tonic he brought from home was the poisoned one?"

"But the dregs of liquid I tested were in the green glass bottle that Elsie retrieved from the room."

"I wonder if they could have been mixed together? The tonic we prepared was quite palatable. If his other tonic didn't taste good, might his manservant have poured it into the sweet-tasting one?" Ela realized she was grasping at straws.

"I suppose Clovis might have mixed the tonics when he put him to bed," said Alice. "I did give him our tonic to take up with him."

"Where is Clovis now?" asked Haughton.

"I suppose he's still at the family castle near Mere, preparing to work for his new master, my husband's oldest son, Peveril."

Ela felt a flush of relief that someone else had been responsible for the bottle. At least if Alice was telling the truth.... "We must summon Clovis to find out what he did with the bottle after dinner. I'll write to his master at once. They live in the far west of Wiltshire but still under my jurisdiction so they can't refuse."

"What was in the other tonic that your husband drank regularly?" asked Haughton.

"I'm afraid I don't know," said Alice. "Our cook prepared it for him."

Ela turned to Haughton. "Let's summon the manservant and the cook here, and they can stay at the castle while you speak with them. I won't be here myself as Alice and I are going to London." She paused to see how this fresh announcement sat with him.

His eyes widened very slightly. "To London?"

"My mother's idea. Just for a few days, as you know I don't like to desert my duties for long. John Dacus can manage in my absence."

"Of course, my lady." She could tell he disapproved but had no intention of questioning her judgment, especially in front of another person.

"Do you have any other questions for Alice before we leave? Our carriage is being readied for the journey to London."

Haughton drew in a slow breath. Ela felt her stomach tighten.

"Would you say your husband was in good health?" he asked.

"His digestion sometimes gave him grief," said Alice without hesitation. "And his gout could be very painful if he indulged in too much meat. But he wasn't prone to falling sick very often."

"Perhaps it was the unaccustomed rich food and drink that sickened him," suggested Ela.

"Perhaps," agreed Alice simply. She really did look as innocent as a newborn babe.

"It seems far more likely that it was the digitalis contained in his tonic that killed him," said Haughton drily.

"Yes, of course," said Ela. "We must ask his manservant if his other tonic contained that substance."

"It's not impossible. It is sometimes used in very small doses to increase vitality in cases of severe dropsy."

"How fascinating. I can't imagine I would dare to experiment with the beneficial effects of a deadly poison. Rest assured that we did not put any digitalis in the tonic we made for him here. We'll continue to investigate how the poison came to be in his tonic, and in the meantime Alice will be safe in my company in London."

She said it as if Alice might be in some immediate danger of being poisoned instead of being the main suspect in her husband's murder. "Did your husband suffer from dropsy?"

"I don't think so," said Alice innocently.

Haughton turned to Ela. "I remain, as always, at your service, my lady." Haughton nodded to her, and then to Alice. Ela wondered if this odd remark was a hint that he recognized his subordinate position to her and that—although he might prefer to continue his interrogation of Alice—he would demur to her request.

"Thank you, Sir Giles. In the meantime I shall send two guards to retrieve Clovis, the manservant, and bring him here to the castle for questioning, along with the cook who prepared the tonic. If you learn anything important from them, please write to me at once."

CHAPTER 6

Alice and Ela set out for London in Ela's carriage, with a retinue of guards riding in front and behind and with their maids Elsie and Minnie riding inside with them. Alianore traveled in her own carriage with her dogs and her own servants.

"I've only been to London one time," said Elsie, peering out the window down the first stretch of the London road. "And that's when the child-slavers bought me and took me there."

Alice looked startled.

"Ela rescued me and gave me a place," explained Elsie to Alice.

"It's true," admitted Ela. "A group of evil men had set up a business in procuring children and selling them on the Continent. I managed to find out where they were hiding the children and set them free."

"Your work as sheriff sounds very exciting," said Alice.

"Not always. Much of my time is spent resolving small disputes between the townspeople and trying them for crimes such as cheating their customers by altering a scale or putting sand in their bread loaves."

"I could never do anything like that," said Alice. "You must have nerves of steel to tangle with hardened criminals."

"I have a strong sense of justice, and I hate to see the weak preyed on," said Ela. "Some crimes light a fire in my belly, and I can't rest until it's extinguished by catching the perpetrator—with God's help, of course."

THE CARRIAGE RATTLED through the Surrey hills as dusk settled over their carriage.

"We won't stop before dark?" asked Alice.

"Not at this time of year. The days are too short and the journey would take three or four days. I prefer to press on. The innkeepers are ready to welcome us at any reasonable hour, and even some quite unreasonable ones. This is a well-traveled route and they're used to accommodating travelers arriving from great distances away."

The horses' hooves clattering on cobbles alerted Ela that they'd arrived in the courtyard of her favorite inn. The Cross and Bell was a great stone structure that loomed over one side of the London road near Bagshot. As large as a bishop's palace, and almost as luxurious, it boasted at least thirty chambers and at suppertime the tables were always laden with fare that wouldn't look out of place in her own hall.

A servant opened the door and helped them down onto the cobbles. Lanterns mounted on the walls lit up the courtyard with shimmering light, and Alice gazed up at the high stone walls of the inn. "It's enormous! I thought it would look like a country tavern."

"It's a very fine inn. I'm not sure if the king himself has

stayed here, but I'd bet a silver mark that most of his courtiers have slept under this roof at one time or another."

"It must be very expensive," said Alice, staring around the courtyard, where servants bustled to and fro, leading horses and carrying wood and leather chests.

Sometimes Alice seemed almost simple, but Ela reflected that she'd been so deprived of life experience that her knowledge of the world was more like that of a twelve-year-old child than a woman in her thirties.

The innkeeper's wife, a rotund woman with a crisp white fillet and veil covering her hair and framing her rosy face, greeted them effusively. "Welcome, my lady. I trust you have traveled well. Your favorite chambers have been prepared and fires laid."

"Our journey has been smooth, thanks be to God," replied Ela with a smile. "My guest and I would like to take dinner in your dining rooms, if we may."

"Most certainly, my lady. There's a fine roast pig just brought out and we have an excellent burgundy wine just arrived from the Continent yesterday. Will your mother be joining you?" Alianore was a regular visitor at the inn both with and without her husband.

"I suspect not." Ela would be shocked if her mother was willing to risk the hurly-burly of the inn's dining rooms. "But perhaps you'd better ask her."

Ela and Alice were led to their chambers by the porters, who carried their traveling chests, leaving Elsie and Minnie with their hands free and their eyes darting in all directions, amazed at the sights and sounds of the busy inn. They climbed a dark oak staircase to the third floor, their way lit by braziers on the stone walls.

On arrival in her chamber, Ela found the fire blazing in the grate. The green damask bed curtains, pulled back with a silken cord, looked reassuringly clean. The wood floors shone, with clean rush matting unrolled next to the bed rather than the strewn herbs favored in less fastidious inns. A sprig of lavender hung from a hook on the wall, filling the room with its scent.

Elsie's eyes sparkled. "What a fine place, my lady. It's almost nicer than the castle."

Ela smile. "There's nowhere as nice as home, though perhaps a bunch of lavender hung in my solar would be a nice addition."

"I shall hang it myself when we return home." Elsie had already unpacked a fresh veil from Ela's chest and shook it out. She pulled the pins from Ela's fillet and removed it, laid the fresh veil, then pinned it back again. Then she gasped. "Oh! I should have asked if you wanted to wash your face first, my lady!"

"I shall rely on your judgment of whether it's clean enough," said Ela, staring right at her.

"It looks very nice, my lady."

"A benefit of traveling in the dry confines of a carriage." Traveling by carriage could be uncomfortable, as one bounced over every rut and pothole in the road on the wooden wheels. It was also very dull compared to riding a good horse, but it had its practicalities.

Ela washed her hands in the bowl of water that shimmered on a side table, and Elsie dried them with a clean linen cloth hanging next to it. She then looked in on her mother, who had commandeered the largest chamber in the inn, just down the hall.

"You know I never eat in a public dining room," protested Alianore. "You might catch something."

"I suspect we'll manage to survive dinner without contracting leprosy," said Ela. "But I wish you a good night's sleep."

Next they went to Alice's chamber, where Alice and

Minnie were still in the early stages of getting ready for dinner. "We couldn't resist opening the window and peeking out. It's too dark to see anything, though!"

"I always make sure to get rooms facing over the surrounding fields. The rooms over the courtyard can be noisy even in the wee hours, with people coming and going."

"Should I change my dress?" asked Alice, looking down at her plain gray-blue gown.

"There's no need. Dinner isn't a formal occasion. In fact there can be some rather strange characters in the dining rooms, so I prefer to look as unobtrusive as possible."

They headed downstairs again, with Elsie and Minnie—who wasn't much older than Elsie—giggling behind them. "I haven't eaten in the dining rooms since my husband died," said Ela. She'd never eaten in any dining room without a male escort, usually in the form of Bill Talbot, if her husband wasn't present, but two guards followed close behind and she knew she could call on them if needed.

They walked across one end of the courtyard, where a party of horsemen were just arriving, and through a great stone archway. A porter bowed slightly and opened one of a pair of great iron-studded oak doors. A wonderful smell of cooked meat assaulted Ela's senses, and she stepped into the first room, where a whole pig lay spread on a long table, its mouth stuffed with figs.

Men milled about, helping themselves to the roasted meat, and to side dishes of mashed turnip, candied carrots and other unidentifiable delicacies.

"We'll take our seats at a table and Elsie and Minnie will fetch our food," said Ela. A porter led them into a room with a shining table of black oak, long enough to seat about eight persons. Sturdy carved chairs stood at each end, and benches ran along each side. Braziers on the walls filled the room with flickering orange light and a fire crackled in the grate at the far end.

"We have our own private room?"

"Yes. Otherwise we might be forced to share a table with masons and ships' captains and goodness only knows who else."

"That might be rather fascinating," said Alice, casting a glance behind her at the men gathered around the great roast.

Ela and Alice sat at the two ends of the table and Ela directed Elsie and Minnie to retrieve platters of a variety of foods and bring them to the table. Servants from the inn, young men dressed in dark attire, entered with a jug of wine and a stack of crisp linen napkins. One servant poured the wine into heavy goblets, and the other gave them each two napkins. Another servant, this time a pretty young woman in a blue dress, brought them bowls of water to clean their fingers in.

Alice stared around the room as if mesmerized by all the activity. "I hope my next husband is a man that travels."

"Be careful what you wish for. When his brother, the late King John, was alive, it seemed like my dear William was never home. The king liked to travel between his various estates and enjoy the hospitality of each with his closest friends. I accompanied William on some of the journeys early in our marriage, but once I was pregnant and had young children I found them too tiring. I stayed home, and he roamed all over the country without me." Ela took a sip of her wine, which, as promised, was smooth and rich without a hint of bitterness.

"I forgot that your husband's brother was King John. I suppose you can't say no to the king, even if he is your brother-in-law! But didn't you miss the amusements at court?"

"I preferred the company of my children and my own hearth to endless nights of revelry."

"I'm sure I should as well if I'm lucky enough to enjoy them."

The maids, grinning and chattering, brought back platters piled high with all the delicacies on the buffet table. "Oh, my goodness some of those men are too cheeky!" exclaimed Elsie. Her eyes sparkled.

Alarm flared in Ela's gut. "Don't encourage them. They might be rogues looking to take advantage of a young girl." Her last chambermaid had become pregnant by a much older rascal who'd seduced her.

The girls looked somewhat chastened. "Yes, my lady," said Elsie. "I'm sure I didn't mean to attract attention."

"I know, Elsie, I didn't mean to scold you." Ela felt a little contrite. Elsie navigated the rowdy garrison soldiers at the castle without a hint of flirtation. On the other hand, the girl was only just starting to come out of her shell these last few months, and was approaching the age when all young girls started to think about men and their marriage prospects, so perhaps she'd have to watch her more closely.

They passed a pleasant and uneventful dinner, enjoying their fill of roast pork and grilled eel and other dishes that would soon be forbidden during the long weeks of Advent, then retired to their chambers to sleep. Elsie slept on a pallet at the end of Ela's curtained bed, and Ela heard her get up at least twice during the night to stoke the fire. The room was toasty warm when she emerged from her curtained cocoon in the morning.

Rather than brave the dining room again, Ela ordered for a small meal to be prepared for them to eat in their carriage, and they were back on the London road less than half an hour after dawn.

Alice and Minnie both had drooping eyelids once the

carriage settled into a rhythm of rolling and bumping down the road.

"Did you not sleep well?" asked Ela.

"Too much excitement," said Alice. "I could hear voices and laughter at all hours. And the prospect of seeing the great city of London tonight has my nerves all a-jangle."

"Catch some sleep on the way, then, as we have a long day of travel ahead of us and will arrive after dark."

THEY REACHED the outer ring of villages around the city just as the sun was setting, and Alice peered out the window marveling over the smoke-smudged skyline of the great city, set against the pink evening sky. "That must be the White Tower," she exclaimed. "And look at all those church towers!"

"My mother's London house is just outside the city walls on a leafy street of houses between the city and Westminster."

Alice looked confused. "I thought Westminster was in the city?"

"Oh, no. It's on Thorney Island, a short distance away. I suppose they wanted room for the king's palace as well as the large hall that houses the law courts. And I suppose the traffic coming and going to conduct the king's business doesn't get held up in the morning and evening crush at the city gates."

Both carriages pulled up outside Ela's mother's house. Servants flew out the front and side doors to welcome them, help them down from their carriages, and carry their luggage indoors.

Alianore's house was large, always impeccably clean, and furnished with beautiful items that Alianore collected from abroad and commissioned from local craftsmen. Alice stared in astonishment at the jewel-colored tapestries on the walls, the engraved silver candlesticks and the painted frieze that ran along the top of the walls. "I can't imagine the throne room in the king's palace is any finer than this room."

"It isn't," said Ela. "And I know that from firsthand experience."

Alianore looked pleased that her decor was appreciated. "We'll have a very light supper, then I'm sure you're all ready for bed."

Alice looked like she wanted to protest but agreed instead. "I am looking forward to seeing the city tomorrow."

"Don't worry, I shall take us on a tour," said Ela. "We'll ride on horseback, or perhaps even walk, so you shall see everything."

THE NEXT MORNING, they rode through the nearest gate of the city on two of her mother's good horses. Smoke filled the air—as always, even in summer—along with the aromas of a hundred different foods cooking.

Men and women bustled around them, shouting, laughing, talking among themselves. Alice stared at everyone as if they were mummers in a play. Once they reached Ela's favorite street market, they dismounted and handed the reins to two guards. "Don't buy anything at the price they tell you," whispered Ela. "There's always room for negotiation."

Ela's favorite stall sold books of all kinds. Some of them were hundreds of years old, copies of ancient texts translated into Latin from the Greek. It was here that's she'd bought some of her most treasured texts, like the medical treatises of Trota of Salerno, which dealt in great detail with matters of pregnancy and childbirth.

"I'm not sure I should buy anything," said Alice. "Since my

life is rather up in the air, right now." Then something caught her eye. Ela followed her over to a stall selling ribbon, and Alice picked up a length of woven silk ribbon decorated with white lilies against a red and gold pattern. "Though I suppose I could add some ornamentation to my gowns. My husband didn't like such fripperies." She looked up at Ela. "My late husband." There was more than a hint of a twinkle in her eyes.

"That ribbon would complement a green gown," said Ela, remembering that Alice had one.

"And perhaps I should purchase some new gowns as well. Of finer stuff." Alice looked up from the stall and glanced around. "Softer wool that would drape better than this old one I'm wearing."

And show off your figure. Alice was already thinking about catching the eye of any eligible suitors.

"I can show you the shop where I've bought some new gowns for myself and my girls. They have striking colors that aren't available locally. I suspect they source dyes from all over Europe and even along the Silk Road."

Alice bought several lengths of ribbon. They walked to a dressmaker in a small, dark shop nearby, where Alice was measured and ordered three dresses, a deep blue, a golden yellow and a rich burgundy. She fondled a deep scarlet red but—to Ela's relief—thought better of it.

"I shall sew the ribbon onto the hems and cuffs when they are finished," she said excitedly. In another shop, run by an older woman whose hands brandished a needle as if it were another digit, Alice bought several diaphanous veils. She tried them on and admired—in the polished brass mirror—the way they wafted around her face, in contrast to the limp linen of her previous ones. She also bought two crisp white fillets, each with a pie crust edge and matching barbettes that were stitched to her exact measurements as they stood in the shop.

"I'm being awfully extravagant," whispered Alice, as they left the store. Minnie and Elsie shared the burden of her purchases, folded and tied with cord into neat bundles. "I should be more careful with my money."

Ela hadn't dared to ask about her finances. It seemed so deeply personal a matter to broach with anyone, and a very sensitive subject for a new widow. She knew she would have been mortified if anyone had pried into her affairs in the weeks after William's death. There were huge debts owed to the king and the imminent loss of profitable wardships that she needed time to navigate—which she did by arranging the marriages of her children to her husband's wealthy wards.

Still...Alice seemed so innocent and unworldly. She would hate for her friend to spend her way into financial embarrassment out of sheer ignorance. "Has your husband's will been read yet?"

"Not yet. His sons will manage that and write to me about it."

Ela frowned. "You should make sure to have your own lawyer review the documents. His sons may try to cheat you if they think they can get away with it."

"I don't have a lawyer," said Alice. "And at least I know I'll have the estate I came into the marriage with. That will suffice for me until I marry again."

Was her friend really so naive? A husband would be every bit as interested in the wealth she brought to the marriage as in the way her new gowns draped over her breasts. Especially since she was a widow and not in the first flush of youth.

"I know an excellent lawyer," said Ela. "Spicewell is his name. He's officially retired but is a good friend of my mother's and has managed some very tricky affairs for me. He has an office at Westminster and with luck we can make an appointment to visit him while we're in London. If he'll take the case I'm sure he'll manage to wring the greatest possible amount out of your late husband's estate for your settlement. You're entitled to a full third as outlined in the Magna Carta."

"Oh, I don't really want his money. I shall have a new husband soon." Alice glanced fondly at her new dresses and ribbons. "At least I hope I shall. Do you think I'll receive proposals?"

Ela wanted to shock some sense into her, but didn't want to frighten her or crush her confidence by spelling out the difficulties an older, not-rich widow might have in gaining a suitable husband. She might even have to accept a proposal from someone who wasn't of noble blood. Ela had heard stories of widowed noblewomen forced to marry a merchant or tradesman out of desperation. "All in good time, dear Alice. All in good time."

CHAPTER 7

After three days of shopping and showing Alice the sights of the city, Ela began to wish she was back in Salisbury, attending to official business.

"You can't leave already!" protested Alianore. "Alice hasn't even attended an entertainment yet."

"I would welcome an opportunity to wear one of my new gowns," said Alice, looking at Alianore. "Ela helped me choose such fine ones and trim that complements them so perfectly. What a waste for only the servants at my remote country estate to see them."

Alice had already expressed considerable trepidation about moving to her own manor all alone—well, except for the servants that would be required to manage the house and grounds.

"I couldn't agree more, my dear. I have an open invitation to dine with the mayor of London. Perhaps we shall see if we might join him at his table tonight. He's a marvelous host with a very talented cook that hails from Paris. I've eaten some extraordinary things at his table."

"How does one invite oneself to dinner with the mayor?" asked Ela, out of genuine curiosity.

"One simply sends one's regards, my dear. I shall dispatch a messenger at once." Alianore called for a boy and had him memorize a verbal message. The boy, dressed in rather fine clothing for a servant, seemed familiar with the task and left at once. "The mayor is wonderfully amusing and has the most unusual guests. Jean enjoys him tremendously as well." Alianore's husband was away on a visit involving a hunting party.

"Does he have a wife?" Ela wondered if her mother was already matchmaking.

"Sadly she died in childbirth some years ago. But I don't recommend him as a suitable candidate for marriage. He's rather too charming to be a safe choice of husband."

Ela didn't find this entirely reassuring. "And are his guests suitable company for two unmarried widows?" asked Ela.

"Of course, my dear. He's the mayor of London!" Ela didn't find this answer entirely reassuring. Still, it might mollify Alice's sense of adventure to have one evening out before they returned to the quieter atmosphere of Wiltshire.

"How do I look?" Alice walked into the parlor, where Ela and her mother were sipping cups of hot spiced wine in front of the fire.

"Resplendent!" cried Alianore. "That deep burgundy brings out the color in your cheeks, and that veil wafts like gossamer."

Alice smiled gratefully. Her eyes sparkled, and Ela could see that she felt beautiful in her new gown and veil. She also wore a new belt made of delicate golden chain that accented her slim waist and made her look younger than her years.

"You look very pretty," said Ela. "The guards might have to beat men away from you with a stick."

"Oh, don't let them do that," said Alice. "I need a husband!"

"I'm afraid it really is too soon to be thinking about a husband just yet," said Alianore. "I know this as I've been in your unfortunate position three times myself, but one must at least make a show of mourning the last one for six months or so."

"Especially when you've been accused of poisoning him," said Ela drily.

"Ela!" cried Alianore. "I won't hear such talk in my house. You don't really think Alice poisoned her husband, do you?"

"Of course not," said Ela. "But we can't ignore the very real possibility that others might think so. The coroner has pronounced it an unnatural death and we have no suspects under arrest yet. That's one of the reasons I'm so keen to return to Salisbury. We sent guards to bring back a servant of Humphrey de Gilbert's who brought a tonic that was also given to him that night and also the cook that prepared the tonic. I look forward to interviewing them."

Alice smoothed the fabric of her dress just below her belt, looking utterly unperturbed by this talk of poisoning.

"It's my duty as sheriff to find and arrest Sir Humphrey's murderer and make sure he's brought to trial," continued Ela.

"We know, dear," said Alianore dismissively. "Though why you wish to spend your time on such unpleasant activities is beyond me. You could be spending the Christmas season here in London with me."

"You know I don't really enjoy that sort of thing," said Ela. Her mother found her lamentably dull, at least in her distaste for festivities and extraneous finery.

"I don't even know if I should enjoy something like that,"

said Alice. "Since I've never attended any entertainments other than my own wedding."

"I'm sure you would and we shall find you a good husband to attend them with once your time of mourning is over," said Alianore. "I have quite a talent for matchmaking, if I say so myself. I'm very disappointed that Ela won't allow me to find her a new husband. Dear William has been gone for nearly two years. With all Ela's advantages we could make a very fine match, perhaps even a prince."

"The last thing I need in my life is some foreign prince who speaks only Rhenish," said Ela. "I'm quite content with my household and children and prefer to be in command of my own destiny."

"Perhaps I should, too, if I already had children to love and raise," said Alice. "But since I don't yet have those blessings I do hope I shan't have to wait too long for them."

"Everything will happen in God's good time," said Ela, trying to convey confidence she didn't entirely feel.

The mayor's private residence was a magnificent house in the city, right on the Thames. It was dark when they arrived but Alice commented on the distinctive wet smell of the river and, as they alighted from the carriage, they could see the Thames shimmering in the moonlight at the end of the street.

Braziers lit up the outside of the house, revealing that the first story was built of cut stone, like a castle, and the upper floors of timber and white plaster constructed in an artful design arranged over several gables.

"What a stunning house," observed Alice.

"The mayor is a man of excellent taste," agreed Alianore.

The grand double doors opened to welcome them, and

serving girls dressed in matching dark red gowns took their cloaks. Candles lined the walls of the entrance hall, illuminating a floor of wood inlaid in different colors like the top of a box. Alice looked half afraid to step on it, so Ela took her arm and drew her in.

"Alianore, my dearest," boomed a loud male voice. "Welcome." A tall man in dark blue, trimmed with black and gold, took her mother's hands and pressed them to his lips. "And Ela."

As her eyes adjusted to the dim light, Ela realized with shock that the man before her was Sir Roger le Duc. She'd relied heavily on his help while trying to find Elsie and the other abducted children more than a year before. "Sir Roger, I hadn't realized you'd traded the sheriff's role for that of mayor."

Her mother had deliberately not told her that their host was Roger le Duc, or she might have protested dining at his table. Charismatic and well-connected, he made her a little uneasy. During her quest for the missing children, she'd sometimes wondered if he was working with her or against her.

Ela offered her hand and he kissed it, his lips lingering a moment longer than was comfortable. Her mother introduced Alice, who was equally flummoxed by their host's effusive attentions.

"Come in, come in! Please be seated at the table. All of our party is here and we shall dine."

Servants ushered them through a carved archway into a room with a long table at the center. The walls were painted in a pattern of rich jewel colors, and candles guttered in a multitude of silver candlesticks as they entered.

From an adjoining room entered two more men, both similarly tall, dark and prosperous-looking, and dressed in fine clothing.

Their host made introductions and Ela found herself greeting two people who she'd never even heard of before, let alone met. They did appear to have titles indicating nobility, even if they were foreign. Ela found herself seated in between one Bernardo Albizzi—a Florentine banker—and their host, who complimented her on her determination and persistence in shutting down the ring of child slavers that they'd hunted together.

The servants brought a first course of roasted quails' eggs in a sweet honey glaze and delicate crisp wafers of bread drizzled with melted cheese.

Albizzi spoke with a heavy accent and explained to Ela that he was here to do business at Westminster. She wondered if he might be lending money to the king himself but was not bold enough to ask. It soon transpired that he was also a keen collector of books and admired some of her favorites, including the works of the ancient philosophers, which he could read in the original Greek.

The length of the table, and the fact that they were both seated on the same side of it made it hard for Ela to see Alice. She did, however, have an excellent view of the third man, who seemed to be regaling Alice with his adventures at sea, including a rather lurid tale of a shipwreck.

"Ela's husband, William, was shipwrecked on the Isle de Ré!" cut in Alianore, who was seated opposite Ela and perhaps wanted to get their end of the table included into this rousing conversation. "He was washed ashore half dead and taken in by the monks at the monastery there. He couldn't even remember his own name! They tended to him for almost a year before he was well enough to return home. Everyone had given him up for dead, except Ela, of course." She smiled at Ela.

Ela felt a wave of sadness. William's happy homecoming had been soured by the fact that she'd just rebuffed a marriage proposal—made on the assumption that William was dead—which she found so insulting that he was forced to take the matter up with the king. The repercussions of these events left him dead—poisoned she was sure—less than a month after his long-awaited return.

The conversation thus turned to the perils of ocean voyages, Alianore lamented over a particularly anxious journey she'd endured on her last return home from Normandy with her husband, Jean. "The sea tossed our ship so violently that we were told to lash ourselves to the masts with rope lest we be thrown overboard or knocked senseless! The cargo included bitter oranges that flew from their baskets and bounced around the hold in all directions. They were forced to furl the sails lest they be shredded to rags, and at one point the main mast creaked so alarmingly we were sure it would break. We made it to Southampton without the ship coming apart, but my stomach was in so many knots I'm sure it was a full week before I could take a bite of food."

"How exciting," exclaimed Alice. "I've never left England's shores. Or even Wiltshire before this week."

The male guests all reassured her that it was far safer to stay home, then entertained each other with yet more harrowing accounts of their many voyages. It was clear that all three men relished travel and perhaps even sought out opportunities to endanger their lives in search of new adventure.

They ate their way through a main course consisting of beaver tail in a savory spiced almond sauce and a colorful array of autumn vegetables. Le Duc insisted that beaver was allowed during the Advent fast, which had just begun, because beavers lived in water and therefore were appropriately fishlike. His explanation was so amusing that Ela almost forgave him for encouraging them to cheat in their fasting.

Ela told le Duc that Elsie, whom they'd freed from her captors in London, was now her personal attendant and thriving in the role.

By the time they'd finished eating delicate cups of gooseberry fool, Ela had drunk far too much wine and laughed too hard and was relieved when her mother announced that it was past her bedtime.

They made their apologies and thanked their host for an excellent evening, and he made them promise to return again soon.

"I ADMIT I am surprised that you associate with such worldly men," said Ela to her mother once they were back in the carriage. "But they are wonderfully entertaining."

"The men of Roger le Duc's family have held the office of mayor and also of sheriff for numerous terms. I've never spent a boring evening at his table."

"The man seated nearest me was most entertaining," said Alice, eyes sparkling. "He's a Breton prince from a very ancient family."

"What was his name again?" asked Alianore. "I didn't quite catch it."

"Adonis d'Ys," said Alice.

"Ys?" asked Alianore. "Is that near Rennes? I can't say I know it."

"He said it's an island off the coast." She looked at Ela. "I suppose it's like the Ile de Ré, where your husband was shipwrecked."

Ela hadn't much liked the look of the mysterious Adonis, who seemed rather too winsome for his own good. "As far as I know, Ys is a place that exists only in legend."

"Apparently the legend is based in fact," said Alianore. "Unless the handsome Adonis is a creature of myth."

Ela peered at Alice. "Did he say what he was doing in London?"

"He has a fleet of ships, and imports and exports goods all over Europe."

Probably just a rich merchant styling himself as some sort of foreign prince to increase his status. "I suppose he must be a descendant of the mythic King Gradlon, whose great palace was built on lands reclaimed from the sea," she said drily.

"Yes," said Alice enthusiastically. "He must be. He asked if he could call on me tomorrow."

Alarm gathered in Ela's chest. "What did you say?"

"I said that I was a guest, so I wasn't sure if I'd be available."

"Good answer," said Alianore. "Some men can be so forward."

"And we'll be gone by then anyway, if all goes according to plan," said Ela. "I've asked the guards to be ready to travel at dawn."

Alice's face fell. "So I won't ever see him again?"

"We don't know anything about him, my dear," said Alianore.

"But he's a friend of the mayor of London. Surely that's recommendation enough." Alice's expression took on an air of desperation. "And he was very handsome."

"Dangerously handsome, I'd say," said Alianore with a lifted brow. "Those flashing dark eyes, that swarthy skin—a touch too piratical for my tastes."

"Especially since King Gradlon died and the entire kingdom of Ys was consumed by the ocean waves."

"When?" asked Alice, in disbelief.

Was dear Alice really gullible enough to believe him related to the mythical king? "Well, according to the legend, which I heard in sung verse from a bard at King John's court, the king's wayward daughter stole the key to the dykes to let her lover into the city. She was so overcome with passion for him that she forgot to close the dykes before the tide came in, and the returning tide swallowed all the land, the palace and everyone in it."

"Surely they drained it!" said Alice. "They'd hardly just abandon the entire kingdom after one mistake."

Alianore was tittering with laugher behind her hand. Even Ela was amused by Alice's abject shock at this unhappy ending. "I'm afraid I don't know," said Ela. "The traveling minstrel who sang the tale didn't continue past all of them being swept far out to sea and never seen again."

Alice looked utterly discomfited, and Ela decided to change the subject. "We're to stay at a different inn on the way back. It's run by the friars at Waverley, and we can attend service in their beautiful abbey. We can offer prayers for the passage of your husband's soul and ask God's blessing for your future plans."

Alice blinked. "That sounds like a good idea."

And we can offer prayers that you won't end up accused of your husband's murder.

Ela didn't want to say that part out loud.

"I don't suppose I can write to him and tell him that I had to leave the city?" asked Alice.

"Write to whom?" asked Alianore.

"The Breton prince."

"Most certainly not."

THE NEXT MORNING their departure was delayed because one of the horses had thrown a shoe. A boy was sent to fetch the blacksmith, but he was already engaged with some other important person's horse, and so was the next one they tried. The bells had tolled for midday service by the time the horse was shod and returned from the forge. The delay meant that they couldn't possibly reach their first inn by nightfall or even by dinnertime, so their departure was postponed until the following day.

Ela tried to persuade Alice to ride with her to a bookshop in the oldest part of the city, but Alice pleaded a headache and sat in front of the fire in Alianore's parlor, gazing contemplatively at the flames. Ela was about to go there by herself—she did crave a new read for the long winter nights ahead—and had already summoned a guard to attend her when a knock sounded on the front door.

CHAPTER 8

Alice immediately awakened from her semi-stupor and, although she didn't turn her head or look toward the door, her whole body seemed suddenly...on alert.

It's probably not him. Ela hadn't really expected a visit by the man from last night. Such a character seemed unlikely to call on a new widow of no great fortune. Though pleasant and pretty, Alice was still over thirty and not exactly the kind of beauty that would launch a thousand ships.

"I'm here to call on the lady Alianore," said a deep voice from the hallway. Ela couldn't see all the way to the door but she knew with immediate conviction that Adonis d'Ys—or whoever he really was—had arrived on their doorstep. Naturally he asked for an audience with the lady of the house rather than her guest. Anything else would be rude.

She glanced at Alice, who now sat rigid with tension, every ounce of her being focused on the events unfolding in the hallway.

"I'm afraid the lady Alianore is not at home presently," said the boy at the door. "She's not expected back until after dark." Alianore had gone to visit a female friend. Perhaps he knew that already. "Would you care to leave a message?"

"Is the lady Ela at home?"

"She is indeed. Who may I say is calling?"

Ela pricked her ears to catch his name.

"She may not recognize my name. I'm of very recent acquaintance, but I'd be grateful to enjoy a few moments of her time."

What can he possibly want with me? Ela couldn't imagine.

The boy appeared in the doorway of the parlor and announced to Ela that there was someone who wished to see her. Ela racked her brain for something to say that would send him away without being impolite enough to cause offense.

"Send him in," said Alice quickly.

Ela stared at her. To his credit the boy didn't jump into action at Alice's request but looked to Ela for confirmation. Reluctantly, she nodded her assent.

Alice sprang to her feet and smoothed out the front of her gown, which, Ela now noticed, was one of her new ones—a deep blue—and trimmed with decorative blue and gold ribbon. She'd changed since they abandoned their travel plans, despite insisting that she wanted a quiet day at home.

The large silhouette of a man filled the doorway to the parlor and—ready to announce him—the servant remembered that he didn't know the man's name.

"At your service, my ladies," said the Breton prince of legend. "As I mentioned to my lady Alice last night, I had business in this environs this afternoon."

"We were supposed to leave for Salisbury this morning," said Alice, with excitement in her voice. "But one of the horses threw a shoe and we had to delay our departure until tomorrow."

"How fortunate...for me," he said slowly. A smile crept across his face, which was exactly the kind of chiseled, handsome visage you'd expect on a legendary Breton prince. His dark eyes glittered slightly as he appraised Alice in the soft light of the parlor. "I did so enjoy your company last evening."

"Me too," said Alice, far too effusively. "I'm so glad to see you again." She clearly had no idea how even the most rudimentary flirtation was conducted.

"I'm afraid I didn't catch your name," cut in Ela, rather imperiously.

"Adonis," he said slowly. He extended his hand to take hers. She really would have preferred to keep her hand unmolested at her side, but that would have required rudeness she couldn't justify under the circumstances. She extended her hand, and he bent his head and kissed her fingers very, very softly.

Ela recoiled from the sudden rush of sensation that shot from her fingers right to her core. She almost snatched her hand back. Adonis was clearly no stranger to flirtation. In fact, she suspected it might be his primary occupation after seagoing adventurer. "Your last name, sir?"

"D'Ys," he said with a wry, almost apologetic look. "It's an odd name because it's a very ancient one."

Alice gazed at him with big moon eyes.

"Where exactly is...Ys?" Ela peered at him suspiciously. "Alice said that you hail from Brittany. I've spent a good deal of time in northern France, and I'm afraid I've never come across it."

"Ys is as remote in location as its origins are in time. It's not the kind of place you'd stumble across."

"Unless you were shipwrecked there," said Alice with a smile. "It's an island, isn't it?"

"Something between a peninsula and an island," he said softly. "Depending on whether the tide is high or low."

"Does it have a complicated network of dykes controlled by a single key?" asked Ela. Now she was being rather rude. Still, she didn't trust this man as far as she could throw him.

He laughed. "No, indeed it doesn't. It does have a single hill with a round tower atop it, that can look out over the ocean for approaching ships."

"Did you grow up there?" Ela asked.

"Sadly no, and I don't live there now. My family has acquired estates in Burgundy that are far larger and more profitable than the remote promontory of my ancestral homeland."

"What brings you to London?" asked Ela. She suspected that both Alice and Adonis—if that was his real name—would strongly prefer that she leave the room, but she didn't trust Alice to conduct herself in a manner becoming to a new widow.

"I'm here on business. My family has shipping concerns at all the great ports of Europe."

"All of them?" Ela lifted a brow. "Goodness. They must have a lot of ships."

"Thirty-two at last count," said Adonis calmly. "I find it necessary to meet with the men who negotiate our customs and excise."

"What do your ships carry?"

"Almost anything you can imagine moving from one country to another, my lady." Adonis lifted his chin, which was darkened by a slight shadow of hair. "Wine, fleeces, woven cloth, live oxen, hides for vellum and parchment, dyes, barrel staves and bands. Last year we even brought three exotic monkeys to London for someone who wanted to give them as gifts."

"So your business is the management of the ships, rather than the trading of goods?" In her work as sheriff, she'd learned far more than she ever wanted to know about the secret trade in opium. The profits of importing the poppy resin proved so great that the importers preferred to hide their cargo among cheaper goods in order to avoid paying taxes on their bounty.

"Indeed it is, my lady, though sometimes we trade in goods as well."

Of course you do. Renewed acquaintance was not warming her heart to Adonis d'Ys. "It's unusual for a prince to be in trade, is it not?"

For the first time he looked the tiniest bit unsettled, a small furrow appearing between his dark brows. "I'm descended from princes but not a prince myself."

"Oh." Ela let her reply sit in the air for a moment. She glanced at Alice. She'd finally caught him in a lie and he'd admitted it.

Alice looked downright annoyed with her. "Ela, why are you grilling the poor man so? I'm sure he didn't come here to tell us all the details of his business and personal life."

"No, indeed," he said with a smile. He pulled something from the leather pouch at his belt. "I came here to give you this."

Ela peered at his hands but couldn't quite make out what the object was.

"Is it a box?" asked Alice, almost breathless with excitement.

"Not quite. Open it up."

Alice plucked at the tiny latch, and it opened to reveal a small painted picture of the Virgin Mary.

"It's a picture of Our Lady," exclaimed Alice. She showed it to Ela.

"It's an icon painted with lacquer and ornamented filigree gold. I bought it in Pskov and credit it with keeping me safe during a great storm that blew up as I sailed across the south coast of Sweden."

"Perhaps you should keep it to ensure your safe passage home," said Alice, gazing at the delicate painting.

"It has already protected me, and now I offer it to you to give you safe passage in your new life as a widow."

Alice blinked, obviously a bit confused. "I hope to marry again soon," she stammered. "I don't intend to take the veil."

Adonis laughed, a deep, throaty chuckle that filled the room. "I certainly hope not. You're far too young and beautiful to lock yourself away in a cloister. But surely the blessings of Our Lady will ease your path through the grief of your recent loss."

"Oh, yes, of course," stammered Alice, remembering that she was supposed to at least pretend to be in mourning. "I'm sure it will bring me solace in times of loneliness."

"May they be few and far between, Mistress Alice," said Adonis in a low, almost tremulous voice that seemed to imbue his words with emotion.

He then presented a similar icon—a picture of St. Anne—to Ela. Though she tried to refuse it he insisted that she keep it as he had another one almost like it.

He's clever. Ela gave him credit for that. She could hardly find fault with him for giving Alice a picture of the Holy Mother, though it was rather too colorful and gaudy for her own tastes.

"I was hoping that perhaps we might walk out together," said Adonis. He looked at Ela as he said it. Naturally he meant that he hoped to walk with Alice. He knew as well as she did that it would be utterly inappropriate for Alice to walk with him without the presence of a chaperone, so the walk could take place only if Ela came too.

"Oh, yes, let's walk. It's a lovely, brisk afternoon." Alice was already calling to Minnie, her maid, to fetch her cloak.

Adonis looked at Ela triumphantly.

"It's quite cold," she protested.

"Well, it is December," he replied with a half-smile. "A time when a chilly walk can heighten the enjoyment of a crackling fire." He looked at the large fire burning in the ornamental stone fireplace of Alianore's parlor. "And perhaps we can buy some roasted chestnuts?"

"I don't think we'll find a chestnut vendor in this part of town," said Ela. "They're all within the city walls or clustered right around Westminster." She glanced at Alice, who looked ready to burst with frustration. "But I suppose it would be churlish of me to refuse a short afternoon walk."

THEY DONNED their cloaks and set out, with two guards trailing behind. "I bring at least two guards wherever I go," said Ela brightly. "Since I'm the Sheriff of Wiltshire, and that has occasionally made me a target."

"I'd imagine that any fine lady might find herself quarry for brigands here in London," said Adonis, with a smile. "So much safer to be in the company of armed men."

Ela wasn't sure she felt so safe in the company of Adonis d'Ys, armed or not. While she could make inquiries into his background and possibly even his intentions, that would take time—weeks or months—and hopefully the name of Adonis d'Ys would not be that long on the lips of anyone, even Alice.

The winter afternoon was chilly and brisk, with a strong scent of wood smoke in the air, even in these leafy streets, sparsely lined as they were with grand houses, many of them with high walls around them.

Curious about what would happen between Adonis and Alice if she left them to their own devices, Ela hung back a little and let them walk ahead. At first their conversation focused on the surroundings: the dry leaves that skittered past them on the unpaved street, the high cut stone wall of a large house, the painted carriage parked outside the gate of one residence, its four matching white horses stamping impatiently.

"I've never seen anything like London," exclaimed Alice. "So many people in one place and it seems to go on forever! I thought Marlborough was a big town."

D'Ys laughed and assured her that London was dwarfed by the sprawling expanses of Paris and Rome and Antwerp and other cities of his acquaintance. He then regaled her with more stories of his travels, and she hung on his every word.

Ela listened, trying to decide if his exploits could truly be that colorful, or if he was embroidering the details or making them up outright. She decided that her husband's life—as brother to the king, a crusading knight, tournament champion, survivor of many battles and of a shipwreck where all the others were lost—made d'Ys story seem almost dull by comparison.

So perhaps he was telling the truth. Alice's cheeks shone pink, partly from the wind and partly from excitement. She laughed and peppered him with questions about his estates and his family, and he answered them all with humor and equanimity.

As she listened, Ela formed the opinion that if d'Ys was telling the truth—if his mother's father was truly a doge of Venice and his father's mother descended from the counts of Anjou—then he was far above Alice in station and must surely be toying with her if he encouraged her any further.

Alice didn't seem at all concerned about her companion's impressive ancestry and continued to inquire in a way that would be downright rude and inappropriate if they were indeed taking careful steps along the well-established route toward a noble marriage.

Having heard enough, and fearful that Alice was making a nuisance of herself, Ela hurried to catch up. "What is your next port of call, my lord?" she asked, annoyed by how breathless she sounded.

"I shall remain here in England for the time being," he said in his deep, sonorous voice. "I intend to strengthen some of our existing trade connections and possibly forge some new ones. Our friend the mayor has made some introductions that I intend to pursue."

"Whereabouts in England will you stay?" *And how much danger will Alice be in from your proximity?*

"I'm not entirely sure yet. I'm renting a house in London, and perhaps I shall take an estate in the country. Do you know of anywhere suitable?" He studied her face with what appeared to be genuine interest.

Ela racked her brain to think of her most remote manors and whether they might be made available for rent. Sadly the most distant were already rented or the house occupied by the steward, so she couldn't think of a way to hole him up far away from Alice.

"You could rent my estate," said Alice. "I haven't seen it since I was married, but I suppose it's still standing."

Alarms rang in Ela's heart. "Alice! Aren't you going to live there yourself?"

"I suppose that's what everyone expects, but I don't want to rot away deep in the countryside."

"Where exactly is it?" asked d'Ys.

"It's hard by Salisbury," answered Ela quickly. She certainly didn't want Alice giving this mysterious character step-by-step directions to her home. "Not remote at all."

"It's a good five miles from Salisbury."

"Which is a short ride, at a brisk trot," said Ela quickly.

"This area is certainly an excellent location," said d'Ys. "I'd be most interested in seeing the property with a view to renting it."

Ela blinked. This was spiraling far out of control. "I don't think—Alice's husband has only just died and the will has not even been read yet. I'm sure it will be some time before the estate is settled enough for Alice to think about what she might or might not do with her manor."

"I'm in no rush. I intend to spend the Christmas season here in London. I hear the festivities are next to none."

"My mother says the same. She spends Advent and the twelve days of Christmas here almost every year."

"I'm staying in the black house on Queenhithe, near the river," he said brightly, thus giving his own address to Alice. Ela resolved to keep Alice far from ink and parchment until her excitement over Adonis blew over. "I shall remain there for the time being, but I do find myself craving the fresh air of the countryside. All the smoke of London does settle in one's lungs and the taste of rich food palls if one is forced to eat it night after night. Sometimes I crave a quiet fireside and a simple meal."

"Oh, yes, me too," breathed Alice, no doubt picturing herself sharing supper with Adonis d'Ys at her own relatively humble fireside. "And I do enjoy long walks and rides in the countryside, as Ela knows. We've enjoyed many in the last month."

"Indeed we have, and Alice was a great help to me in giving alms to our neighbors."

They had reached the end of the street and had to choose whether to turn around and head back the way they came, or forge onward, toward Westminster.

"We really should be getting back," said Ela, ready to end this encounter. "We leave London tomorrow early and must make our final preparations."

"But we did that this morning," protested Alice. "I'm all

packed. I would love to see the Palace of Westminster and the great hall."

"It's still quite a walk from here." A gust of cold wind carried the smell of the river. "I'm afraid I feel rather tired." Her gut instincts told her that Adonis d'Ys was not to be trusted.

"Why don't we head into this church?" said Adonis, stopping suddenly in front of the arched doorway of St. Peter and St. Paul. "We can offer prayers for the poor departed soul of Alice's late husband."

"That's a wonderful idea," said Alice, with far too much enthusiasm, as usual. "I can light a candle for him."

Ela couldn't find a good reason to protest prayer. Hopefully the good Lord would intervene to put a stop to Alice's troubling flirtation. The door, dark oak banded with iron, was open, as if to welcome visitors as well as the cold winter air. The church, like most of the buildings in this prosperous neighborhood, was fairly new. Ela could still smell the rich scent of carved wood over the incense that wafted toward them.

They made their way into the nave through arches and past columns decorated in bright paint. Ela spotted a side chapel with a statue of St. John the Baptist. She turned to one of the brothers who hovered nearby clearly wondering what this party of a man and two women, plus their guards, were doing in their church between services. "Might I buy two candles to offer prayers for the souls of our dear departed?" she asked softly.

The brother looked at one of his fellows, and the second man hurried away, lifting his brown robe at the hem with one hand. Alice had walked into the side chapel and now knelt at one of the wooden prie-dieus that sat in front of the carved statue of St. John the Baptist, who was holding up his hand as if to bless them.

Ela wanted to kneel at the other prie-dieu and offer prayers for her husband, but that would mean that Adonis might decide to kneel directly next to Alice. As she was wondering how to prevent that from happening, Adonis indeed knelt on the same prie-dieu as Alice, and so close that his knee was actually on the cloth of her gown.

Panic rushed Ela's chest. Could she tug him away from Alice and push him toward the other prie-dieu?

You're overreacting. Most likely he'd never see Alice again after today. He was hardly going to rent a house in Salisbury for the sole purpose of chasing a middle-aged widow of unimpressive fortune. He'd forget Alice as soon as their carriage departed London, and there was no need to take a bellows to the fire of whatever was happening in Alice's heart by making a fuss over where he prayed.

Ela knelt at the second prie-dieu and started to murmur the words of the Hail Mary under her breath. She realized that instead of focusing on the words of the prayer, she was focusing entirely on listening intently for any words passing between the two people at the next prie-dieu. Worse yet, soon she found herself peering through squinted eyes at them.

She chastised herself for fussing over worldly matters in God's house instead of tending to spiritual ones. *Let God's will be done.* She tugged her attention back to her prayers and to the journey of her husband's soul toward paradise.

The monk cleared his throat when he returned, which jerked her from her prayer. Soon they were all lighting fine beeswax candles to place on iron spikes that stood in the side chapel for that purpose, and dripped their wax down onto an iron platter below.

After some more prayers they departed the church and walked back to Alianore's house. To Ela's relief, Adonis d'Ys did not try to come in but asked Ela to send her mother his regards and bid them both a good afternoon.

Alice stared after him as he rode away on a thick-built black horse with a long, wavy mane. "What a kind and charming man."

"He does have a lot to recommend him," said Ela charitably. She felt considerably warmer to him now that his broad shoulders were receding safely into the distance.

"Do you think he'll write to me?" asked Alice, seemingly unable to take her eyes off him.

"How would he do that, without your address?"

"Oh, I shall ask your mother to give it to the mayor, who can pass it on to him."

As Ela suspected, her mother would have nothing to do with passing Alice's address to Adonis through their mutual friend. "You're in mourning, my dear," said Alianore. "It would be unseemly."

Alice pouted and protested and even brought up the subject of her aging womb, but Alianore wouldn't budge. They traveled back to Salisbury without mentioning the subject again.

Ela and Alice had visited Spicewell, the lawyer, who had advised the services of a colleague who might intervene if the terms of her husbands will or its disposition were found to be unfavorable. They now discussed plans to visit Alice's manor and see what repairs might be needed before she could move there and start her new life as a widow of—hopefully—independent means.

Unfortunately, on their return it was necessary to address the unpleasant matter of who had poisoned Humphrey de Gilbert.

CHAPTER 9

As soon as the party arrived back in Salisbury, well into the night, Ela inquired whether Clovis, Humphrey de Gilbert's manservant, had arrived from Mere. She was informed that he had, and that he was now imprisoned in the dungeon. The cook, however, had apparently been relieved of her position directly after Sir Humphrey's death. She was no longer at the castle and no one knew where she'd gone.

The next morning she summoned Giles Haughton. She left Alice sleeping in her chamber and met with him in private so she could understand the implications of this new twist in the situation without alarming her friend.

"Clovis did indeed bring a tonic from the de Gilbert castle," said Haughton. "He said it was for Sir Humphrey's gout. He also admitted that he mixed the two tonics together, the better to get them into his irascible master."

"That seems foolish. How did he know the ingredients of each wouldn't interact to form an unpleasant taste, let alone a deadly poison?"

"He does not seem to be a man of high intelligence, my lady."

"Yet you've put him in the dungeon, so you suspect that the poisoning was deliberate rather than accidental."

"I'm not sure what to think, but I didn't want to risk a murderer going free in your absence. John Dacus called a jury and they all agreed there could be no harm done by detaining him until your return. Since it's clear that the tonic killed Sir Humphrey de Gilbert, and was administered by either Clovis or by Sir Humphrey's lady wife, it seemed only prudent to wait until you and she return to address the matter."

Ela swallowed. "I suppose the jury should have an opportunity to interview Alice."

"That would be conventional."

"I think she's recovered enough from the shock of her husband's death to face them. Please call a jury for tomorrow morning, and they can interview both Clovis and Alice about the tonics."

Ela hoped that having Clovis there would at least take the focus off Alice. She didn't imagine that the jury would suspect Alice, whose greatest crimes were likely innocence and naiveté.

AT BREAKFAST THE NEXT MORNING, Ela tried to explain to Alice how her interview with the jury of the Hundred would proceed. Alice seemed astonished by the whole concept. "They can just ask me any question they like?"

"They can."

"And they're just random villagers? The butcher and the baker and the candlestick maker? Not even nobles?" She blinked as if this was impossible to imagine.

"They are mostly tradesmen or farmers, but each of them is an upstanding and respected local resident, and some of them have been on the jury for decades and have almost as much experience as the coroner himself."

"And there are a hundred of them, all at once? Where do they sit?"

Now Ela laughed. "No, for a serious trial we strive to get a full dozen, but if they are called to witness a crime that's just occurred, two or three suffice. In reality the same handful of stalwart and reliable jurors attend to most crimes in Salisbury. Some of the others may have been on the rolls for years and never set foot inside the castle."

"Will there be a dozen here today?" Alice looked a little nervous.

"Half that is more likely. If they decide to try you for murder"—Ela crossed herself and muttered *God forbid*—"then you'd have another trial before the judge at the assizes. All capital offences are judged by an experienced traveling justice who moves from one town to another hearing the more serious cases."

Alice inhaled. "They won't think I killed him, will they?"

"I certainly hope not."

ALICE GREW anxious as the jurors filed into the great hall. She'd worn one of her new, ribbon-trimmed gowns—the deep yellow one, hemmed in black and wine-red—and kept fiddling with the end of her chain-link belt.

Ela was glad to see familiar faces, including Peter Howard, the stalwart baker; Stephen Hale, the cordwainer; and Hugh Clifford, the young wine-seller who had largely taken the place of his aging father on the jury as he had in their family business.

As always, the jurors arranged themselves on benches along three tables placed in a U-shape. The din in the hall seemed especially cacophonous today. The usual throngs of soldiers and petitioners milled about and stood in the corners and around the doorways.

Ela couldn't help thinking that more eyes than usual glanced toward Alice, arrayed in her finery, standing like a lost lamb in the middle of the great hall. No one approached her or spoke to her. Ela, busy dealing with various local matters that petitioners laid at her feet, watched with growing alarm from her dais, until she finally excused herself.

She didn't necessarily want everyone to know that Alice was a dear friend of hers. Then she might be seen to show bias which could even prejudice the jurors against Alice. However, she didn't want her friend to feel abandoned or even terrified in the midst of all these strange men.

Ela seated Alice along the edge of the table where she herself sat, rather than on a chair in the middle where the accused were usually brought in chains. Then she asked for Clovis to be brought from the dungeon. Ela had deliberately avoided asking Alice for her opinions of Clovis and whether he might have killed his master. Again, she didn't want to lay herself open to accusations of perverting the course of justice.

She decided to start the proceedings by introducing Alice as something of a victim in the situation. "And this is Alice de Gilbert, wife of the late Sir Humphrey de Gilbert, who found him dead that fateful night in their shared bedchamber. You may ask her any questions you have."

Ela found herself holding her breath as she sat and looked around the jurors. Eventually one raised his hand: Will Dyer, the barrel maker, a youngish man with black hair and piercing blue eyes, who'd lately become more active on the jury. Ela gestured for him to speak.

"My question is for you, my lady. If this man was found dead in your castle, why was a jury not called as soon as his body was discovered?"

Ela swallowed. "Sir Humphrey de Gilbert was a good deal older than his wife, past middle age. Finding him dead, we assumed that he died of natural causes."

"If that's the case, then what later made you think that his death was unnatural?" he continued.

Ela glanced at Giles Haughton. "The coroner conducted an experiment that suggested his evening tonic contained the deadly poison found in the leaves and flowers of the foxglove plant."

"And who gave him his evening tonic?" asked Will Dyer.

Ela hesitated for a moment, then drew in a steadying breath. "His wife, Alice de Gilbert, gave him some of the tonic in the great hall during dinner, then his servant Clovis mixed that tonic with another one that he'd brought from home and administered the rest in his bedchamber before he went to sleep."

The cooper and all the other jurors looked at Clovis. The servant was a small, thin man with a slightly stooped posture and wispy brown hair. His skin had fine wrinkles that made it clear he wasn't a young man, but nothing about him suggested great age, either. Ela suspected he was probably about her age.

The jurors also peered at Alice, who stiffened under their accusatory gaze.

"Alice and I made the first tonic together," Ela said. "It was intended to increase her husband's...vigor, that they might conceive a child together." Again, she hoped that the mention of future hopes would dispel the idea that Alice wanted her husband dead.

Will Dyer looked at Alice. "And when you made it, did the tonic contain foxglove for some therapeutic reason?"

Alice looked to Ela, who answered. "It did not."

"Did it contain comfrey?" asked Timmy Watkins. Watkins was a farmer who served on the jury only occasionally.

"It did not. All the herbs were from my own herb garden inside the castle walls, which is carefully tended and weeded almost daily, and most certainly did not harbor a foxglove plant. Alice picked the herbs with me, and I use them all regularly to make tonics and possets and teas for my household and myself. She also did not have access to woods and fields at any time that she wasn't in my company, so if she'd picked some for any reason, I'd have seen her do it."

No one had actually accused Alice of anything, so Ela wasn't sure if she'd overstepped by vigorously protesting Alice's innocence. She had also revealed that she and Alice were companions.

The jurors probably noticed these things and reflected on them as there was a prolonged silence.

"If there were two tonics, then there were two bottles," proffered Stephen Hale, the cordwainer. "Did both contain the deadly poison?"

"I'm afraid we only had access to the bottle that Alice and I prepared," said Ela. "The other one presumably having been removed during the night."

"So the one she prepared had the poisoned dregs left in it," said Peter Howard, the baker, slowly. He turned his gaze to Alice, who shrank under it.

"Clovis, Sir Humphrey's manservant, has already admitted that he mixed the two tonics together in the larger bottle, which is the one that Alice and I made. So the dregs that Giles Haughton tested, and found to be poisonous, were in fact a mix of the two tonics."

"Why was the first bottle removed?" Will Dyer peered at Clovis.

The servant paled visibly. "It was empty, so I took it outside to wash it so I could pack it to take home the next morning. We were all supposed to leave at dawn."

"My Lady, were these people guests at the castle?" asked Miles Crabbet, a farmer in late middle age, of Ela.

"Yes," she said quickly. "Alice had stayed with me for some weeks after attending her father's funeral in Marlborough. Her husband had arrived just that night in order to take her home to their manor in Mere."

"So you expected him that night and had prepared the tonic for him?" asked Will Dyer, of Alice.

"Oh, no," burst Alice. "I didn't know he was coming at all. I'd hoped to stay several more weeks with Ela." There was a rather tense silence.

"But your husband arrived to take you home at once?" asked Will Dyer.

"Well, yes," said Alice. "I'd written to him, asking him if I might stay longer, but instead of replying, he came to fetch me home."

"Was his sudden arrival, with the intent of removing you immediately, perhaps an unpleasant surprise?" continued the cooper.

Alice glanced at Ela, who could see the panic in her eyes. "It was a surprise," she stammered. "But not an unpleasant one, of course."

"We prepared the tonics more than a week prior to his arrival," said Ela. "So there's no question of an intent to poison him that night. We even bought nice bottles for them, and she was intending to take them back to their castle with her and give them to him there."

"If I may be so bold, my lady," said Will Dyer. He hesitated, and Ela felt her shoulders tighten.

"Yes?" Ela wondered just how bold he was going to be.

"How long have you known Alice de Gilbert?"

"She and I spent a summer in each other's company at my mother's house fifteen years ago. We've since maintained an occasional correspondence, and I attended her wedding to Sir Humphrey de Gilbert. I hadn't seen her face-to-face since the wedding party, but I still consider her a friend." It had to come out sooner or later.

"And Alice was a good deal younger than her husband?" asked Dyer.

"She is thirty-three. He was fifty-four," said Ela. "So not exactly ancient, but old enough to die of natural causes without causing astonishment."

"But," Will Dyer looked at Alice. "If she was tired of her husband and possessed of a desire to become a widow, what better place could she think of to commit a crime than under the jurisdiction of her longtime friend, the Sheriff of Wiltshire?"

Ela rose to her feet. "I must protest!" Will Dyer had gone too far. "You seem to imply that she might expect me to cover up any crime she would commit. As you can see from your presence here, and from the fact that the coroner was called to attend the death, that is most certainly not the case."

"Begging your pardon, my lady." Dyer did actually look somewhat cowed. He was a young and confident man of keen intellect, but he'd overstepped his bounds into rudeness by essentially accusing Ela of being willing to pardon a crime.

Which she wasn't.

Was she? Ela didn't like how this was going at all.

"While I most certainly don't wish to bolster Master Dyer's accusations of partisanship by insisting on my friend's innocence, may I draw your attention for a moment to the second tonic—the one I didn't have any hand in making, and which I know nothing about. Perhaps you might care to question Clovis about it?"

Clovis twitched visibly.

"Clovis," said Peter Howard. "Were you a servant of the dead man?"

Clovis nodded.

"How long were you in his employ?"

"More than twenty years." Clovis's raspy voice was hard to hear. "Been with him since I was a lad."

"And you prepared the tonic that you gave to your master that night?"

"Oh, no. I wouldn't know how. I just packed the tonic in the chest to bring on the journey. It kept his gout flareups from being so painful."

"What is in the tonic?"

"I don't know, sir." Clovis shifted nervously from foot to foot.

"Who did prepare the tonic?"

"I suppose it was the cook, sir. She usually prepared it."

"How long had the cook been at the castle?"

"Her whole life, I suppose. Three score years at least. I think she was there when Sir Humphrey was a child."

"So she was an older woman?"

"Oh, yes."

"Did she have any reason to despise Sir Humphrey or to want to kill him?" asked Peter Howard.

"I can't imagine she did, sir. She seemed happy enough in his employ. He liked plain and simple cooking."

"Did she leave of her own accord?"

"She did not," said Clovis quietly. "I'm not sure exactly what words were said, but she packed up her belongings muttering about how her food didn't need a lot of seasoning or pepper, because it was good, plain cooking."

Ela frowned. "So the cook, who'd prepared Sir

Humphrey's tonics for years, was suddenly sent away in the wake of his death."

"Yes, my lady."

Ela found this quite suspicious. Did this cook know something about the household that made her a liability to whoever had killed Sir Humphrey?

"So Sir Humphrey drank this tonic regularly?"

"Every morning and night. He drank it after dinner so he might be comfortable enough to sleep."

"So the cook prepared the tonic, as far as you know, and the serving girl brought it to you, and you packed it for the trip?"

"Yes." Then he paused. "No, wait, it wasn't the serving girl who brought the bottle this time. It was Sir Peveril." He blinked rapidly a few times, as if trying to peer back into his memory. "Yes, Sir Peveril brought it that time."

"Who is Sir Peveril?" asked Ela.

"Sir Humphrey's oldest son, my lady."

Ela glanced at Alice, who now stared at Clovis.

"Was Sir Peveril in the habit of bringing you the tonic for your master?" asked Ela.

"No, my lady. Though Sir Humphrey asked me to pack in a hurry that he might get to Salisbury before nightfall. It sent the household into a bit of a frenzy of people running hither and yon. It didn't surprise me that much when his son brought it, as perhaps the girl was busy packing food for the journey."

Did the son have reason to kill his father? Ela's brain churned with new thoughts. *And perhaps hope to have Alice blamed for his death?*

"Did Sir Humphrey have a close relationship with his son?" she continued.

Clovis blinked and looked around. "Well, they were father and son. I don't suppose there's any relationship closer than that." His face took on a hopeful expression as if he was praying he'd given the right answer.

"I didn't mean close in kinship," said Ela. "Were they affectionate toward each other?"

Clovis's face took on an expression of mild panic. "I—I don't know, my lady. They weren't hugging and kissing if that's what you mean."

Some titters and rumbles of laughter rose from the jury.

Ela drew in an exasperated breath. "Would you say that Sir Peveril felt...love toward his father?"

"I don't know, my lady."

"Let me try another approach, Clovis." Ela fixed her eyes on his face. One of his eyelids twitched. "Did Sir Peveril have reason to hate or resent his father?"

Clovis shuddered visibly and for a moment she thought he might lose his footing. "I don't think so, my lady. I-I-I..." He didn't continue.

Ela looked at the jury. "It appears that we have a new potential suspect in the person of Sir Humphrey de Gilbert's son Peveril, who provided the tonic."

"But how do we know which tonic was the poisoned one?" asked the cordwainer.

"We don't," said Ela.

"Why were you in such a rush to rinse out the bottle?" Stephen Hale asked Clovis.

"I hardly want to put it in my master's trunk still soiled with dregs," said Clovis. "It might have leaked on his spare cloak or shoes."

"I shall summon Sir Peveril here to Salisbury and answer the jury's questions," said Ela. She signaled for John Dacus, who sat at her right, to attend to the matter, and he rose from the table to send a messenger to Mere.

"Perhaps we might ask Mistress Alice about the relationship between father and son?" asked Peter Howard, looking at Ela.

"A good suggestion," she replied. She glanced at Alice to see her reaction. Alice had returned to her usual expression of placid good cheer, perhaps because the finger of accusation was pointing away from her—at least for now.

"Mistress Alice," said Howard, in his gruff voice. He was a man in late middle age, with a good deal of experience on the jury as well as in baking bread. "How would you describe the relationship between father and son?"

Alice looked up and to the side slightly, as if the answer might be found somewhere in the embroidered tapestry on the wall above. Then she looked at Howard. "Sir Peveril never said a word against his father, at least not that I heard. However, he rankled at his father's tight purse strings. He wanted to spend time as a scholar at either Oxford or the new university at Cambridge, and study the works of the ancients, but his father thought it a foolish expense and wouldn't pay for it."

"What did Sir Humphrey want his son to do?" asked Howard.

"To run his estates. My husband found the day-to-day practicalities uninteresting. He preferred to spend time in his library at work on translating ancient texts. He instructed Sir Peveril to take over the duties of steward and manage the manors himself."

"With a view to one day running the castle manor as his own, I suppose?" asked Howard.

"No doubt. Peveril was his oldest son and heir."

"Does Peveril show an aptitude for running the estate?" asked Howard.

Ela thought that an odd question and looked at Alice while she answered.

"I'm not sure," said Alice. "He might also rather be

hunched over a candle trying to make out a sentence in Greek than deciding which ram to put to his ewes."

"So Peveril and his father shared this passion for books?" continued Howard.

"I suppose they did," said Alice. "Though they each pursued it in a solitary fashion. I never saw them read together or discuss books."

"Did Peveril live in the castle with you and Sir Humphrey?"

"No. He lived in a manor at Chicklade. He rode over about once a week to see to the running of the castle manor, but he rarely slept there unless the weather was very bad."

"And have you seen this other manor?"

"No, but he complained a lot about the house being squat and drafty and infested with vermin."

"Surely that was his fault if he lived there?" said Howard.

"That's what his father always said."

"So we have a son who resents his father." Will Dyer's voice boomed out. "And who's perhaps waiting impatiently for him to die so he can take up residence in the ancestral castle." He looked at Alice. "Is it a pleasant castle?"

Alice blinked. "It's not very comfortable but I suppose castles rarely are." She glanced around the great hall.

Ela felt a little discomfited. She found her home castle to be a very pleasant place to live and wouldn't trade it for even the most commodious and draft-free new manor house that money could buy.

"But I suppose we can assume that Sir Peveril would be glad to take up residence in the castle if his father should happen to die?"

Alice stared at him for a moment. "I'm sure I don't know."

"The will has been read?" asked Giles Haughton.

Ela hesitated. "Alice has not yet received word of it. Or have you?"

Alice shook her head.

"Alice will remain here until she receives word of her portion." Ela saw no reason to mention that she'd written to Spicewell's lawyer friend, instructing him to intervene if matters proved unsatisfactory. She did wish Alice would show at least the tiniest hint of grief. She didn't expect her to sob and rend her clothes, but the occasional tear or even a downcast expression wouldn't have gone amiss. "I'm glad that I can comfort her in her grief."

Alice smiled gratefully, which didn't exactly produce the intended effect.

"It does seem that Sir Peveril has at least some motive to poison his father," said Haughton. "He was not at the castle when I visited in search of Clovis. I look forward to questioning him at the earliest possible opportunity."

Ela stood. "We shall adjourn this jury until Sir Peveril arrives."

CHAPTER 10

Ela and Alice walked in the herb garden among the dried heads of flowers and the bare stalks of dormant herbs. They both wore cloaks with hoods pulled about their ears to keep out the winds that always buffeted the castle mound, penetrating even deep inside the walls. The bees were silent, it being too cold for them to ply their trade. "How would you prove that Peveril killed his father?" asked Alice.

"It would be most difficult, I'm afraid," admitted Ela. "If he did poison the tonic, then it was cunning of him to arrange to have his father fall ill during a night away from home."

Ela remembered her husband arriving home, then becoming violently ill after his "reconciliation" visit with the king's justiciar. He'd become ill on the journey and now she suspected that perhaps the food or wine that had been packed for him to eat after he left the justiciar's house had been poisoned so he might not sicken until he returned home.

Perhaps Hubert de Burgh had carefully planned for the

illness to be delayed until he was far from his own residence in order to avoid suspicion.

"Even if circumstances suggest that the poison originated in the de Gilbert household, it might be hard to secure a conviction without witnesses that saw him prepare the poison. Unless we can find compelling enough reason to convince the traveling justice that Peveril de Gilbert murdered his father. It's a wonder that half the great men of England aren't murdered by their eldest sons. They must all surely be at least somewhat impatient to assume control of their lands and titles," mused Ela.

"Does your son William feel that way?" asked Alice.

"What?" Ela startled. "I'm sure he doesn't. I mean…his father is dead but he's far too young to take control of such a great estate."

"But he is the Earl of Salisbury now that his father is dead, I suppose," said Alice, stopping to pluck a dried seed pod.

Ela blinked. "He isn't. I am the Countess of Salisbury and intend to hold the position until such time as I feel he is ready to assume the role of earl."

"I suppose you couldn't be sheriff if you weren't countess."

"I'm sure you're right." Ela found this whole discussion quite unsettling. "But I hardly feel I have to watch my cup in case my own dear son was to slip a tincture into it."

Alice laughed. "Of course not! Because William loves you. I suppose that's why most sons don't murder their fathers, isn't it?"

"It must be. Otherwise older sons of the nobility have considerable motivation to patricide in England, where they often spend much of their life waiting to take up the mantle of their inheritance."

"And younger sons have motive to kill their older brothers so they can inherit in their stead."

"God forbid." Ela couldn't imagine Richard and Stephen harboring fratricidal thoughts toward their older brother. "I thank Heaven that my younger sons are both capable young men and will make their own way in the world without the title of Earl of Salisbury. Richard wishes to be a bishop, and I'm sure Stephen will distinguish himself on the battlefield as he already shows skill and bravery worthy of a knight of the realm."

Alice's sighed. "You're so blessed with your children. All charming young individuals in their own right. And the little ones are so sweet."

Ela had forgotten Alice's pain at being childless and now regretted bragging about her boys. "I am blessed indeed. And you shall be too, in the Lord's good time."

"Unless the Lord wishes to punish me for not loving my husband and being a more dutiful wife," said Alice softly. Ela glanced around to see if anyone was within earshot. She did not need Alice planting such thoughts in the minds of anyone at the castle. Even the staff could alight a spark of gossip that could grow into a mighty conflagration among the residents of the castle and of the entire town within the walls.

"I'm sure that's not the case," she said quickly. "The Lord is merciful and loving, and no doubt he has great plans for you."

Alice bit her lip for a moment, then a smile crept across her mouth. "I think Adonis d'Ys might be in his plans."

Ela almost tripped over a cobblestone. She'd half forgotten about the dark-eyed charmer that they'd left behind in London. "I suspect the Lord is preparing someone more...sensible. A nice Englishman from a good family. Someone kind and patient and—"

"Boring," said Alice with a smile. "Someone more ordinary, I think is what you're trying to say."

"Perhaps it is. A nice, suitable husband to enjoy creating a family with."

Alice sighed. "He'd have to be a widower. No reasonably appealing and solvent man would be single at my age unless he was a widower."

"That's not true at all," protested Ela. "Some men spend their formative years abroad fighting, or establishing trade relations for their families or diplomacy for their king."

"Name one unmarried, non-widowed man over thirty that you personally know." Alice stared at her, eyes shining with her challenge.

Ela racked her mind. Not Bill, he was widowed, although it was so long ago that hardly anyone remembered his poor dead wife. She ran through all the single men in her inner circle—there weren't many—and then in the noble circles she moved in, and was forced to admit that they had all been married except for two or three who were so utterly unsuitable or undesirable as to be the exception that proved the rule.

"See? You can't think of any. So he has to be a widower, probably still pining over his lost love, and with a host of grown children who'll resent me in their house, let alone in their father's bed."

Ela couldn't argue on this point, since Alice had already experienced it in both her own household and her father's.

"There's nothing wrong with a widower. He's learned how to treat a wife, for one thing."

"Or how to treat her wrong. What if I had died rather than my husband? He'd have trapped another poor woman in that grim and remote castle of his and ignored her—preferring the company of his dusty books, just as he did me."

"Why do you think he married at all?"

"Because he needed a housekeeper to manage the servants. Far better to take on one who comes with an estate and takes no salary than hire one who must be paid and is mistress of her own destiny and might abandon her post for greener pastures at any time."

"Such a cynical view," mused Ela. "But put like that, I see your point."

"I suspect most widowers marry more from habit than from love," Alice continued. "If they don't have a wife, their fellows will constantly question them about it or try to find one for them. They find it more convenient to keep a wife tucked away to prevent such unpleasantness." Alice laughed. "I've had far too much time to myself to reflect on the bland realities of many marriages."

"Then I'm surprised that you seem in such a rush to plunge right into a new marriage. You already know that the sweet-smelling bouquet of roses that tempts you conceals a bristling thicket of thorns."

Alice stopped walking for a moment. Then she leaned in close. "Were there thorns in your married life with William?" She spoke in a whisper.

Ela regretted her unaccustomed frankness. "All marriages have their thorns. In addition to traveling constantly with his brother, King John, William could be given to excess in food and drink. He loved tournaments and even battles and sometimes I felt that he risked his life unnecessarily by taking a role in conflicts he could have left to others."

Surely that was enough. She didn't want to admit that she knew he had mistresses and had even sired children by at least one of them. Such things were better left unsaid, even to oneself.

"No man is perfect," said Alice. "No mere mortal is perfect, least of all me! But I would like my next husband to be more...exciting." Her eyes sparkled as she leaned close again. "Including in the bedroom."

Ela smiled. "That's not too much to hope for. And the good thing about widowers is that they have practice, unlike callow youths who don't know what to do with a woman when they get her into bed."

"I bet Adonis d'Ys knows what to do with a woman," said Alice with a dreamy look in her eyes.

"I'm sure he does. Probably learned from the courtesans of Constantinople, or worse. A man who's bedded a lot of women is often poxed and to be avoided at all costs."

"He did say he'd been married before at a very young age. His wife was lost at sea, washed overboard on a voyage from France to England."

"I can imagine that would be a terrible shock."

"He said he'd never recover." Alice bent over and picked a half-dried sage leaf and held it to her nose. "But perhaps all he needs is the tender solicitations of the right woman to help him heal and enjoy life again." A sly smile crept across her mouth.

"And you think you're that woman." Ela couldn't help but smile at her friend's romantic optimism. "Does he have children?"

"He didn't mention any."

Adonis d'Ys struck Ela as the kind of man who might have married four different times and have a dozen children. Or perhaps one who found the paid attentions of whores more convenient. Hopefully Alice would never find out either way. "What other characteristics would you like in a husband?"

"I'd like a man who's handsome," said Alice with a smile. "Though not in a pretty, boyish way. A man with character in his face appeals to me more. And tall, of course."

"How tall?" asked Ela, humoring her. "Is six feet tall enough, or do you prefer taller?"

Alice laughed. "Your husband was one of the tallest men in England so don't you dare mock me."

"I'm just trying to make a mental list of your wants so I can scour the men of England for possibilities."

"In that case, let's give him a strong build with broad shoulders," said Alice, plucking at another seed pod. "And a full head of hair."

Ela laughed. "The man you describe sounds more like a hero from a French romance than a sensible Englishman."

"I don't mind if he's French. Didn't you grow up in France?"

"I did indeed. I'll be sure to search the halls of Normandy for your future husband as well as the hills and valleys of Wiltshire and the surrounding counties."

"Or perhaps I really will marry Adonis d'Ys," said Alice, not looking at Ela. "After all the Lord did put him in my path most unexpectedly."

"Perhaps the Lord was just opening your mind to the possibilities," said Ela. "With a plan to present you with more suitable candidates once your period of mourning has passed."

"Though I don't suppose there's any harm done by keeping my eyes open while I'm still officially in mourning."

"I suppose you can look about you, but it would be unseemly to show too much interest in another marriage. Especially while your husband's murder remains unsolved. If rumors start about your husband's death and that you seem to be enjoying your widowhood, gossip about you might seriously shrink the pool of interested candidates."

"People won't really think I killed him, will they?"

"They absolutely might, so don't grow overconfident. As

sheriff I know how suspicion can guide public opinion and even influence the decision of the jurors over whether someone is innocent or guilty. I'm sure more than one innocent person has hung because public opinion decided that they were guilty."

"While you were sheriff?"

"Not while I've been sheriff, God be praised, but I must constantly guard against letting myself be swayed by public opinion so I can guide the jurors to look at the facts of each case, not at the stories about it."

"I suppose my husband's son grew impatient to assume his inheritance," said Alice, walking again. They were taking their fourth or fifth turn around the herb garden.

"Ah, but that is the story being told. As of right now it's not based in fact. The facts of the case are that your husband died from digitalis poisoning—in the opinion of the coroner, at least—and that his servant Clovis administered the poisoned tonic."

"Do you trust the coroner?"

"With my life. Giles Haughton is wise and thoughtful as well as experienced. Every now and then I do find him leaning toward a predictable conclusion, but he's quick to listen to my thoughts and those of others."

"I don't imagine Clovis would want to kill his master. After all, what will happen to him now?"

"Perhaps young Peveril will want him in his own household. Would Peveril be a better master than Humphrey, do you think?"

"I doubt it. He seems more capricious and impatient. I'd imagine he'd be hard to please. My husband was dull as a stone but predictable and steady, at least."

"So the servant has no motive to poison his master," said Ela. "Which makes it seem all the more likely that the son placed the poison in the tonic, in the hope of claiming his inheritance sooner."

"I suppose that makes life safer for me, anyway. Do you think the jury will allow me to leave the castle and go to my manor?"

"I suspect so, but first you need the inheritance confirmed and your manor restored to you."

~

ALICE'S INHERITANCE of only the one small manor and a modest annual purse to sustain herself with was confirmed by letter from Mere.

"We must contact your lawyer to protest," said Ela on hearing the news.

"Why?" Alice had carried the letter into the cramped accounting room, where Ela sat on a stool, going over the steward's books.

"You were married for thirteen years and should inherit a greater portion of your husband's estate. The Magna Carta states that widows should get a full third of the estate's assets. At the very least your stipend should be a hundred per year. With twenty pounds a year you could barely keep yourself in embroidery thread."

"I shall manage just fine. I'm sure the manor will make money and hopefully I'll be married before two years are out." Alice looked positively cheerful about her small inheritance. Probably because her independence and future prospects were far more important to her than the coin and property she'd inherited.

"You don't even know the condition of the manor. The house may need money poured into it just to make it habitable. And the land might require a great deal of effort to become productive again. Do you know what uses the land is under right now?"

Alice shook her head.

"Well," Ela smiled. "Now that we know it's yours, we shall ride out today and see for ourselves."

~

ALICE'S SMILE vanished from her face as they rounded a corner in the overgrown track and saw that part of the thatch had fallen into the main structure.

"Oh." She slowed her horse to a halt and surveyed the grim scene of her manor.

Ela pulled up her horse, Freya, and signaled to the guards behind them to go on ahead to the house. "Don't worry. The roof timbers are still in place. The thatch will soon be replaced by an experienced thatcher."

"But surely all the furniture inside is ruined."

"That may well be true," Ela was forced to admit. "Let's go see."

They dismounted outside the front door. Sheep grazed on the ragged lawn, suggesting that the property wasn't entirely abandoned. "Hello!" Ela called. "Is there anyone here?" She glanced around for any sign of a cottage where the steward might be living.

She heard some shuffling from behind the door, and it creaked open. A stooped man with a shock of white hair stood before them. "What d'ye want?" he snarled.

"This is your mistress, Alice de Gilbert," said Ela sharply. "Who are you and what is your role on this manor?"

The man's rheumy eyes darted to Alice. "Begging your pardon I'm sure, my ladies. I'm old Egbert and have been tending sheep here since I was a lad."

"From the color of your hair I suspect that's a very long time," said Ela. She tried to look behind him into the house but couldn't make out much in the dark interior. The house had few windows considering its size, and apparently light wasn't pouring in through the roof, even in its decrepit state.

"Nigh on four score years, my lady! Always been faithful to the family, I have."

Ela turned to Alice. "You've never been here before?"

Alice, apparently struck dumb, merely shook her head.

"We'd like to enter," said Ela bravely. She grew afraid of what they might find behind the doorway. Possibly flapping chickens or inches of filth from decades of neglect.

"No one told me you were coming," he said, not moving. "Or I'd have tidied."

"Never mind. We can see that the thatch has rotted and fallen in so we're prepared for the worst."

He stood aside, and Ela took Alice's arm and tugged her forward. The sight that greeted them made even Ela gasp. The thatch had indeed fallen entirely in at one end of the roof and lay in a heap on the floor like a pile of manure. Leaves and dirt blew about on the floor like it was a courtyard rather than an interior room.

Alice let out a small whimper. "It will cost a lot to repair."

"I tried to patch it," said old Egbert, his voice tinged with regret. "But it's rotten and slimy and just won't hold."

Alice made another small sound. Ela could tell she was on the brink of tears, possibly even hysterical sobbing.

"What's happened to the furniture?" asked Ela, peering around the gloom. There didn't seem to be a single stick of it.

Egbert cleared his throat. "Woodworm. I burned it in the fireplace. That were more than five years ago."

Now Alice did start sobbing. Ela wanted to wrap her arms around her and comfort her, but there were more important things to establish first.

"Does the house itself have woodworm, in the timbers?"

"I don't know, my lady." Egbert seemed to stoop and

shrink before her eyes. "My eyesight isn't very good these days."

"How will I live here?" wailed Alice.

"Don't worry about that," said Ela. "Everything's fixable." *With enough money.* Though possibly not if the house was riddled with woodworm. Alice's annual income left to her in her husband's will was very far from allowing her to build an entirely new house and furnish it fit for a lady. In some ways it truly would be easier to just find her a new husband, with his own well-established home.... "I have a carpenter who does a lot of work around the castle, and he's an excellent judge of timber. He'll let us know what work needs to be done." Ela turned to Egbert. "And where do you live?"

He looked down at the floor. "I used to live in a cottage at the top of the meadow—" He paused.

"Used to?"

"The roof caved in and one of the walls fell down in that very wet spring we had a few years ago. Since then I've been living here since there wasn't anyone else in the house."

"Did you report to Sir Humphrey de Gilbert that the structures were deteriorating?"

He blinked at her with his bleary eyes. "Report to him how? I've never even laid eyes on him."

"Did his steward come here to oversee the management of the property?"

"Yes." He wobbled a little on his unsteady legs. "He came once a year to collect the fleeces and gather up the spring lambs to sell."

"Who sheared the sheep?"

"I did, my lady. And stacked the wool. My hands are getting stiff, but I can still shear six sheep in a day!" he said proudly.

"Goodness, that sounds like a lot." Ela couldn't believe that the manor had been almost totally abandoned in the care of one elderly man. "But the steward didn't inspect the buildings or fences or other structures?"

"Never did. Always in a hurry. This is good land for growing, but they never did anything but graze sheep on it. In the old days there were good orchards of apples and pears and rows of carrots and cabbages galore. That was a long time ago, though. I could show you where they were, if you like. Some of the old trees are still there."

"No, thank you," said Alice quickly. She looked uncomfortable, almost as if she had an itch. "Perhaps I shall sell the manor and move to London."

CHAPTER 11

"Please do show us around," said Ela to Egbert. "As then we'll know the most fertile land to develop when you bring this manor back to its fullness." She stared pointedly at Alice.

"The vegetables were in the place where the lambing pens are now. I'm sure the soil's richer now for having the pens on it!" Egbert looked quite animated at the prospect of improvements. "I grow enough to keep my body and soul together on a bit of earth I scratch out behind the kitchen door."

Egbert's tour sent Ela's mind spinning with plans to rebuild both the house and the necessary outbuildings and to make the land productive again. After they'd said goodbye to him and remounted their horses, she found herself quite cheerful about the prospects for the manor, which was both well drained and well supplied with water, two benefits that did not always go together.

"...and then you can direct your steward to breed for better wool and—"

"I don't want to manage a manor!" wailed Alice. "I

couldn't tell a good lamb from a bad one, and I don't want to know the difference."

"I suppose you had that in common with your late husband," said Ela drily. "For it's clear that he didn't spare a thought for the management of his manors and has let this one run to rack and ruin when it could have been turning a profit every year."

"He left the management to his steward and then to his oldest son," said Alice, staring off into the distance. "All he cared about were his books of Latin and Greek."

"Perhaps his steward skimmed off the cream and poured the rest on the ground. That happens if you don't go over the books and examine the details."

"You have a head for these sorts of things. I just want to be a wife and mother."

Ela wanted to scold Alice's own mother for neglect of her education but reminded herself that the poor woman had not enjoyed good health and had likely been too ill to oversee it properly. "It's a wife's job to oversee the management of the household. The availability of cabbages and parsnips and spring lambs for the kitchen is essential to the happiness of the family. I schooled all my girls as well as my sons in the importance of good husbandry. Even when you have the means to hire the very best stewards in the land, you should watch over them with a keen eye and suggest improvements where you see room for them."

Ela couldn't believe that anyone would just drift through life leaving such things to chance.

"We shall turn this manor back into a silk purse, and your husband will be pleased with it as well as with you. Men appreciate the enticement of a well-managed property almost as much as the elegant figure of a beautiful woman."

"I suppose I do see the sense in that," said Alice. "I need all the enticements I can get. And it would get me a better price if I sell it."

"You can't be seriously considering moving to London."

"Why not?"

"Well, for one thing, you don't know anyone there."

"I shall soon enough! The city is bristling with people."

"And almost none of them is suitable for a young widow to associate with. You must manage your future carefully. My mother can dine with odd and eccentric people because she's already older and established. Her reputation is chiseled in marble and unlikely to be dinged or dented by laughing in the company of a rogue at the mayor's table."

"But my reputation is easily tarnished and my prospects ruined by such things?" Alice challenged her.

"Yes!" *Not to mention that accusations of murder still hover around you like a bad smell.* She didn't want to raise that right now, though. Alice was clearly shaken by the deplorable conditions of her only asset. "You must choose your company very carefully and cultivate yourself like a delicate flower in your garden. Trust me, I have considerable experience in planning the marriages of my own children. There's a dance involved, and it revolves around reputation and property before all else, far before beauty and wit."

"Then am I to share this crumbling hovel with crusty old Egbert?"

"No!" Ela wanted to laugh. "Egbert shall be removed to some other residence, which will have to be built from the ground up if none of the structures can be repaired. All of these expenses give us arrows to put in your lawyer's quiver. He shall press your late husband's estate to provide the funds for repair of your property that he let fall into such neglect."

Alice looked somewhat mollified by this news. "How long will all this take?"

"Several weeks for the repairs. Perhaps several months

for the legal affairs to be settled. But you shall stay with me in my castle until the repairs are made and the manor and gardens staffed." Her heart sank a little at the prospect of babysitting Alice—for that was what it now felt like—for several more months. "So take heart."

Alice didn't look entirely thrilled by the prospect of living under Ela's roof for an extended period of time. "I thank you for your kind hospitality. I must write letters to such kin as I have and to my lawyer. Is there a way to deliver them?"

"I have messengers at the ready for such things. You shall use them whenever you need."

SIR PEVERIL DE GILBERT arrived in Salisbury riding his own horse—a sturdy bay—and with a substantial entourage. His entrance through the castle gates looked more like that of a valued guest than a man under suspicion of murder and the stern gaze of eight armed guards.

The de Gilbert heir was a tall, thin man with wavy brown hair and a long, narrow nose, pinkish red at the tip. He was put up in a decent chamber, rather than the dungeon in the bowels of the castle, and Ela invited him to join the family for meals. She did this more because she wanted to tease him out, perhaps once he was in his cups, than out of any warm feelings toward him. Perhaps wiser than he looked, he refused.

"I played no part in my father's death," he announced when she came face to face with him. "And being accused of such is an outrage."

"I appreciate your coming here," said Ela, referring to the fact that he had come of his own free will, rather than in chains. "And you'll have an opportunity to discuss matters before the jurors tomorrow morning. In the meantime, please enjoy my hospitality."

He looked like he'd prefer to shove her hospitality down her throat until she choked on it, but he held his tongue. Ela looked around for Alice to reintroduce the two, but her friend had made herself scarce.

"I brought my own supper and shall remain in my chamber until such time as I am required to appear before the jury," said Peveril.

Ela nodded her assent. As soon as he and his servants had gone upstairs, with a considerable commotion of wood and leather chests, rolls of bedding and other sundries, Alice appeared.

"He's angry, isn't he?" she whispered.

"Were you hiding out of sight?" asked Ela.

Alice nodded. "Behind the columns over there. He's never liked me. I don't think he wanted his father to marry again. He was probably worried I might bear Humphrey another son that he'd like more than his firstborn."

"But father and son seem quite similar."

"That does not necessarily endear men to each other."

"True. Happily you won't be seeing him again tonight, as he refuses to join us for dinner."

"Good. Perhaps he'd try to poison me, then insist over my dead body that I killed his father." Alice spoke without whispering.

"Don't say such things! You must remember that I'm the sheriff and such wild speculation is unseemly."

"Will I have to testify before the jury tomorrow?"

"Quite possibly."

An ice-cold wind whistled around the castle on the morning of Sir Peveril's appearance before the jury. Ela felt it sneak in through her bed curtains and tug at her toes, and she called for Elsie to stoke the fire before she even got out of bed.

"Christmas is coming and that's a fact!" said Elsie cheerfully. "I like this time of year, when everyone huddles around the fires and wraps themselves up in cloaks."

Elsie's hands looked rather red and chapped as she pumped the bellows to bring the blaze to a welcome inferno.

"Don't you mind the cold?"

"It's never too cold here in the castle. There's always a fire somewhere nearby. You wouldn't believe how cold it got out on the farm. Often we ran right out of wood and kindling and had to run out into the woods to scavenge some. We were stealing it, of course. If there was anyone about we had to hide and sometimes we didn't manage to get any wood at all."

"How did you cook with no fire?"

"We didn't." Elsie put down the bellows and gave Ela a satisfied smile. "Went whole days without eating a morsel. I've eaten bark off the trees more than once to stop the hunger pangs."

"God be praised that you're safe now," said Ela. She knew that others in the district were likely suffering the same privations now that winter had all of Wiltshire in its icy grip. She'd have to visit some of the poorer villagers with a wagon of wood and some provisions from the castle pantries.

Elsie helped her dress in a soft wool gown and a contrasting overtunic trimmed with fur that kept her neck warm. Ela had a similar garment that was entirely lined with fur, and a fur-lined hood and cloak—more than one, in fact—so she rarely suffered the discomfort of the winter season, no matter how stiff the winds that buffeted the castle mound.

Ela broke her fast with her children, and with Alice, who was unusually quiet.

"Is something troubling you?" asked Ela, after noticing that she seemed absent from the conversation. "Are you worried about today's trial?"

"I suppose I am," she replied quickly. Ela got the distinct impression that she was…lying. Which made her realize that she'd never had that impression before.

"What concerns you?"

Alice hesitated for a moment. "I don't like to say."

Ela didn't feel she could press her in front of the family and servants, so she let the matter drop. Instead she helped Petronella master a difficult stitch for an embroidered bookmark she was making, then quizzed Richard and Stephen about their study of the Psalms that they'd been making with their tutor.

Before they'd finished their oat porridge and berry compote, the jurors started to arrive, straggling in through the great front doors and streaming toward the tables set up for the trial.

Local gossip about the poisoning, and the coroner's interesting study of the poison, had once again yielded an unusually good turnout of jurors. When Giles Haughton arrived, Ela excused herself from the breakfast table and went to greet him.

"Where's the defendant?" he said, looking around the room after they'd exchanged their initial pleasantries.

"He hasn't emerged from his chamber yet. I shall send a guard to bring him when we're ready. He seems to have brought his own food. Perhaps he's afraid that I shall try to poison him."

Haughton chuckled. "And what motive would you have to do that?"

"I can't imagine. I'm hoping his guilt will prove the innocence of my dear friend Alice, though naturally I must remain entirely impartial." She wanted to make it clear that she wouldn't let friendship subvert the cause of justice.

Once the jury was assembled and Sir Peveril summoned, they took their seats around the tables. Peveril looked peevish and uncomfortable, with dark circles under his eyes as if he'd passed a sleepless night. He, too, wore a fur-trimmed tunic against the cold of the hall. The room was too large to heat effectively even with the great fire that roared at the end farthest from the doors.

Ela stood and cleared her throat. "Today we meet again in our efforts to uncover the mystery behind the death of Sir Humphrey de Gilbert, who was poisoned while a guest in this house. We've heard from his wife, Alice, who found him dead in the middle of the night, and from his servant Clovis, who served him the two tonics found in his room. You'll recall that the tonics were mixed in a single bottle before he drank them, and that Giles Haughton determined that the dregs from that bottle contained a deadly dose of foxglove that caused his heart to slow until it could no longer sustain his life. Under questioning, Clovis revealed that the tonic he'd brought from home had been provided to him by Peveril de Gilbert. Sir Peveril now stands before you." She turned her gaze to Peveril, who twitched visibly under it. "Sir Peveril, do you admit that you provided the tonic that Clovis packed in your father's bags?"

Peveril flapped his hands slightly. "I provided it in the sense that I handed it to the servant, but I did not prepare it."

"Who did prepare it?"

"How should I know? Someone in the kitchens, I presume."

Ela turned to the jury. "When guards were sent to fetch Clovis the manservant they were also asked to bring the cook, who prepared the tonics. It was found that she'd already left the household."

Paul Dunstan, the miller, raised his hand to speak. "If the cook had left her position so quickly, is that not suspicious? Perhaps she poisoned her master for reasons of her own?"

Ela spoke up. "We've learned that the cook had served the family for decades and was sent out to fend for herself in her old age, so that seems unlikely. It has been suggested that Sir Peveril let her go because he found her cooking too plain."

"Is that true?" asked the same juror, of Peveril.

Sir Peveril looked mutely furious.

"Sir Peveril, please answer the question," said Haughton.

"Well, I..." Peveril sucked at the air. "She never seasoned anything. Her food was tasteless as the table it sat on."

"That's how his father liked it," whispered Alice, who stood behind Ela. Ela swung around, having half forgotten that Alice was there, and prompted her to repeat her words louder for all to hear. Alice added. "Sir Humphrey was a man of simple, plain tastes who didn't hold with using spices or even salt."

"Did you live in your father's household?" asked Ela of Peveril.

"Nay. I lived over the hill in Chicklade."

"Did you own the property you lived on, or was it one of your father's manors?"

"One of my father's manors," he said quietly.

"Could you tell us about this manor?" asked Ela. "How many virgates of land? How large is the house? Is the house new and in good repair?

Peveril looked at the floor. "The house is large enough. It's on about eight hundred acres with a village near the valley floor. The house could be better but could be worse."

"We've discovered that the manor that is now in possession of Alice de Gilbert had been left to fall into extreme disrepair. In fact, most of the outbuildings had deteriorated to ruin and the roof of the main house had fallen in. Was your father in the habit of neglecting his manors?"

"I wanted to repair them, but my father wouldn't spend money where he didn't see the need for it," said Peveril without much expression. "The profit from that manor was in the crop of spring lambs that were sold each year, and he saw no need to put money into the house or orchards."

"How many manors did he own?"

"Five at one time, including the one from Alice. He left the management of the manors in the hands of his stewards, and then in mine, with strict instructions that no coin be wasted where it could be saved."

Ela hated lords like this, who gathered properties to their bosom like so many gold pieces, then didn't even trouble to visit them but took pleasure in simply owning them. Unlike gold coins, properties often suffered badly from their lord's neglect.

"Did you offer him advice for making improvements?"

"Naturally I made suggestions, but my father was set in his ways."

"So it's possible that you were waiting with some impatience to inherit the properties and improve the management of them?" Ela spoke calmly and pleasantly, as if she were offering a compliment.

Peveril did not fall into the trap she'd laid. He stared at her for a moment with his beady eyes, then said, "I most certainly was not eager for my father's death, and I resent the implication."

Even though he'd denied her accusation, she suspected that she'd planted the thought firmly in the minds of the jurors.

"It must be frustrating being an older son," said Ela. "While a younger son must of necessity pursue a career of some kind, it is an older son's lot to wait patiently to inherit his father's estates, no matter how long that may take."

"I wasn't in any rush to inherit them," protested Peveril. "My father had already charged me with the management of them. I wasn't any more interested in fussing over heads of ram or sheaves of wheat than he was. And the castle is almost impossible to heat in winter."

"That's true," muttered Alice softly. Too softly for anyone but Ela to hear. Ela realized she hadn't asked Alice whether she thought Peveril might have had a hand in his father's death.

"Do the jurors have further questions for Sir Peveril de Gilbert? And you may also ask questions of Sir Humphrey de Gilbert's widow and his manservant that pertain to their knowledge of Sir Peveril."

Ela felt Alice stiffen behind her. Surely she had to realize that Peveril looking guilty was good for her own exoneration? Clovis, the servant, sat mutely off to one side.

"I'd like to ask Sir Peveril about his own thoughts on who might have killed his father." Ela recognized the juror as Peter Hogg, an older man who'd turned the management of his prosperous farm over to his oldest son.

Peveril looked flustered. "I don't know who would want to kill him. I can't see what his manservant or the cook would have to gain from his death. I suppose his widow may have hoped to claim her inheritance and a measure of freedom. I don't believe they were a happy couple."

Alice gasped and Ela felt her grasp the back of her chair.

"Mistress Alice," continued Hogg. "Were you happy with your husband?"

Alice hesitated and Ela felt her chair vibrate as Alice gripped it. "No."

Peveril sat up in his chair. "See?"

"Just because she didn't enjoy wedded bliss doesn't mean

she killed her husband," said Ela quickly. She regretted the words instantly. She needed to maintain at least an appearance of impartiality. If she seemed to show favoritism to Alice that might even turn the jury against her friend.

"No, indeed," said Hogg. "Those who enjoy a long happy marriage are blessed indeed. Though it does seem that these are the only two people who stood to benefit from the death of Sir Humphrey."

"I didn't kill my husband!" The words burst from Alice's mouth. "I won't say I didn't ever wish he was dead—of natural causes—but I'd never stoop to poison him. I don't want to burn in the fires of hell!"

Murmuring broke out among the jury and around the hall.

"I have a question for Clovis," said Will Cooper. Ela sat up, as he tended to ask thoughtful and probing questions. Clovis seemed to shrink into himself as everyone turned to look at him. "Who do you suspect of killing your master?"

"I—I don't know, sir."

"Did your late master, Sir Humphrey, ever complain about either his wife or his eldest son?"

Clovis hesitated. His eyes darted around, and Ela noticed his hands starting to shake. "I—I dare say he complained about them both from time to time."

"And what were his complaints?" asked Cooper.

Ela felt her breathing grow shallow as tension gripped her.

"I—I do recall him muttering about his wife being too silly. He blamed himself for marrying a foolish young woman."

"He said this to you?" Ela asked because she couldn't believe cantankerous old Sir Humphrey would share such observations with his servant.

"He muttered them to himself, more like."

"Did you overhear him say anything else about his wife?"

Clovis hesitated and glanced at Alice. "He did huff and puff about her wanting to go places and do things, which he thought was a waste of time and money."

"Where did he think she wanted to go?"

"Just to the local markets, if I recall. And to church. Nowhere that wasn't quite sensible."

"And your master didn't want her doing those things?"

"He preferred to stay home and wanted his wife to do the same."

"Did he object to her going by herself?"

"Said it was wear and tear on the horses' shoes or on the cart wheels or some such. And when she offered to walk he said he couldn't spare an attendant to accompany her."

Poor Alice. No wonder she longed to be liberated from her prison of a marriage. Ela had certainly never asked anyone's permission to go to the market or to Mass at the cathedral. The very idea of such constraints made her breath quicken.

"Did you agree with your master that she was better kept at home?"

Clovis looked confused, as if this might be some kind of trick. "I can't say I did, my lady. I don't see any harm in a lady going to the market or to worship in the local church."

"No indeed." For some reason Ela wanted the jury to know that Alice's marriage to Humphrey had involved considerable forbearance. After she'd said it she realized that perhaps she'd also made it clear that Alice had a motive to kill her solitary and miserly husband. "Did you ever hear Alice complain about her marriage?"

"She wasn't one to mutter aloud, my lady, and I never heard her complaining to her husband. She did look sad a lot of the time."

Some of the jurors glanced at Alice.

"What did you think of your late master, Clovis?"

Clovis shifted from one foot to the other. "He wasn't a well-liked man, mostly because he kept to himself and didn't much like other people. I don't have reason to gripe about him as a master, though. I didn't have to do much beyond dressing him and bringing him his meals from the kitchen. Easiest job I've had, and that's the truth."

"What other jobs have you had?" Ela was curious.

"I've worked in the castle since I was a lad tugging at my mother's apron. She was a kitchen maid and then a chambermaid. I used to help her sweep the floors and weed the kitchen gardens and—"

"You weeded the herb gardens?"

"For many years, my lady."

"And could you tell comfrey from foxglove even if there was no flower on the plant?"

"Of course, my lady. You'd have to be a right simpleton to confuse them. The edges of the leaves are quite different."

"So you've worked in the castle your whole life, and the pinnacle of your career has been serving as manservant to your lord, Sir Humphrey de Gilbert."

Clovis puffed out his chest very slightly. "That's the God's honest truth, my lady. I counted myself lucky to have clean indoor work and not too hard, either."

"And what will you do now that your master is dead?"

Clovis half turned, as if he was going to look at Sir Peveril, but caught himself just in time. "I don't know, my lady. Naturally I hope to continue in service to the de Gilbert family, as my mother and father did before me, and my grandfather and grandmother...." His voice tailed off, and he looked at the floor.

Ela reflected that his answer to her next question might be shaped by concerns for his future prospects. "Do you think Sir Peveril capable of poisoning his father?"

CHAPTER 12

No one moved a muscle, except Clovis, who swayed a little, "I—I—no, my lady. I can't imagine such a terrible thing. I'm sure Sir Peveril is a man of honor with a concern for his immortal soul who would never stoop to endanger it with such a terrible act." When he stopped speaking an odd shiver took hold of him.

"Thank you, Clovis." She looked at the jurors. "As a faithful manservant, Clovis can hardly be expected to speak ill of his new master." She looked from one juror to the next, hoping that they'd take her meaning. "Do any of you have questions for him?"

Will Dyer leaned forward and fixed his eyes on poor Clovis, who was starting to look quite unsteady on his feet, probably terrified of whether he'd have to choose whether to risk his soul in a lie or his body in losing his lifelong job and being turned out to starve. "You served Sir Humphrey for some years, as I understand it."

"Aye, that I did."

"So I would hope that your loyalties lie with your late

master rather than his son, if you had to choose between them."

Clovis didn't say anything, but Ela could see his chest rise and fall quite fast. "I suppose they would."

"And that if Sir Peveril had indeed had a hand in his father's death, that you'd honor the memory of your late master by putting him where he belonged—on the end of a gallows rope."

Ela's gaze darted to Peveril, who whitened.

"—rather than shaving his chin and emptying his slop bucket for the rest of his life or yours."

Clovis swallowed.

"Do you have a question?" asked Ela, growing uncomfortable and impatient with these statements of opinion that weren't based in knowledge of either man.

"I do, my lady," said Dyer pleasantly. "But I'm seeking to establish the absolute honesty of the manservant Clovis before I ask it."

Clovis looked like he was about to pass out.

"Would you tell a lie before all the jurors assembled today?"

"No, master," stammered Clovis.

"Would you tell a lie before the Lady Ela, High Sheriff of Wiltshire, or Giles Haughton, the coroner of our county?"

"No, I would not." Clovis spoke louder, clearly anxious to be believed.

"Would you tell a lie before the Lord your God, who sees all and hears all and holds a place for the virtuous in his heavenly kingdom?"

"Indeed I would not, sir." Clovis spoke with increasing conviction.

"Then, having established that, do you think there is even the tiniest possibility that the defendant standing here today might have slipped a few drops of poison into his father's tonic in order to hasten his own possession of the castle, lands and other inheritance awaiting him?"

Clovis hesitated, looking at the table, the floor, the tapestried walls, anywhere but at Peveril. "I shrink from thinking ill of any member of the de Gilbert family. And I didn't see him do such a thing. But I suppose it's not entirely impossible."

"Did Sir Peveril often bring your father's tonic from the kitchen?"

"No, sir." Clovis didn't hesitate.

"Had he ever done such a thing before?"

Clovis did pause now, seeming to search his mind. "I don't believe he ever did, master. He only visited the house about once a week, sometimes less."

"But he knew of his father's habit of drinking a tonic before bed every night."

"Oh, yes. Sir Humphrey drank the same tonic in the morning also. I dare say that everyone in the household knew of it, what with all the fuss over straining the herbs and washing all the bottles."

"And who usually brought it from the kitchen?"

"Either one of the kitchen girls brought it, or I went to fetch it myself."

"But that day you were busy packing Sir Humphrey's belongings to prepare for the sudden journey to Salisbury."

"Aye."

"Then I can't help but wonder—" Dyer looked around the jurors. "If Sir Peveril, impatient to be master of his own domain, didn't seize his chance to remove the obstacle between him and his inheritance."

Ela watched the jurors study Peveril for his reaction.

"I didn't, I swear it!" he burst out.

"Then what made you bring the tonic from the kitchen that evening?" asked Ela.

"I—I don't know." He looked around, his gaze imploring them to believe him. "I don't even remember how it came to be in my hands."

"What do you mean by that?" asked Ela.

"I mean that I didn't go to the kitchen and fetch it. It was just there in the great hall, on the small table near the fire where my father kept a pile of his books. I suppose it was an instinct to carry the tonic up to his chambers, where he usually takes it."

"Who would have put the tonic in the great hall?" asked Ela.

"One of the kitchen servants, perhaps? I can't think of anyone else who would have. The cook would never have done such a thing herself."

"Were there any new servants who might not be familiar with your father's routines?"

"No, my lady. It's been more than three years since my father hired a new servant."

"You said that you live in your own manor at Chicklade, is that correct?" continued Ela.

"Yes, my lady."

"But you were there that day, in the castle at Mere, when your father was preparing to go on a journey?"

Peveril looked uneasy. "I was there when my father got the news that his wife wished to extend her stay with you. I visited the manor at least once a week, as Clovis observed, to visit my father. And it was my duty as steward to make sure the castle was kept in good order and didn't fall to ruin. My father didn't enjoy managing the household, and his wife didn't seem to know much about it either. She's an empty-headed thing."

Alice stiffened and gripped the back of Ela's chair tighter. Ela could feel her muscles tensing.

Ela turned to her. "Alice, did Sir Peveril come regularly to your father's estate for the purposes of keeping it running well?"

"Yes, my lady," said Alice mildly. "And he's not wrong that I wasn't very clever about managing the household. Every time I tried, my husband told me that I would waste money or cause a disturbance or that what I suggested was unnecessary and frivolous. Eventually I just gave up trying."

"And was Sir Peveril more effective in convincing your father to make necessary repairs and other such matters?"

"Yes, my lady. He could grow quite agitated about it and would keep pressing the matter and wear his father down. Eventually my husband would crave solitude so much that he'd agree to the repair or purchase or some such."

Ela turned to Sir Peveril. "So you were paying one of your habitual visits, but this time your father's wife was absent. Was your father upset about this?"

"I don't think he missed her very much," said Peveril coldly. "But when I pointed out that she'd been gone for weeks, and intended to be gone for several more weeks, I told him that if he wanted to keep his wife he'd better go after her." Peveril shot a pointed glance at Alice, who twitched noticeably, jerking Ela in her chair.

"You told your father to venture to Salisbury after his wife?" Ela now sat up, her mind working through the ramifications of this new information.

"Yes."

"Were you afraid that she was trying to escape him?"

"I thought it a possibility."

"And why did this concern you?" asked Ela.

"Naturally I was concerned for his health. A man in his later years needs the ministrations of a wife." Peveril glanced nervously around the room. "And given that she'd never seemed happy and that she was staying with a very independent-minded widow—" He stared at Ela. "I wondered if she might be encouraged to sue him for a divorce and bring scandal and shame on the house of de Gilbert."

"I would never encourage such a thing," said Ela quickly. "Marriage is a commitment until death. I resent the implication that I was a dangerous influence on Alice."

"I beg your pardon, my lady," said Peveril, looking chastened. "I didn't mean to offend, just that I thought there was some urgency to the situation."

"So you sent your father out in the cold winter winds to chase after his wife—who was only on the other side of Wiltshire with an old friend, not absconded to the Continent with another man?"

"Perhaps it sounds foolish, my lady, but I did. And he must have thought my urgings made sense, as he wasn't a man to leave the warmth of his fire and the comfort of his books for no good reason."

"And what did you do with the castle at your command?" Ela stared hard at him.

"Very little. I spent some time in the library looking for an edition of Virgil, which I found and then read that afternoon. Then my wife and I had supper in the hall, where I sat at my usual place, not at the head of the table where my father is accustomed to sit, then I went to bed. It was a cold and blustery night, and I wished I was at my own manor house, which—being smaller—is a good deal easier to heat."

"Did your father let you borrow books to take to your manor to read?"

"Yes, though he was very particular about the weather conditions if I wanted to take a valuable old book with me. His books were his children in many ways."

Ela felt a tiny tug of sympathy for these book-loving men. She prized her own collection that was both inherited from her father and his father before him, and—to an increasing extent—purchased during journeys to London.

"Do you have children of your own?"

"Yes, my lady. I'm blessed with a boy and a girl." A smile creased his grayish visage. "My father was very fond of them."

Ela found this hard to imagine, since the late Sir Humphrey cherished his time alone with his books above all else. "Did you bring them with you to visit the castle?"

"Rarely, my lady. We find it more convenient for them to stay at home during our brief visits. Since my father was away my wife did bring them to the castle that day so we could all be there together in case he was detained in Salisbury."

"And were you still at the castle when you were notified of your father's death?"

"Indeed I was, my lady. I had intended to remain there until he returned with his wife. No sense leaving the servants to run the place!" He said that as if they might immediately feast on the fatted calf and cavort in the great hall. Ela found this ludicrous. On the other hand, it usually fell to the lady of the manor to manage the staff, and clearly Alice had done a less than stellar job of this.

"What was your reaction when you heard the news of your father's death?"

"Shock at first. I couldn't believe it. He was in excellent health, or I wouldn't have encouraged him to ride across Wiltshire in late November. Then the grief hit me, with the realization that I'd never see him again."

"Did you immediately suspect foul play?" asked Ela.

"No, my lady. I assumed he had died of an apoplexy or similar. It's not unheard of in men of his age." She couldn't blame him. She'd thought the same herself. Although not elderly or infirm, Sir Humphrey wasn't exactly robust and ruddy the way some men of his age—and older, like Bill Talbot—were, who seemed younger than their years.

Ela turned to Clovis, who she knew had accompanied the body of Sir Humphrey back to his castle. "How did Sir Peveril respond to the sight of his father's body?"

Clovis glanced nervously at Peveril. "He looked sombre, my lady. He'd been informed of the death by messenger, so it wasn't a shock. He and the whole family came into the courtyard to watch the wooden box containing the master's body being unloaded." Ela had provided a carpenter to hammer a box together. "Sir Peveril watched in silence and his wife and the little girl shed a tear, if I remember right."

"So you and your family had moved into the castle already?" Ela said it curtly. She hoped to provoke a reaction of some kind.

"I suppose so, yes." His answer was polite, almost apologetic. Ela had to admit that she was having a hard time finding fault with Peveril. But he was the only person—other than Alice, of course—with any discernible motive to kill Sir Humphrey de Gilbert.

"Do the jurors have any further questions for Sir Peveril?"

Stephen Hale, the cordwainer, raised his hand. "I'd like to know if the will was read and if there were any heirs other than Sir Peveril."

"It was read," said Peveril. "And my father's widow, Alice, retained the manor that she brought into the marriage and an annual stipend to support her in widowhood. Other than that, the estate remained intact to pass to his oldest son and heir, myself."

He spoke matter-of-factly, as if this wasn't incriminating in any way but a simple statement of fact. Which perhaps it was.

Any lord with an estate at his disposal and his wits about him kept a current will that his estate might pass into the right hands. Ela's husband had refreshed his last will and testament every time he set out to fight in a war or even to take a long and difficult voyage. It would have been irresponsible for him not to.

Peveril was likely familiar with the content of his father's will as well as the management of his estates, the way a miller's oldest son would be familiar with the operation of his family's grindstone. No doubt the disposition of his father's estates gave Peveril motive, but how could they prove—or disprove—that he was the killer?

"You have a younger brother?" asked Ela.

"Yes. He's married and lives in Shropshire on a manor that was his wife's dowry, so he's well provided for." Ela couldn't see any reason why this younger son might be a suspect. He had nothing to gain from his father's death.

"I'd like to ask some questions of Mistress Alice," said one of the jurors, a short, wiry older man with a thatch of white hair. Ela recognized him as Clement Dawson, a retired blacksmith who used to shoe horses at the castle.

"Alice, why don't you come around the table and face the jurors," said Ela softly. It was awkward having Alice stand behind her chair, clinging to it, as if she and her chair were a piece of driftwood in a storm at sea.

Alice moved hesitantly around the tables and went to stand at one end of the U-shape they made. She clearly didn't want to move into the middle, where the defendant stood. Instead she hovered near Clovis.

"I don't mean to upset you, my lady," said the blacksmith softly. "As I'm sure your husband's death came as a great shock to you."

Alice nodded silently, lips pressed together. Ela was glad that the juror didn't seem to be about to accuse her of killing her husband.

"But you and Clovis here seem the most likely witnesses to testify as to the nature of Sir Peveril's character and the likelihood that he killed his father. Since the servant is clearly motivated by a desire to keep his living, and perhaps cannot be trusted to be completely frank, I hope that we can count on you to give us honest answers to our questions."

"I'll do my best." Alice's voice shook a little.

"Do you think young Sir Peveril capable of poisoning his father in order to inherit his estates?"

All eyes turned to Alice, whose knees buckled slightly. Ela prayed that she would give a good answer if only to shift the blame from herself. "I—I don't know." Ela glanced at Peveril, who was peering at her through narrowed eyes. She shrank from his gaze. "I wouldn't have taken him for a killer. He's a man of books and learning, like his father, not a man of action."

Ela's heart sank. Alice had just said that Peveril was unlikely to be the killer, which put her back under the shadow of suspicion.

"Thank you, my lady, for your thoughtful answer," said the blacksmith. "I wonder if, among his collection of books, we might find some volumes filled with remedies and... perhaps...poisons?"

"I wouldn't know," said Alice simply. "Though I suppose you might."

The blacksmith turned to Clovis and asked him the same question.

Clovis, now shaking visibly, muttered that there were a few books filled with herbal remedies and medicines of various kinds. On further questioning he admitted that it was possible that at least one book contained information on how to make a poison to kill vermin, though since he couldn't read, he had no way of knowing for sure.

"Did your master, Sir Humphrey, ever gather the ingredients to make his own tonics?" asked Dawson.

"No, sir, he didn't. They were gathered from the herb garden by one of the kitchen girls."

"And how long had she been in the household?"

"Her whole life, sir."

"Could she have any reason to despise Sir Humphrey?"

"I can't think of any. She didn't really have much to do with him other than serving meals."

"Might he have…er…tampered with her?"

"Sir Humphrey? Fiddle with a young girl? Never!" Clovis looked deeply shocked. "He wasn't that type of man at all."

The blacksmith turned to Alice. "It pains me to ask you, but would you agree with that assessment?"

"Yes," said Alice without hesitation. "My husband was not disturbed by lusts of the flesh."

Dawson turned back to Clovis. "Did Sir Peveril ever gather or handle the herbs for his father's tonics?"

"Not that I know of. I never saw him do it."

"Did Sir Humphrey's wife, Alice, ever gather herbs or prepare his tonics?"

Clovis hesitated. His gaze darted toward Alice. "I believe she did. Not all the time, but on occasion she would."

Alice looked unperturbed by this new revelation. The jurors, however, seemed stirred by this news and one or two of them started to fidget. Peter Howard raised his hand. Ela nodded for him to continue, her chest tightening.

"Mistress Alice, were you familiar with all the ingredients of your husband's tonics?"

"No, the cook always made it for him and only she knew the exact recipe."

"Did he take the tonics the entire time you were married?"

She paused and frowned slightly. "No, he started after we'd been married about three years. That's when his toe started to swell and the doctor told him he had gout and should try taking a tonic made with sour cherry for it."

"And did he find the remedy helped?"

"He had to eat less meat as well, but, yes, it did seem to give him some relief from the pain and swelling."

"And the cook had the responsibility of making this healing concoction?"

"Yes." Alice blinked. "She'd hang the herbs to dry in the kitchen, then grind them to a fine powder. Once a week or so she'd boil water and brew the herbs into a tea, which was sealed into a brown glass bottle."

"Was the bottle kept in your husband's bedchamber?"

"No, it was kept in the pantry and he usually drank it at dinner."

"And who had access to the pantry?" asked Dawson.

"The cook and her kitchen staff," replied Alice.

"And you?" pressed Dawson.

"Well, yes. Except that I wasn't there that day. I was here in Salisbury."

Ela took the cue. "It seems that Sir Peveril is the only person who had both access to the tonic and sufficient motive to commit the crime. I therefore suggest that he be held here until such time as the traveling justice can try the case."

She didn't use the word "dungeon." Locking Sir Peveril up down there in the slimy cavern under the castle on rather slim evidence might provoke an outcry that could work in his favor. "I propose that Sir Peveril be kept under guard in the tower, where there's a room with an antechamber suitable for the purpose. The servant Clovis can remain with him."

Peveril looked as if he'd been struck by lightning. "But that's impossible! I must see to the management of my estates."

His response drew a round of stern gazes from the jurors.

"Guards, please remove him to the tower."

CHAPTER 13

"Surely you want to spend Christmas here at the castle?" protested Ela. It was less than two weeks before Christmas, and Alice had announced her intention to move immediately into her house, which was still in the process of being renovated.

"I've prevailed on your hospitality for long enough. And it's hard to sleep under the same roof as my husband's murderer."

Ela found that a bit rich since Alice had been hoping and praying for her husband's death. "I understand that it must be awkward having Sir Peveril here, but you have had no interaction with him. His meals are taken to his room, and he hasn't left it except to stand before the jury."

"Still, I feel like I need to begin making my own way in the world."

"But the walls are still being plastered!" Ela couldn't believe Alice's sudden resolution to leave the warm, busy castle—all abustle with Christmas preparations and the great hall smelling of hot spiced wine—for her manor that was only halfway to being habitable.

"The roof is fixed so the inside is dry. Once a fire is roaring in the grate it will be quite warm. I've secured some staff from a local family."

"How?" Ela could hardly believe her ears.

"I spoke to the thatcher and the plasterer to ask if they could recommend a cook and kitchen maid or lads for cleaning and gardening. They produced two likely young lads that are nephews to the plasterer, and the thatcher brought his daughter and her husband to be cook and steward. I liked them at once and hired them."

Ela stood blinking in shock. Alice had made a few journeys to the manor without her in the past few days, mostly because Ela had been busy with preparations for the annual Christmas festivities as well as village and county business and the planning for the monasteries at Lacock and Hinton. Christmas was always one of the more hectic times of year in the castle.

"Does your intended steward have experience? A poor steward can ruin a manor in a few months if he makes bad decisions regarding the livestock or planting. It's essential to have someone with knowledge and good judgment."

Alice smiled. "He's from a farming family and said he's experienced with the management of cows and sheep."

Ela inhaled slowly. There was much potential for disaster here but also perhaps the germ of success and joyful independence for Alice. She should think twice before trying to plow under the seeds Alice had sown to build her new life. "Well, that's all very exciting. I'm sure I can prevail upon you to stay in the castle until after Christmas, though. We have such gaiety planned. I'll be hosting a party of guests on Christmas Eve. It would be far better if you waited until the house is finished and comfortably furnished for you."

"I've ordered furnishings from a local carpenter. The

price was very reasonable, and the thatcher recommended him highly."

"Is he a relative of the thatcher?"

"Yes! He's his cousin. How did you know?"

"Just a guess." Ela didn't know the thatcher personally, but he'd come highly recommended by Thomas Pryce, who—along with his sons—was responsible for maintaining many of the roofs in Salisbury.

"What about bed linens and curtains and rush matting for the floors? Your new bed will be ice-cold without curtains to keep the heat in, and those stone floors—"

"All ordered already," said Alice brightly. "A seamstress is making the curtains out of blue-dyed linen stamped with a pattern of leaves and the thatcher's daughters are weaving the rush matting."

"Goodness, I had no idea the project was so far along. I almost feel like you've been keeping me in the dark." Ela wondered why Alice hadn't boasted of any of these accomplishments.

"You've been so busy lately that I didn't want to fill your head with my trivial concerns. It's not as though you ask me for advice about your sheriff duties."

"Well, I'm most impressed that you've made such progress and I admire your industry and independent spirit."

Alice glowed. "I take my inspiration from you."

"That's a kind compliment. And if at any time you find that you've rushed into your new life too fast, you must feel yourself welcome back at my table and hearth."

"That's so kind of you."

Ela wasn't available to accompany Alice on the day of her move or visit her for several days after it because a crime involving two farmers and a mysteriously missing calf kept her busy in Salisbury. Once the calf was located and returned to its true owner and peace restored, she found her thoughts returning to her friend.

Leaving the chapel after morning prayer, she turned to her daughter. "Petronella, why don't we ride out to visit Alice and take her a baked ham and some of the cook's sweetmeats? She may have found the novelty of her new home is waning after a few cold, dark evenings there."

"I bet she'll want to jump on a horse and ride back with us," mused Petronella.

"That wouldn't surprise me at all. And I'd be happy for it. I miss her gay company."

"Rather too gay, if you ask me. The Christmas season should be a time for reflection on the life of our Lord."

"This is a time to celebrate his birth and rejoice in the gift of faith. There's nothing wrong with making merry at Christmas. We have plenty of time to reflect and mourn during Lent."

"I suppose you're right," said Petronella with uncharacteristic agreeability. "And I wouldn't mind a ride. I like this brisk, icy weather that mortifies the flesh."

THEY LEFT as the pale sun rose to its highest point in the bright December sky. A light dusting of snow had frosted the trees with sparkle that fit the festive season. Bright berries glowed among the holly bushes and the fields glittered like cloth of silver.

They took a route that led them around the edges of fields, where stubble pricked from the frosty ground or sheep grazed on icy grass. They urged their horses to canter up the hills and watched their breath steam in the cold winter air. The guards—bearing their gifts of food—stayed at a discreet distance, and Ela almost forgot they were there.

"It really isn't far at all," said Petronella, as they spied the newly thatched rooftop of Alice's house from the slope of a nearby hill. Smoke rose from both chimneys, presenting a picturesque and encouraging view.

"It's a roundabout journey by road, which makes it feel remote. But if you head straight across the countryside, it's an easy ride."

They rode down through a stretch of sunny woodland. The bare branches of the trees shone with ice and dry twigs and leaves crackled under their horses' feet.

They emerged from the woods right near Alice's manor.

"Do you think she'll be surprised to see us?" asked Petronella.

"She'll be thrilled. I suspect she's dying to show us all the work that's been done on the place. You should have seen it when we first came here. It was quite derelict and neglected."

They dismounted and handed their horses to one of the guards, then took hold of the baskets. One contained a small smoked ham and a clay jar of fig preserves. The other held a well-aged fruit cake wrapped in bright blue cloth and a round glazed pot of brandy butter.

The bare ground in front of the house was much disturbed with hoofprints. "Looks like there's been a lot of activity here since it snowed last night," said Ela. "I do hope Alice hasn't ridden off to Salisbury to see us!"

"That would be funny."

At that moment Ela heard Alice's characteristic tinkling laugh and the trotting of a horse on the packed earth of the lane.

"Alice!" she cried out. She couldn't yet see Alice's horse. The naked branches of large oak trees shrouded the lane in dappled light. "Alice! We came to see you."

A broad-shouldered black horse came into view—and stopped, as its rider pulled on the reins. Behind it, she could see Alice on a gray horse.

"Who's that, Mama?" asked Petronella. "Does Alice have a brother?"

"That man is not her brother."

CHAPTER 14

A full half of Ela wanted to run back to her horse, mount and bolt for home. But she stood, transfixed in the yard in front of the house, too shocked to move, a basket of ham and fig jam weighing heavily on one arm.

"Ela!" Alice's shocked voice and aghast expression jolted her from her trance. Ela could see that Alice was also tempted to turn and bolt.

"My lady Ela," said Adonis d'Ys, with a nod of his tousled dark head. "What a surprise."

Ela was mindful of Petronella standing right next to her. She knew nothing of Adonis d'Ys and his unsuitable flirtation with Alice. "Good afternoon," she said stiffly. "Petronella and I thought you might enjoy some treats from the cook's kitchen."

Alice rode closer, peering at Ela as if not sure what to do. "How lovely. Do come in." Her voice was flat, as if she'd strongly prefer that Ela do anything but.

"We don't have much time," said Ela, her voice trailing off. She still couldn't believe that this man had the gall to come visit Alice at her remote manor. She had no one here to chaperone her! As far as Ela knew, she was entirely alone here with her servants.

"I would like to see what you've done with the house," said Petronella eagerly. Ela looked at her. Petronella must have sniffed out that something odd was going on, as she'd never shown any interest in a house interior before. "Mama told me it was quite dilapidated, but it looks very snug now."

"Oh, it is," said Alice brightly. Still, her face looked pale as she glanced around the assembled company.

"I'll take the horses to the stable," offered Adonis, jumping down from his black mount. He took the reins of Alice's horse, and she slid gingerly down. Once she was on the ground he marched off around the house, leading both horses.

"What's going on here?" asked Ela, unable to contain herself.

"Adonis came to help me settle into the house."

"I can see that," said Ela coolly. "You're an unmarried woman and it's not seemly for you to entertain an unmarried man in your home, especially with no one else here to act as chaperone."

"I didn't really have a choice," said Alice, opening the front door. The door was freshly painted in dark green paint and the door surround in red. "Since I have no suitable relatives to come live with me."

Ela followed her into the hall. The floor was scrubbed clean, revealing smooth stone flags. A fire burning at one end in a large fireplace accounted for one of the smoking chimneys. The other must belong to the kitchen, which was hidden from view.

"The thatcher did a marvelous job with the roof," said Alice, sweeping into the room. "Luckily the woodwork is still in good condition so few repairs were needed. He replaced nearly all of the reed." Ela could see the exposed underside of the thatch, still the warm color and fresh scent of new reed. "And look at all the nice furniture that young Ned built for me."

Ela looked at the sturdy table with two chairs near the fire. There was also a high-backed armchair large enough for two to sit in. Neither featured any carving or ornamentation but they looked serviceable enough.

"I intend to paint them when I have time to make some paint," said Alice.

"Adonis d'Ys isn't staying here, is he?" asked Ela softly. She really didn't want Petronella to think that Alice was carrying on a love affair with a man she barely knew.

Alice hesitated. "No, of course not." The words rushed out, and Ela got a distinct impression that she was lying. "He's staying with a friend nearby. He just visited so we could ride together."

Ela wanted to feel relieved but didn't. "How did you communicate with him?"

"I wrote to him at his address in London, on Queenshithe," said Alice, with a determined expression, as if she challenged Ela to tell her not to. "He was the most interesting person I'd met in years, and I didn't want to let our chance meeting fizzle away to nothing."

"You are certainly showing a tremendous amount of initiative," said Ela. "Which normally I would commend."

"I know, I know, I'm not supposed to even glance in the direction of a man until I've been widowed for a year and a day," said Alice impatiently. "But I'm hardly parading with him through the streets of London so no one will be any the wiser."

"May we see the bedrooms?" asked Petronella.

Alice's eyes grew wide with alarm. "Uh...they're still in some disarray." Ela had a horrible vision of her clothes mingled on the floor with Adonis d'Ys discarded hose.

Ela fervently wished that Petronella wasn't standing right beside her. She wanted to warn Alice how very easy it was to become pregnant and how very difficult it could be to force an unwilling man to marry her if that happened, with both of her parents dead and her brothers indifferent at best. But the less Petronella suspected about the awful possibilities, the better. She certainly didn't want any rumors catching fire at Salisbury castle.

Adonis himself still hadn't appeared in the hall. "Do you have a groom to put the horses away?"

"There's a stable lad who does most of the work. But perhaps Adonis is helping him. He's a very skilled horseman."

Ela fought the urge to cross herself at the thought of Adonis's prodigious riding skills. She suspected he was hanging back, wanting to avoid any probing questions about his presence here. No man with honorable intentions would arrive at a respectable woman's isolated country house without so much as an attendant and with no chaperone—even his own elderly mother or similar—in place.

Which meant that Adonis d'Ys did not have honorable intentions.

"Petronella, you stay here with Alice for a moment."

She turned back to the front door.

"Where are you going?" cried Alice.

"I want to get something," said Ela. "From my horse." A bald lie, but she didn't intend to leave without giving Adonis d'Ys a piece of her mind. She hurried outside and around to the stable yard, where she found a lad rubbing down both horses. Adonis d'Ys was nowhere to be seen.

Ela walked into the stable building, where the saddles sat on trestles waiting to be wiped clean. The stable showed signs of recent repair, including a new roof of much thinner thatch than the house.

She walked back out and around toward the back of the house.

"Are you looking for me?" D'Ys stepped from behind a tree. Dark eyes shining with amusement rather than concern, and thick dark curls tossed by the wind, he looked even more disreputable than he had in London.

"Why are you here?" asked Ela rudely.

A half smile lifted one side of his mouth. "Let's not play games, my lady," he said softly. "We both know why I'm here."

"I believe you are here to take advantage of my dear friend's innocent nature."

"She's willing. I'm not forcing her to do anything."

"She's spent her life locked up with a pinched old man. She knows nothing of the world. She thinks you're going to marry her and sweep her off to your palace in France."

"And who's to say I'm not?" he asked, gazing at her defiantly. "You think you know my intentions better than I do."

"I'm concerned for my friend's character and reputation, not to mention her spirits. She's suffered greatly already, and I don't want her crushed by despair."

"Don't be so quick to assume I'm a villain. Alice is a beautiful young woman. Why do you assume I couldn't possibly want her as my wife? This suggests that as her friend you have no appreciation for her good qualities and don't think anyone else would either. Perhaps she'd be far better off without your friendship."

He didn't look in the slightest bit perturbed during this speech but might have been discussing the bright afternoon sky or the price of beef in Marlborough.

Am I being churlish regarding Alice's prospects? Perhaps it did make sense for a woman of her years to enter another marriage as soon as possible. Still...

"Have you been married before?"

"Of course. It would be strange if a man of my years have never been married."

"How many times?"

He shifted his weight slightly, which somehow emphasized the breadth of his shoulders. "Ah, 'tis sad, but I've buried four wives."

Ela felt a frisson of unease. "That is a great number."

"It's not so unusual. Your mother, the Lady Alianore, is on her fourth marriage."

"That is true, but husbands tend to die in war. Women aren't availed of such opportunities."

"No indeed, but I think most would agree that childbed is far more treacherous than war."

"I can't argue with that, though I've been blessed to bear eight children myself without adverse incident."

"Lucky you! To enjoy the comforts of home, hearth and a large brood of healthy children. Would that we could all congratulate ourselves on such riches."

His wistful expression gave Ela pause. "Do any of your children live?"

"Alas, no." His gaze dropped to the hard, frozen soil. "And beyond the tragedy of such great loneliness, I find that I yet have no heir to inherit the ancient name of d'Ys."

"Perhaps you have a nephew. Or a niece. Although I'm female I was my father's heir."

"And to one of the greatest fortunes in all England," he said, looking her directly in the eye. "You are lucky indeed that he valued you as much as a son. I would do the same, of course. I don't expect Alice to bear me eight children, not at thirty-three."

Ela was surprised that Alice had confessed her true age. Most women would have shaved off five years or so. But Alice was not one to prevaricate.

"So your main interest in Alice lies in starting a family?" She still couldn't bring herself to believe he was genuine.

"Indeed it does. And at my age—I am forty-seven—I find I no longer have the patience for stripling girls fresh from their mother's teat who have no experience of the ways and wearinesses of the world."

Forty-seven! Ela could hardly believe it. Adonis d'Ys's black hair had few strands of silver. His face was weathered rather than lined. "I appreciate your honesty about your age and intentions. I must confess I thought you were younger and inclined to toy with Alice's affections. Still, you must see that it's inappropriate for you to court her out here alone at her country manor."

"Where else might I court her? You hardly showed an inclination to invite me to sup with you all at Salisbury castle."

True.

"Perhaps I can prevail upon my daughter Petronella to join Alice here as a companion. A young woman of quite severe morals, she would provide an appropriate chaperone."

There was no danger of Petronella being prevailed upon to keep anyone's dark secrets. She had eyes like a hawk for mischief and a bloodhound's nose for sin.

"How delightful that would be." Neither his gaze nor his voice revealed much enthusiasm for this suggestion.

"Where are you staying, exactly?"

"With my friend...Wilfred." He held her gaze as he spoke, but she had a distinct impression that he was plucking a name out of the air. He must be staying here with Alice. Which was appalling beyond all measure and made her doubt all his honeyed words.

I'd be putting Petronella in danger by leaving her here with Alice. The prospect of dear, pure Petronella being tampered with by a rogue brought a sudden flash of fear to her mother's heart.

"No, this can't work. I can see no alternative than for both of you to remove yourselves immediately to Salisbury castle, where you can be chaperoned by my entire household." Odious as the idea seemed, it was better than Alice being seduced and abandoned out here at the mercy of this virtual stranger. If she could have whisked Alice away she would have, but she could only be sure Alice would come if she invited him, too.

To her surprise, he didn't immediately protest. "I'd be most grateful for your hospitality, especially during the Christmas season, when I'd imagine your castle is most busy."

"Indeed it is, but we are fortunate to enjoy a great many chambers to accommodate a variety of guests. You and your manservant shall have a suite of rooms in a tower at the opposite end of the castle from the family quarters where Alice shall dwell." She said it with a sense of prim satisfaction and watched his face for a reaction.

To his credit there was none.

"My manservant is in the barn." He tilted his head toward it. "I shall instruct him to return to Wilfred's and gather my few trifles and hie at once to Salisbury Castle."

Ela's gut suddenly churned with misgivings. So much could go wrong when she invited a scoundrel under her roof. She remembered the disaster of opening her home and hearth to Drogo Blount, a one-time battle comrade of her husband's who'd proven lusty and incorrigible.

Still, at least she could keep an eye on them. If they were to be married, then it could be arranged properly and with all the legal protections that Alice would require. Alice's family was not of great consequence and it was quite likely that her marriage to an obscure French noble would go almost unremarked by the world at large.

"You'd better come with me to break this news to Alice," she said.

"I'd be delighted."

They walked back around the house, hard ground crunching slightly underfoot, in an uncompanionable silence. Everything about this man set Ela's teeth on edge. His handsome face, his easy manner, his tall, broad physique, his claim to an ancient lineage—all the things that would normally be seen as assets, seemed like liabilities in him.

When they reached the front door he held it open for her with a gracious gesture and she walked through. Alice chattered gaily away to Petronella about her further plans to furnish the space and the decorative items she hoped to acquire. Petronella listened silently. Her gaze immediately latched onto Adonis d'Ys when he entered the room.

Alice halted mid babble and stared at her suitor. Then she looked at Ela with alarm. "What's happening?"

"I bumped into Sir Adonis out in the courtyard." Not really a lie, though not the whole truth. She assumed he was a knight—a chevalier—though it hadn't been stated. "We discussed the possibility of both of you coming to stay at Salisbury Castle over Christmas, and he agreed that it was an excellent idea."

"Really?" Alice looked incredulous. "He'd be staying at the castle, and I'd be staying at the castle?"

"Yes, though not in the same quarters. It's not appropriate for him to be calling on you out here where you have no chaperone." Or protection. "I'd feel much better about him courting you in the well-peopled terrain of my great hall."

"Well...goodness..." Alice looked at Adonis, expectant but also a little nervous, as if she thought he might reject the idea. Which he might have, if he was solely interested in bedding her. Spending time alone with her would be all but impossible in the busy atmosphere of the castle. "What do you think?" she asked Adonis.

"I agreed that it was a most pleasing plan and I accepted Countess Ela's gracious offer of hospitality." He beamed his winning smile at Alice, then turned it on Petronella. "And who is this lovely young lady?"

Petronella's face tightened. She was as likely as not to take a compliment as an insult. She looked deeply suspicious of this dark-eyed stranger.

"This is my eldest unmarried daughter, Petronella," said Ela stiffly. It would certainly be revealing if he suddenly turned his attentions to Petronella. Her daughter was niece to the king and belonged to one of the richest and most influential families in the country. If a man was motivated by ambition and greed he'd certainly show more interest in her than in poor, sweet Alice.

He strode toward Petronella and took her hand. "I'm most honored to make your acquaintance." He kissed the back of her fingers. Petronella looked stunned—horrified, even—and snatched her hand back at the earliest opportunity.

Alice simply looked pleased by what she no doubt interpreted as a friendly gesture to the daughter of his host. "Well, isn't this exciting! I did miss the festive atmosphere of the castle. I've never stayed anywhere that really celebrated Christmas. My husband wasn't one for frivolities and my parents didn't hang boughs of holly in their hall, either."

"Good! Then we shall set out at once. Sir Adonis will return to his friend Wilfred's house with his manservant to collect his belongings, then will meet us at the castle later."

Alice looked at Adonis in confusion. Had he not bothered to pretend he had a local friend called Wilfred? Did he even have a manservant? So many questions...

Alice ordered Minnie to pack her clothes and to instruct the stable boy to tack up her horse for the journey. Adonis excused himself to make his own preparations but shot Alice a starry-eyed glance just before he exited the front door.

Alice sighed once the door closed behind him. "Isn't he handsome?"

No one answered.

"I admit that I did question him about his intentions toward you and he sounded genuine," said Ela. "So I thought it best for me to step into the role of your late mother and make sure he doesn't have the opportunity to take advantage of you."

"You don't mind him courting me?"

"Well, naturally I would have preferred for you to wait, but under the circumstances perhaps that's not for the best."

"I am getting older, after all."

"Speaking of which, are you aware that he's forty-seven? He's a good deal older than you. Not that much younger than your late husband." She didn't want to come out and say that he might not be able to get her with child and that—if that was her main goal—a man closer to her own age would be a much better choice.

"Is he really? He doesn't look it."

So he hadn't told her his age. Or he'd lied to Ela about it for reasons unknown. "Did you know he's been married four times?" Ela was fairly sure that Alice only knew about one wife the last time they'd spoken of it.

"Yes. Poor man! He's had his heart broken so often. His disappointments make my own easier to bear."

Ela wondered just what maudlin stories he'd told her. She lowered her voice, in case he was lurking nearby, listening. "Perhaps the two of you shall find joy together in marriage, but until then let's proceed with caution. We still don't know much about him, and we must make sure he's a suitable match who'll serve well as your protector and defender."

"He has a good and pure heart," said Alice with a smile.

Petronella rolled her eyes, which was happily visible only to Ela since Petronella stood right next to Alice. Ela was inclined to agree with Petronella's assessment of the man. She certainly intended to send out urgent inquiries to learn what she could about him.

CHAPTER 15

Back at the castle, Ela penned a letter to her mother, reporting on the day's shocking events. She rather blamed her mother for taking them all to dinner at the mayor's house in the first place. While Roger le Duc himself was undoubtedly a clever and fascinating man from a fine family, his guests came with no guarantees. As a man of business and politics in what was arguably the world's greatest city, he was as likely to dine with a wealthy mercenary as with a scion of ancient nobility.

After she'd sealed her letter and given it to Elsie to send, she headed to the chapel to pray. She prayed for compassion and kindness toward Alice—whose behavior she thoroughly disapproved of—and generosity of spirit toward Adonis d'Ys, who might yet prove to be her perfect match. Then she said another decade to offer penance for her dark thoughts about the prospects for their marriage.

It was well after dark by the time she ventured into the great hall. There she found Adonis and Alice sitting side by side at the table nearest the fire, gazing deep into each other's eyes, though admittedly from a reasonably chaste distance.

She ignored her instinctive distaste and forged toward them. "I trust you dined well?"

"Yes, thanks to your hospitality. Why didn't you join us for dinner?" asked Alice.

"I felt called to spend time in prayer," said Ela. "Although this is one of the holiest seasons of the year it's also the busiest, so I must steal myself away so that I don't neglect my prayers."

"Ela's very devout," explained Alice to Adonis. "She's planning to found two monasteries even as we sit here. One to honor her husband's memory and one for her own."

"I'm sure such generosity will not go unrewarded in God's heavenly kingdom," said Adonis. His eyes glimmered with something that might possibly be amusement.

Ela felt instantly offended. Did he suspect that she was trying to buy herself a place in Heaven?

Was she?

"I hope to support communities that will provide a haven for men and women in England who wish to devote their lives to the glory of God," she said stiffly.

"That's most commendable, I'm sure," he said. He looked at her warmly. "Though sometimes it seems there's a monastic community in every hamlet."

"Better that than a brothel, surely," said Ela. Her reply came out rather curter than she'd intended.

Adonis didn't immediately agree, which suggested that he was silently considering whether a brothel or a nunnery might offer more benefits to the residents of a community. Alice giggled.

"Ela suggested that I join a nunnery," she said.

Adonis laughed heartily, which further irritated Ela.

"Why is that so amusing? I intend to take holy orders myself once my children are grown."

"Now that does surprise me," said Adonis. He studied her

face. "Ela, Countess of Salisbury, a woman of action and substance on all accounts, wishes to lock herself away behind high stone walls and quit the world and all its cares?"

Ela's stomach shriveled at his words. "The religious life does not always require utter seclusion." She hated that this arrogant man seemed to have seen right through her. She did enjoy taking an active part in the affairs of Salisbury and all Wiltshire. If she could have found a way she'd gladly play a role in the affairs of all England, like her powerful neighbor Bishop Richard Poore and her nemesis, Justiciar Hubert de Burgh. "Besides, life has its seasons. I'm sure I shall be glad of the peace of the cloister when the time is right."

At least she hoped she would. She rather envied Petronella's fervent craving for the monastic life, even as she disapproved of it in someone so young.

"I'm not cut out to be a nun," said Alice brightly. "I crave the world and all its pleasures far too much. And I've missed out on them for too long already. I was practically living the life of a nun with my husband, except for all the singing and praying."

"Such a terrible waste," said Adonis, gazing at her with apparent adoration. "Such a gay and bright spirit shut away like a light under a bushel."

"Speaking of shut away," said Alice. "What has become of my late husband's son Peveril, who's suspected of killing him to claim his inheritance?"

Ela wondered if she'd spelled out the story for Adonis's benefit. "He's still confined to his chamber, where he's receiving meals. I'm afraid the traveling justice won't come before Epiphany at the very earliest."

"I suppose the traveling justice wants to enjoy the comforts of his own hearth in the dead of winter and toast Christmas at his own fireside," said Alice brightly. "I can't blame him."

"Well, I, for one, consider Sir Peveril to be a brave knight who has delivered you from the prison of your marriage and back into the warm bosom of life," said Adonis with a cheeky half smile. "I'd like to meet him and shake his hand."

Ela blinked, not sure how to respond. She was beginning to seriously regret inviting him here, even for Alice's sake. His audacity seemed to know no bounds. A fire of indignation flashed in her chest. "Sir Peveril is not guilty until the traveling justice finds him so." She leaned in and spoke under her breath. "In fact, Alice herself is still under suspicion, for the reasons you so boldly state. She had little to lose and much to gain from her husband's death. So if I were you I would watch your tongue lest it start fires you can't put out."

"I beg your pardon, my lady," he said, with a look of sudden contrition. "I didn't mean to cause offense. My overbold tongue has certainly made trouble for me in the past, and I will take your advice and counsel it to remain still."

Alice, who didn't look at all troubled by this last exchange, smiled at him and said, "I do hope not. I so enjoy your conversation." A little silence suggested that she might have enjoyed his tongue in other ways as well.

Ela swallowed.

"Mama!" Her youngest son, Nicholas, came barreling toward her from the main entrance to the hall. "Carolers are at the gate! May they come into the hall?"

"Yes, Nicky. I shall send for some sweetmeats from the kitchen for them." Ela smiled after him as he pelted back across the hall, setting the dogs barking. She summoned Elsie and sent her to alert Cook.

"I strongly suspect this is the most festive place in all England!" said Alice.

"I doubt it comes close to the amusements at Westminster, but the children do enjoy the Christmas season."

The great double doors to the hall creaked open, and a

large group of men, women and children of all ages shuffled into the hall, cheeks red with wind. When they reached the center of the room, a young boy with windswept blond hair and a worn blue tunic stepped forward and burst into a beautiful sung version of the Ave Maria prayer. His voice, clear, bright and strong as a ray of sunshine, rang through the hall and bounced off the stone walls and the wood roof.

Ela felt emotion flood through her at the beauty of his voice, and the gift of its presence right here in her hall.

Before the notes had died down from his last verse, the assembled group joined their voices in one of her favorite carols, "Rejoice, for Christ Is Born." She stood, rapt, quite forgetting about Alice and Adonis and all her other cares. They sang several more songs, then a little boy with a mop of reddish-brown hair ran forward and asked if it was time for figgy pudding yet.

Ela laughed. "I think it must be!" and she gestured for them to approach three tables that had been hastily cleared of garrison soldiers and stacked with sweetmeats and dried fruit. Cook always kept an excellent supply of such delicacies on hand at this time of year. Ela often swore she could serve a dinner fit for a king with a quarter-hour's notice.

The assembled group fell upon the platters of marzipan and candied fruit and tiny spiced cakes, and Elsie and two of the other serving girls poured cups of ale and passed them around.

"Oh, I'd like my house to be this cheerful at Christmas-time," said Alice, gazing in wonder on the merriment.

"You'd better move it into the middle of a town, then," said Adonis softly.

"I wish I could. I don't really like living tucked away in the countryside. Perhaps because it's all I've ever known. I'd like to live somewhere exciting."

With you.

Her unsaid words rang loud in Ela's mind. Ela glanced at Adonis's face to gauge his reaction. He smiled pleasantly but didn't say anything. He's humoring her, thought Ela. She still had very deep doubts about his intentions.

"Where do you usually reside, Sir Adonis?" she asked brightly, as if it were just a casual question.

"I live wherever my cloak has room to air in front of a fire," he said with a twinkle in his eyes. Alice blinked, looking just slightly alarmed. "Because the Burgundy estate that is my home base is inconveniently located for my trading activities that take me from Venice to Sevilla to Antwerp and all points in between."

"It doesn't sound like a very easy life to negotiate with a wife and children in tow," said Ela, looking mildly at him.

He stared at her for a moment before lifting his mouth in a smile. "Indeed not, and as I grow older I find myself more inclined to settle and enjoy my own hearth."

Alice looked pleased by this. "Is your Burgundy estate in a town or near one?"

"Oh, no. It's remote as a hermit's lair. The mountain passes can become so treacherous in winter that not a soul can get in or out for months at a time."

"Goodness. I suppose you won't be settling there, then. What about your ancestral lands in Brittany?"

"Ah, they're all but under water now," he said with a wistful look. "Time and tide can wreak such change on a landscape. And the old castle was at the far end of a forlorn promontory, chosen for its inaccessibility, which made it a safe stronghold in times of war."

"Oh." Alice had taken a cup of wine from Elsie, and she sipped it, looking a little nervous.

"If you could live anywhere you wanted," said Adonis, looking at Alice, "where do you think it would be?"

Alice's lashes fluttered as if her brain was making a great

effort to tackle his question. "Goodness…I've traveled so little that I hardly know. I did enjoy the excitement of London."

"Paris is a far finer city than London," he replied. "But so cold in the winter! Venice is a magnificent ethereal city rising out of the marshes, furnished with all the luxuries of the Silk Road, but the mosquitoes in summer are thick as fog and breed sickness among the people."

"Oh, dear, I shouldn't like that. What about Antwerp?"

"Ah, the Flemish, sturdy but dull as their flat lowlands. Now Sevilla…there's a city with a heart!"

"Do you speak the language?" asked Ela, wanting to pour cold water on Alice's new Continental fantasies.

"Alas, no," admitted Adonis. "But the language of numbers makes it easy enough to conduct business anywhere I go, and contracts are often in Latin."

"It would be difficult to settle somewhere that you don't speak the language, though, I suppose," continued Ela, a sweet smile pressed her lips.

"It can't be that hard to learn a new language, can it?" asked Alice. "I mean, most of us speak English and French and know at least a passable amount of Latin from our prayer books."

"You could hire a tutor to teach you, I suppose. And once you're living there, surrounded by chattering servants and visiting neighbors, I suspect you'd pick it up fast enough."

"I think I should enjoy the adventure," said Alice.

Adonis regarded her with amusement. "You're a spirited woman," he said softly. "I like that." His husky voice was barely a whisper. It was the kind of tone and talk best saved for behind the bed curtains—between husband and wife.

Did he intend to propose to Alice? Or was he merely seducing her for his own entertainment? Ela couldn't shake the suspicion that it was the latter.

The carolers, having enjoyed their food and drink, burst back into a final song of praise for the house and its residents, and Ela graciously accepted their thanks and presented her own thanks for their joyous song. When she turned back to Alice and Adonis, they were nowhere to be seen.

CHAPTER 16

The next morning, Ela knocked on Alice's chamber door. No answer. She knocked again, louder. "Alice, it's Ela! Are you within?"

"Yes," came a muffled voice, that sounded like it was both behind the bed curtains and underneath the covers.

"Please let me in, I need to speak with you." She tested the door to see if she could let herself in, but it was locked.

"I'm coming."

After what seemed an eternity, she heard Alice fumbling with the latch and pulling it back. Then Alice cracked the door open, blinking like a creature startled from its burrow. Her hair was wild as if she'd been out doing cartwheels in a windstorm, and her wrap appeared to have been pulled hastily over her nightgown. They stood in the doorway for a few moments.

"Are you going to invite me in?" asked Ela, suddenly suspicious. Was Alice bold—or insane—enough to sneak Adonis into her room at night?

"It is your house, isn't it?" said Alice, with a wry smile. "So you may do as you please."

Ela ignored this rather odd comment and pushed past her into the room. Was he under the bed? She bent and lifted the curtains from the floor, but saw nothing but dusty wood planks. Her attention turned to the window, and she hurried to it and unlatched it, and peered down at the courtyard below. There were no signs of anyone exiting it, and the cobbles below were a good thirty feet away.

"What are you doing?" asked Alice, shivering in the icy breeze that rushed in through the open window.

Ela closed the casement and latched it. "Did Adonis d'Ys visit you here last night?"

"No!" Alice looked shocked. "I can't believe you would think such a thing."

Momentary guilt tugged at Ela. Then her suspicion overwhelmed it. "Where did you go last night while the carolers sang their last song?"

"To the chapel," said Alice quickly. "Their sweet song inspired me to spend some time in prayer."

Ela blinked at her. While Alice had attended chapel with her many times in the past, and even prayed in what appeared to be a devout manner, Ela couldn't recall a single instance where it had been her idea to go there.

"Was Adonis d'Ys with you in the chapel?"

"Yes."

"And no chaperone?" Ela felt her blood heating again.

"Surely one needs no chaperone under the eyes of God?"

He put these words in her head. "God sees you everywhere. He hears your words and sees your actions whether you're in the chapel or not. I'm worried that you're being tempted into sin by a man whose intentions are not honorable."

"His intentions are very honorable," protested Alice.

"Has he proposed marriage?"

"Not yet." Alice's mouth worked for a moment. "But I feel sure that he will soon."

"Has he kissed you?"

Alice hesitated. *Yes.* Ela could hear the answer as loud as if she'd just said it.

"Why would you let him do that without proposing marriage first?" Ela couldn't keep her incredulity out of her voice.

"I'm in love with him!" gushed Alice. "I've fallen madly and deeply in love with him. How can I not kiss him?"

Ela's heart sank. "You barely know him. All we know of his past and his fortune is what he told us. His only references are in his relationship to the mayor of London. I've sent out inquiries about him and asked my mother to do the same, because neither she nor I know anything about him and as far as I know he's a stranger to the king's court."

Alice stared. "You've been asking people about him?"

"Well, I only started yesterday so all I've done so far is write letters. I have been most discreet, I assure you."

"Why would you have reason to doubt his own accounts of his family and his life?"

"I'm the sheriff, Alice, and before that I attended many juries and trials while my husband was sheriff. I have much experience with the crimes men commit and the lies they tell."

"He hasn't committed any crimes!" protested Alice loudly. Ela glanced at the door to make sure it was shut.

"How do you know? We don't even know if Adonis d'Ys is his real name. And if he's kissed you, then that is certainly a crime. As sheriff I've upheld a father's right to force a young man to marry his daughter after he's kissed her and spurned her."

"So you could force him to marry me?" said Alice, with what appeared to be genuine curiosity.

Ela stared at her. "I suppose I could compel him if you were to press a suit against him. I wouldn't advise it, though.

A marriage begun under duress would not bode well for your happiness. And he could just flee my jurisdiction. I couldn't put him in prison for refusing to marry you."

"Oh. Well, I'm sure that won't be necessary, anyway."

"Because he's going to marry you and take you to live in Sevilla," said Ela drily.

"I wouldn't mind living on his remote estate in Burgundy," said Alice with equanimity. "I'm used to the quiet."

Ela fought the urge to roll her eyes. Hadn't Alice complained of being stuck far out in the countryside? "You'd be there alone a lot while he travels."

"Hopefully I'll have children to keep me busy." A dreamy look came into her eyes and a smile played around her mouth. She looked so young and pretty at that moment that Ela could almost believe Adonis d'Ys to be besotted with her.

She also had to admit that his previous wives dying in childbirth suggested that he was at least able to conceive children, even if he hadn't successfully brought one into the world yet. "I sometimes think women are more courageous than knights of the realm. We marry and leave our family home to follow our husbands to parts unknown, where we'll have to run a household of strangers, and willingly risk our lives to bring forth children. Setting out on a crusade seems safer."

Alice laughed. "I hadn't thought of it that way. I suppose we grow up knowing that we're going to do those things, just like your sons are being raised to fight for their king. Though I suppose you could be enjoying a quiet widowhood sitting by the fire but instead you are managing the affairs of Wiltshire."

"I'm sure some people must think I'm mad and others frown on my ambition. But God gave me the gifts to manage the castle and the county and also the desire to do so, and who am I to disobey his will?" She frowned. "But why are we talking about me? The more urgent matter is your conduct regarding Sir Adonis d'Ys. You must promise me that you'll not see him in secret."

"I promise!"

"And you must behave with decorum and set a good example for my children. The boys are young and impressionable. I don't want them to get the idea that open flirtation is acceptable."

Alice hesitated at this scolding. "I'm sorry. I just get all flustered when he's about! I'll do my best to maintain my composure. Hopefully we'll be betrothed soon."

"I hope so, too, or you'll risk a scandal."

THE LAST DAYS before Christmas were a frenzy of preparation for the guests that Ela had invited to celebrate at the castle. Her dear friend Helene de Montfort was arriving with her husband Ernest, and her husband's old friend Alain de Hanisse had traveled all the way from Flanders with his wife Marguerite, to spend time in Salisbury before continuing north to Yorkshire to visit kin.

The guests arrived, including Isabella, the youngest daughter of Sir Alain from his first marriage. Isabella was a striking beauty of sixteen, with a joyous manner and a gift for entertaining the children. Ela hoped that Petronella might strike up a friendship with her and talk about something other than God's will on earth or the correct manner of storing the Host to prevent depredation by mice or mold.

"A letter for you, my lady." Ela was sitting by the fire, chattering gaily with Helene about horses, when Albert the porter approached with a sealed parchment in his hand.

Ela recognized her mother's seal as he handed it to her. "Thank you, Albert."

She broke the seal and unfolded the parchment covered with her mother's neat hand. "My mother likes to spend the Christmas season in London," she explained to Helene. "Otherwise I'm sure she'd be here to meet you. She can't resist the rounds of parties and amusements, especially when the king spends Christmas at Westminster."

Dear Ela, I've made inquiries into the unfamiliar man who shared the mayor's table with us. I was alarmed to hear that he pursued Alice all the way to Salisbury without an invitation, as I'm sure you were, too. The information I've gathered about him—or should I say the lack of it—is most worrisome.

Ela stopped reading and excused herself. She didn't want Adonis d'Ys to sneak up behind her and peer at the letter over her shoulder as she sat reading it in the hall. Folding the parchment, she hurried to her solar, where she quickly opened it again and continued reading.

First, I inquired of the mayor, who was responsible for our making his acquaintance. I had presumed that he knew the man well, to entertain him at his own board, but it turns out he had only been introduced to him the week before! The man who supposedly wrote the letter of introduction that he brought with him now claims he has never heard of any Adonis d'Ys and knows nothing about him.

Ela stopped reading. Her heart beat rapidly and alarm bells rang in her mind and body. Who is he?

He ingratiated himself with the mayor with a very generous gift of Burgundy wine and Venetian brocade. He spoke of bringing a large amount of trade, and the resulting tax revenue, to the city. The mayor found him entertaining and personable and invited him to dinner, quite by chance on the very night when I decided to impose our merry little group on his hospitality. Sir Roger admits that if he'd known in advance that I would be dining with him, he would have entertained only entirely respectable and well-known company, as I would naturally expect of him.

Further enquiries have revealed that no one knows anything about this man.

Ela stopped reading, alarmed by her mother underscoring several of the words to emphasize this new and very disturbing fact.

Who had she invited to spend Christmas under her roof?

And how could she pry Alice away from him?

THAT NIGHT AT DINNER, Adonis d'Ys was already showing his true colors by flirting outrageously with young Isabella de Hanisse. A bubbly and cheerful girl, she enjoyed his attentions and answered his outrageous questions with charming frankness.

Ela, seated at the head of the table and fairly far away from them, could only catch the occasional snippet. Alice, seated at Ela's right hand and also too far to intervene, watched with increasing consternation.

"What are they saying?" she whispered to Ela, as the remains of a roast goose stuffed with apples and raisins was removed from the table.

"Nothing of consequence, I'm sure," said Ela politely. She didn't want Alice causing a scene. She'd seated Adonis at the children's end of the table hoping to steer him clear of her rather distinguished guests, and now she could see the error of her ways.

Alice kept trying to catch his eye with a simpering smile but now he only seemed to have eyes for Isabella.

"Who is that man speaking with my daughter?" asked Alain de Hanisse, with no small amount of concern, as their cups were filled with Rhine wine to accompany the sweetmeats.

"Um..." Ela tried to come up with a reasonable reply. "I met him in London during dinner at the mayor's house. He's doing business in Salisbury, and I offered him a bed for the night."

"Oh." Sir Alain peered at him, clearly as doubtful of the mysterious stranger as she was. "I suppose that as Sheriff of Wiltshire you must run across all sorts of people."

"Indeed I do." She steered the conversation deftly to the planned Christmas festivities, which included a visit by mummers the following day. Still, she kept a close eye on Adonis d'Ys during the rest of dinner and decided to have a very blunt chat with him at the earliest possible opportunity.

AFTER DINNER the assembled company sat in comfortable chairs near the fire while a minstrel played traditional Christmas melodies on his lute. The dogs curled up at their feet, and even the children gathered around and listened to the lovely music.

Ela decided this was a perfect moment to slip away and give Adonis d'Ys a stern talking-to. But when she rose from her chair and looked around the hall, she couldn't see him anywhere.

"Are you looking for something, my lady?" Elsie, waiting nearby, hurried over.

"Come with me," said Ela, ushering her away from the group. "Have you seen Adonis d'Ys anywhere?"

"No, my lady. Not since dinner, I don't think."

Another realization dawned on her, and she searched the hall again. "Where is Alice?"

"I think she might have gone up to her chamber, my lady.

I saw her walking upstairs when I came down from putting fresh washing water in your room for tonight."

Sudden anxiety clutched at Ela's heart. "I shall go check on her and see if she's feeling well."

"Shall I come with you, my lady?"

"No, thank you, Elsie." The girl wasn't naturally inclined to spread gossip and rumor, but there was no need to put an irresistible temptation before her. "You stay here until I come back."

Ela hurried out of the hall, away from the music and warmth and the gentle bustle of the servants clearing and breaking down the trestle tables. In the chilly darkness of the hallway beyond, lit only by occasional braziers, she let her full panic overtake her.

He's bedding her right now.

She was as sure of it as she'd ever been of anything.

Poor foolish Alice would end up pregnant and abandoned and her dreams of motherhood would end in a lifetime of recrimination and isolation forced by her scandalous behavior, which would make both men and women shun her.

She lifted her hem and took the stairs two at a time. At the top of the stairs she looked around. When she slept up here, a guard was always stationed at the end of the corridor to protect her from intruders, but he hadn't taken his post and—rather neglectfully—none of her guards had shadowed her up here.

She approached Alice's door on the balls of her feet, careful to avoid the creakier floorboards. This time she intended to surprise them in the act, the better to warn her away from her foolish behavior and to seize the opportunity to banish d'Ys from her home.

Once at the door, she leaned in and listened. Silence. She listened again. Nothing.

Then she tried the latch and to her surprise the unlocked

door flew open. A shriek made her jump, and Minnie scrambled up from a bed roll unfurled on the floor near the fireplace.

"Alice?" Ela peered at the closed bed curtains. A lady's maid was privy to the most intimate details of her mistress's life, but surely Alice wouldn't commit a carnal sin with this young girl in the room?

"She's not here, my lady. She's downstairs in the hall listening to the music. She told me that I could come up here to get some rest if I wanted."

Of course she did.

She must have gone to Adonis's room with him. Or, the castle being a sprawling space with an almost limitless number of rooms spread across several buildings, she might be somewhere else altogether, casting shame on herself and ruining her prospects for future happiness.

"Thank you, Minnie. I'll find her in the hall."

ELA ABANDONED Alice as a lost cause. She could hardly leave her guests unattended while she searched the castle for her, and even if she found her it would likely be too late to prevent whatever mischief Adonis d'Ys had planned.

She rejoined the group in the hall, trying to distract herself with the usual amusements, including a game of chess with her son.

"Mother! I can't believe you just let me take your queen like that." Richard, who'd been improving his chess game steadily all year, crowed triumphantly. "Didn't you see my bishop was perfectly lined up with her for the last three moves?"

"Perhaps I've had one too many cups of wine," said Ela.

"Don't make excuses now," teased Richard. "You've always schooled me not to."

"You're right, of course." She had no excuse but to continue the game and at least pretend to put up enough of a fight so he could enjoy the honor of winning.

THE NEXT MORNING—THE Nativity—Ela would have dearly loved to devote the whole day to celebrating Christ's miraculous birth, but duty called. Taking two guards with her in case of trouble, and Elsie—sworn to secrecy—to carry the supplies she needed to achieve her goal, she approached Adonis's chamber door shortly before dawn and rapped on it sharply with her knuckles.

There was no answer. She took the knife from the small ornamental sheath at her belt and used the wooden handle to bang on the door even louder.

"Who's there?" called a muffled voice from inside.

Ela knew Alice wasn't with Adonis in this room. She'd assigned Elsie to sit up waiting for Alice's return to her room, and Elsie had alerted her to Alice's presence in it some hours earlier.

"This is your host, Ela of Salisbury. Please attend me at once." She wasn't afraid to sound imperious.

There was a pause, then she heard some shuffling and the movement of footsteps toward the door. The lock scraped and he pulled the door open, running his fingers through tousled hair.

"You and Alice crept away from the hall last night."

"What of it? She's in her majority and can do what she wants." He leveled a shining stare at her.

"This is my house, and I will not have any woman taken advantage of and ill-used within its walls. I've made inquiries about you to the mayor of London, among others, and the general consensus is that you are unknown, a stranger, a ghost...possibly a demon."

The hint of a smile tugged at his mouth. "Come now, my lady, such flights of fancy."

"Your charms have worn thin on me, and I require you to leave my castle at once."

"And break Alice's heart?" one dark brow lifted slightly.

"You're going to do that anyway." She leveled a steady gaze at him.

"True," he admitted, with an infuriating twinkle in his eye.

Fury surged in Ela's chest. "I knew it. Is any of your story true?"

"Not really." His handsome face looked unperturbed by her accusations. She fought the urge to slap it. "Though I am a man of means."

"From piracy?" Profiteering seemed a likely trade for a man who engaged in international trade, and she did believe that part of his story.

He didn't answer her question, but a dimple in his cheek deepened slightly. "I believe in seizing opportunities that cross my path."

"But why Alice?" Ela still didn't understand why he'd pursued her all the way to Salisbury.

"A plum, rich and sweet, softened almost to the point of over-ripeness, ready to be plucked and enjoyed before it withers and molders."

Ela fought a wave of sadness for her friend. "Alice is still just young enough to marry and have children, but now you've blighted her prospects and she'll likely spend the rest of her life alone."

"How? No one knows what happened between us."

"Don't be a fool!" Ela found her voice rising. "Everyone knows what happened between you. The castle is packed with guests and servants and the garrison soldiers. The very least you can do is be gone before she awakens."

He looked a little confused. "Should I not say goodbye to her?"

"Absolutely not. She's besotted enough to try to come with you. You don't want that, do you?"

He had the decency to look a little sheepish. "I confess that I do not."

"No, because you've plucked her and sucked all her juices, and now your appetites crave a new dish," she said angrily. "But she won't believe that, so I require you to write her a letter."

"Saying that I've gone to find another lover?" He tilted his chin.

"Of course not." Ela gestured for Elsie to hand her the parchment that she'd brought with her. She pushed into the room and spread the parchment on the small table near the remains of the fire. Elsie handed her the pen and ink, and she dipped the pen in the small vial of ink.

She held out the pen and he took it. "I suspect you've already planned the words for me to write."

"If need be, I can dictate, but I'm happy to let you compose the letter if it's close enough to the truth to kill her passion for you but not so close as to crush her spirit."

"A delicate balance," he said with a sigh. "But I shall walk the plank like a man." With that, he put pen to paper and started scratching.

CHAPTER 17

Ela waited until dawn to give the odious Adonis d'Ys time to make himself scarce. He hadn't even tried to argue and defend his right to a relationship with Alice, because he'd already enjoyed all the love he wanted with her. He was probably glad of the opportunity to make an escape without causing a scene.

With the letter folded in her hand and her heart beating hard beneath her gown, she approached Alice's door, anxious to get the heartbreak over with before the castle awoke.

Alice opened the door with a dreamy smile on her face. "Oh, Ela, this is the best Christmas ever!"

"Thanks be to God for the roof over our heads and the bounty we shall enjoy," she said quietly. The letter burned her fingers. "May I come in?"

"Yes!" She flung the door wide for Ela to enter, then closed and bolted it behind her. "Now I know you're going to be angry with me for flirting rather shamelessly with Adonis, but I just know he's going to propose today. He almost did last night." Her dark hair was a wild tangle and her face flushed.

Ela struggled to control her face. "I have a letter for you, from him."

"What?" Alice stared at the parchment in her hand, her face darkened by a sudden frown. "Why would he give his proposal to you?" She took the offered letter, still folded. Her smile returned. "Oh, I suppose he sees you as my guardian—since my parents are dead—and thought to ask your permission first."

"Not exactly."

Alice broke the seal—set with his thumbprint in the red wax—and opened the paper with fumbling fingers. Her expression darkened as she read his words.

"No!" she cried. "What is this? He didn't write this."

"I'm afraid he did," Ela said softly.

"I don't believe it." Alice's hands shook, and the parchment rattled. "Where is he?"

"He left the castle before first light. He's doing you a favor by not prolonging his mischief where all and sundry can see him do it. At least you still have a chance to salvage your reputation."

"My reputation! All you care about is my reputation. I couldn't give a fig about my reputation. Did you make him write this?"

Ela swallowed. "I told him it would be best, and he agreed."

"I don't believe you. You forced him into this somehow. Did you give him money?"

Ela had contemplated offering money, but he'd had the decency to leave before she'd felt the need to. Still, the question opened the door for Alice to have doubts about him. "Do you think him the kind of man who'd take money to abandon a lover?"

"No! I don't. He's a man of honor and great passion. He'd

never run away like a coward, leaving a letter in the hand of another."

Ela didn't know what to say.

Red blotches formed over Alice's throat as she read the letter again. She looked up at Ela. "Did you write this?"

"You know my hand. He wrote it himself, though I provided the pen and ink. He freely admitted that he wanted to enjoy you and that he had done so."

"And I enjoyed him, too!" protested Alice. "Why is it always assumed that the man is using and despoiling the woman? Does no one think that she enjoys the act, too?"

"Lovemaking within the sanctity of marriage is a blessing for any woman to enjoy. Lovemaking outside the legal and financial protections of that institution leaves a woman open to scandal and scorn and destitution."

"Did you read the letter?" asked Alice.

"I glanced at it to make sure he'd written what he promised."

Alice folded it and tucked it into the neckline of her gown. Ela found herself wondering what exact words the scoundrel had chosen. He clearly didn't mince them too much.

"Try not to fret. Perhaps few people noticed your absence last night. We shall attend chapel and pray together and enjoy Christmas with hope in our hearts. Christ's birth is a day of celebration," she said as cheerfully as possible. Alice's childlike enjoyment of feasts and amusements might help Ela to distract her.

"I still don't believe it. Some trickery is afoot. Last night he promised to propose marriage today."

Ela sighed. "I've heard of men promising such to win the prize they crave. Though that prize is not a lifetime of togetherness but a night of passion."

Alice stared at her. "We did share passion. I've never known anything like it."

Ela took her hand. "You shall know it again, with the right person." She hoped and prayed that this foolish affair wouldn't ruin Alice's chances of marriage. A woman's dreams had been blighted for far less. Even a stolen kiss might make her an object of ridicule, especially when she was a seasoned matron like Alice, not a silly young girl.

"Get dressed and we shall go to the chapel."

ALICE MOVED WOODENLY through the first service and sat mostly silent through breakfast. Her thoughts seemed to be spinning behind her eyes. She managed token replies when the children or one of the other guests addressed her, but her mind was clearly elsewhere.

The younger children played games and ran around shrieking while the adults enjoyed cups of spiced wine and honeyed delicacies. Another group of carolers came and filled the hall with their joyous song, then some of them acted out the story of Mary and Joseph arriving at the inn and being turned away, then settling in the stable to have their baby. Older men in turn played the shepherds and the three kings, arriving from afar to offer their blessings. They were onto the second king when Ela realized, once again, that Alice was nowhere to be seen.

She scanned the hall, looking from one table to the next. In an instant she was on her feet, panic flashing in her chest.

She's fine. She's probably just gone for a walk to clear her head. She tried to calm herself. Why had Alice slipped away without saying anything?

Ela excused herself from the assembled company and headed for Alice's chamber.

ALICE WASN'T in her chamber, where Ela found Minnie dozing in a chair. Once awoken she had no idea where her mistress was, but said she'd been told to wait there for her. She also wasn't in the herb garden or the walled orchard—which might have been a good choice for a secret tryst.

Ela hurried along the paths inside the castle walls with increasing alarm. She went to the chamber Adonis had stayed in, in case Alice would go there to look for him. The door was unlocked and the chamber stripped as Ela had requested, and there was no sign that Alice had been there.

She was descending the stairs, wondering what could have become of Alice, when a scream tore through the air.

Ela's gut clenched. The scream sounded like it came from outside the castle walls. She hurried to the nearest guard tower and climbed the stairs to the observation platform, then peered down at the landscape beyond the castle walls.

Another scream, this time longer and more emphatic, drew her gaze to a figure just on the far side of the moat. A woman in a dark red dress who, on further study, was definitely Alice. She stood over something that looked like a dead animal, a cow perhaps, but it was hard to see due to a patch of long grass and the shade of a great oak tree.

For a moment, Ela wondered about calling out to her, but decided the potential for confusion and further alarm made that a bad idea. Instead she rushed down the steps, past the startled guards.

"Did you hear those screams?" she asked one, an older man.

"Aye, my lady. A woman's scream. Should I go investigate?" He spoke so slowly that she thought he'd just slow her down.

"Go up the tower and watch down below."

She hurried along the inside of the castle walls to the gate and exited through it onto the road out of the castle.

"Do you need attendants, my lady?" asked a guard stationed there.

She hesitated. "Yes." She wasn't supposed to even walk about the castle without armed guards, due to a series of menacing events that had befallen her. "Come with me."

The guard had also heard the scream but not thought much of it. The festive atmosphere of the castle, and the copious quantities of ale that had already been consumed, had dulled any sense of urgency he might have felt at the sound.

But now, seeing Alice running toward the castle, her face in a mask of horror, he grabbed his sword and pulled it from its sheath.

"What's amiss?" called Ela, as Alice ran toward her.

"He's dead!"

Ela looked over at the oak tree. "Is it a cow?"

"A cow?" Alice stared at her, cheeks trembling. "It's Adonis! He's been murdered!

Ela noticed at that moment the dark stain spreading across Alice's dress. The dark red color of the cloth obscured it at first, but now she could see that the sleeves, the chest and parts of the skirt were wet with it.

Ela turned to the guard. "Call for the coroner and a jury to attend us at once! And send more guards out here."

Alice screamed again, piercing Ela's ear with the sound and making her jump.

Ela looked at Alice's hands, and found them also red with fresh blood. Had Alice killed her wayward lover?

Four guards came running toward her and Ela gestured for them to follow her. Alice seemed half inclined to run in the other direction, which gave Ela pause. Should she have Alice arrested?

No. She couldn't do that. Not without proof that she'd done this horrible deed. "You must stay with me, Alice."

"But I can't look on him again!"

"You must."

She hurried purposefully toward the spreading tree and the dark shape sprawled beneath it. As she grew closer she could see that it was indeed the form of a man, clothed in a black cloak and dark hose, slumped over forward, with his face hidden from view.

"Don't touch anything!" she called to the guards. "The coroner must see the body as it lies fallen."

"I touched him already," said Alice. "I thought he was sleeping so I bent to wake him up. Then I shook him and turned him over and—" She let out another piercing scream that rattled Ela's teeth.

"What were you doing out here?"

Alice hesitated. Her hands were now shaking and her teeth chattering. "You're going to be so angry."

"Never mind that, what happened?"

"Last night...when we were together—" She burst into sobs. Ela wasn't sure whether to comfort her or to try and slap sense into her.

"What?" she asked impatiently. She wanted to get a sense of Alice's story before they were mobbed by jurors and the coroner.

"He said to meet here, under this spreading oak tree that stands outside the castle walls. Even though it's very close to the castle it's hard to see from anywhere. I know you told me he'd left already, but when the time came for our meeting I came here as planned."

Ela's fury at the man was tempered only by his lifeless state. "Was he alive when you found him?"

"No, he was dead. And there's a knife in the grass somewhere. I trod on the handle."

Ela looked down at the grass, which grew in long tufts. "Did you move it?"

"No."

"Then leave it be until the coroner gets here," said Ela, mostly to the guards.

More people were already coming through the castle gate and out toward the tree.

Ela thought of her guests and her children, inside by the warmth of the fire, enjoying Christmas merriment. She realized at that moment that she wasn't wearing a cloak and that the December chill went right through her finely woven wool dress. She called to one of the guards to find Elsie and have her bring cloaks for both of them.

"Did you see anyone else nearby when you came out and found him like this?" Ela asked Alice quietly.

"No one." Tears now streamed down Alice's face. "I thought maybe he was lying down under the tree, waiting for me where no one would see him in the tall grass. I called out his name and he didn't answer."

"How did you get blood all over you?" whispered Ela.

"I shook him when I tried to rouse him."

"When did you notice the blood?"

"I s-s-saw it coming out of his mouth." Alice started gasping for air like she was drowning.

"Try to steady yourself," whispered Ela urgently. "It's far better that all these people don't know you were...carrying on with him."

"Carrying on?" wailed Alice. "I'm in love with him! And he's in love with me, which is why he still came to meet me even after you told him to go."

Ela glanced around and saw that eyes were indeed turning toward Alice, who provided quite a spectacle near the dead body with her blood-stained dress and frenzied weeping.

Giles Haughton arrived, jogging across the grass from the castle gate. He hurried right to the body and studied its placement and position. "Has anyone moved him?"

Ela cleared her throat quietly. "Alice found him here and tried to awaken him."

Haughton seemed to notice Alice for the first time, with shock in his eyes. No doubt he was wondering how this woman might find herself in the company of two different dead bodies within the space of two months. "What were you doing out here?"

Alice glanced nervously at Ela. "He'd asked me to meet him here."

"For what purpose?" Haughton stared right at her, almost disbelieving. Ela wished there weren't so many people around to hear the shameful truth.

"To say goodbye," said Alice. She looked at Ela as if hoping this was the right answer.

"Who is he?"

"His name is Adonis d'Ys," said Ela. "Or at least that's what he called himself. Alice and I had the misfortune to meet him at the mayor's house in London and he followed us to Salisbury, where he managed to ingratiate himself into the affections of poor recently widowed Alice."

Alice sobbed quietly.

"He pursued Alice…with a view to marriage?"

"That's what he led her to believe," said Ela quietly. "Though I suspected that his intentions weren't so honorable. I'd told him to leave the castle, and he had signed a letter saying goodbye to Alice very early this morning. I thought he'd had time to leave the area by now, but it seems he hung around hoping for another encounter with her."

Haughton's brows knitted. "So he had wooed Alice, and now decided to abandon her?"

"I doubt he would have left if I hadn't pressed him to. He

was enjoying Alice's company far too much." Ela did her best to keep her voice low enough that no one should hear. But she didn't want to tell the coroner half-truths or try to cover anything up. Giles Haughton was far too sharp for her to get away with that, and it might make him more suspicious of Alice. "I ordered him to leave at once and told him that if he didn't I'd have my guards throw him off the property."

"Did you know this?" Haughton asked Alice.

Alice nodded mutely.

"I gave her the letter he wrote saying that he couldn't marry her and apologizing for taking advantage of her kind and generous nature," said Ela.

Haughton turned to Alice. "Then why did you think he'd still meet you?"

"I knew he wouldn't just leave," said Alice. "He loves me. He told me so just last night!"

It hurt Ela's heart to see Alice still talking about him in the present tense. "He had a good deal of charm," she said quietly to Haughton. "But was very definitely a scoundrel."

Alice let out another wail. Ela, aching to keep Alice safe from herself, wished she could clap a hand over her mouth and tug her away.

The jurors started to arrive, with Peter Howard the baker first on the scene, as he often was, since his shop lay so near the castle. Ela apologized for pulling them away from their homes on Christmas morning.

Ela was forced to explain who Adonis d'Ys was—not that she believed a word of his inventive personal history—and how he happened to be under a tree outside Salisbury castle. She noted with alarm that each of the jurors regarded poor, sobbing Alice with a mix of disdain and suspicion.

The jurors examined the body and the surroundings. "The knife was found right here by the body?" asked Peter Howard.

"Yes," said Ela.

"And in your opinion was that the murder weapon?" asked Howard of Haughton.

"Indeed it was. The width of the blade matches the lacerations on the victim's neck and torso. It also appears to match the leather sheath on the victim's belt, so I believe he was killed with his own knife."

Ela jolted a little at this realization. Did Alice pull his knife from his belt and stab him when he told her he was leaving?

Impossible. She tried to shake the ugly thought from her mind. Her sweet friend could never kill anyone.

Could she?

It was a horrible coincidence that first her dull and miserly husband and now her wayward lover were found dead within reach of her.

Was it too much of a coincidence?

Alice wept, face in her bloodstained hands, looking every inch the guilty murderess who now mourned the lover she'd dispatched to the fires of hell.

"What did you say to him, when you found him here?" asked Stephen Hale, the cordwainer.

"I called his name, thinking to waken him," stammered Alice. "But after that I didn't say anything. I think I screamed when I realized he was dead."

"I heard the scream," said Ela. "I have no doubt that others did, too."

A murderess would hardly announce her crime with a scream, would she? Unless she was trying to deflect suspicion...

"Did the castle guards see anyone else near this tree?" asked Peter Hogg. A flurry of inquiry went among the guards, and the ones posted at the nearest tower were sent for. No one had seen anyone—including Adonis or Alice—arriving at or leaving the spot.

"My castle could be under attack by the Saracens for all you notice," cried Ela with frustration. "Your job as sentries is to guard the castle!"

The guards had the decency to look sheepish.

"You didn't see anyone? Even a passing shepherd?"

"It's Christmas Day, my lady," mumbled one of the older guards. As if that explained their inattention to their duties.

"I suppose Christmas Day would be a good day for our enemies to attack the castle," mused Ela.

He had the good sense to keep his mouth shut.

"It's a shame that the morning sun has melted the frost," said Haughton. "Or we might see footprints in it that would let us know who was here."

"How long has he been dead?" asked Ela.

"Only a very short time," said Haughton. "Rigor mortis has not set in yet."

"So the killer is still nearby?" asked Ela.

"Yes."

All eyes turned to Alice. Ela's heart sank. She knew she had no choice. "Alice, I'm afraid we'll have to take you into custody while we investigate."

CHAPTER 18

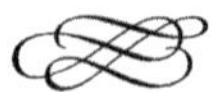

Ela instructed the guards to take Alice to a chamber in the highest part of the castle, where she could be kept under guard privately, like Peveril de Gilbert, whom she sometimes forgot was still locked up awaiting the assizes.

She couldn't even meet Alice's eyes as they took her away. Part of her was angry with Alice for putting herself in this predicament by throwing herself into a situation that had no possible happy outcome.

"I don't think Alice killed him," she said to Haughton, once Alice was out of earshot. "But in the absence of other suspects I couldn't let her go free."

Especially since this is the second time she's been found next to a dead body.

"Why was mistress Alice out here in the first place?" asked Stephen Hale.

Ela hesitated. There really was no way to preserve her friend's reputation and pursue the truth at the same time. "He had started a flirtation with her, which I vocally disapproved of, so she came to meet him out here in secret."

"Perhaps he scorned her, or ill-used her, and she killed him with his own knife in a fit of rage," suggested Hale.

"A woman aroused to anger can possess the strength of three men," said Will Dyer, looking down at the lifeless form of Adonis d'Ys.

"What do we know of this man?" asked Giles Haughton. "Who else might have reason to kill him?"

"Unfortunately, my inquiries have revealed that no one knows much about him. He's certainly involved in international trade and approached the mayor of London with generous…gifts." Bribes, really. "He seems to have been trying to establish himself in London, but he's not well known here. I don't believe he speaks English at all. We spoke to him only in French. He describes himself as owning an ancestral estate in Brittany and a remote manor in Burgundy, but I don't know how much of that is true. I had banished him from the castle and forced him to pen his goodbye to Alice. I had no idea he'd lie in wait for her outside the walls."

"But how did she know to come here to meet him?" asked Dyer.

"It seems they had planned the meeting last night. I only threw him out this morning just before dawn."

Giles Haughton had moved away from the group slightly and was walking around the grassy area near the tree. "The grass is crushed flat right here, and broken in such a way that it appears to have happened while the grass was stiff with frost." He moved further toward the wall. "The pattern continues here, right up to the outer edge of the ditch." He kept moving. "As if someone was keeping so close to the berm around the ditch that they could hide behind it and not be seen from behind the castle walls."

"They could have been made by the victim himself. He had good reason to hide," said Ela.

"I don't think so," said Haughton. "The stride of this person is short, similar to what we see of a woman walking in her long skirt. The imprints themselves also suggest a smaller foot."

Ela swallowed. This did not look good for Alice. "So, if it was a woman, do you think she crept around the wall and sneaked up on him?"

She followed Haughton at a distance, as he traced the pattern of crushed grass blades around the ditch. The jurors tagged along, keeping far enough away so as not to destroy the evidence. The trail led around the castle ditch all the way to the other side of the castle, where there was a well-trodden track leading to several nearby villages.

"The person came down this track, or left by it, but not both." The crushed grass didn't provide a detailed enough footprint to tell which way the person was headed.

"So the person might have come from inside the castle, on the track we've obliterated in coming to find the body, then left around the outside of the moat."

"Or they came around the moat, killed him and then—" Haughton lowered his voice. "Stood weeping over his body."

Ela hurried to catch up. "You think Alice killed him?"

"She has blood on her hands and dress, the murder weapon was lying there in the grass, and she was right there at the scene of the crime."

"But surely if she did it, she would run away?" said Ela.

Haughton leaned in. "I don't mean to cause offense, as I know she's your friend, but she does not strike me as a woman of keen intelligence."

"She's naive, to be sure, but not a half-wit. She's also gentle and kind and entirely incapable of stabbing a man."

"Do you think her capable of poisoning one?" He peered into her eyes.

Ela hesitated. "No, but that at least is a less violent crime.

I absolutely cannot picture her raising a knife against a large, muscular man, especially one that she's still starry-eyed over."

"I do value your opinion, my lady," said Haughton. "You know her better than any of us. Still, you can see that she'll have to be tried at the assizes, along with Peveril de Gilbert."

"I fear that she'll find herself on trial for both killings."

"Finding herself in the company of two dead men is certainly terrible luck. The only way to prove her innocence is to discover another killer." His voice held skepticism that such a person existed.

"Then clearly that's what we must do." They'd lost the track of crushed grass where it met the much trampled path out to the villages. There was no point following the trail on foot. She'd have to mount up and ride out there looking for anyone who might be capable of killing Adonis d'Ys.

Ela felt some compunction abandoning both her children and her guests on Christmas Day. The jurors were excused for that reason, and she vowed to herself not to summon them again that day unless there was a very pressing reason.

Mounted on Freya, and with Haughton riding another one of her horses, she set out with four guards down the track to the villages, in hope of catching a scent of an escaped murderer.

There were three villages along the track, each a hamlet of fewer than five houses. In the first one, they found villagers surprised to be roused from their fireside on Christmas Day, but none had seen a stranger. In the second one someone mentioned seeing an unfamiliar woman walking along the road earlier that day.

Ela's heart leapt. "How old was she?"

"Well, I can't say," said the older woman, standing in her doorway. "I just caught a glimpse of her as I was throwing out the peelings, and she had a hood over her head."

"How do you know it was a woman?" asked Haughton.

"She wore a long cloak over a dress. Green, they were."

"Fine fabric? Or faded and worn?" asked Ela.

The woman thought for a moment. "Fine, I'd say, though not flashy. I saw no gold braid or nothing. No holes or tears or trailing edges, though."

"Which way was she headed?" asked Haughton.

"She came the same way you did, from the castle. She didn't stop here in this village but kept walking at a brisk clip, off toward the main road. Looked like she was in a hurry."

"Did you notice any…stains on her clothes?" asked Ela. The murderer would surely be covered in the victim's blood.

"Stains? Not anything out of the ordinary. Her hem was damp with the dew, to be sure. But then I didn't get a good look at her."

They thanked her for her time and continued in the direction she'd pointed.

"If she escaped in this direction, she must have come from another. From inside the castle," said Ela.

"The castle is thick with people this Christmas, my lady. Would your servants have noticed one extra unfamiliar woman amid the throngs of guests and all their strange servants?"

Ela hated to admit that a strange woman might pass unnoticed among them, but he was right. "I suppose a woman is more likely to go unremarked than a man."

"If this man was a scoundrel, perhaps he left a broken-hearted and vengeful woman in his wake?"

"I think that's very likely," agreed Ela.

In the third village, several people had seen the woman.

In fact, they'd seen her circle around the village to a grove of trees where a man was waiting with a spare horse. She had mounted, and they had ridden off in the direction of Southampton.

"How long ago?" Maybe they could still catch them.

"Before the bells for Terce."

She looked at Haughton. "They're long gone."

"Aye, my lady, but it seems almost certain that she's the one we seek."

"Did you see stains on her clothes?" asked Ela of the small group of villagers.

"I don't know, my lady, but she left them over there." They pointed to a copse of poplars. "None of us wanted to go near them in case she was coming back for them and would accuse us of theft."

Ela rode over to the trees, and she and Haughton dismounted. The pile of clothes contained a green cloak and a green dress—matching the description from the previous village. On inspection the inside of the cloak was indeed stained with blood that had started to soak through to the outside, even though the lining was made from a separate layer of felted wool.

"She turned her cloak inside out after killing him," said Ela.

"And wore green to hide easily in the landscape," said Haughton.

"And she had an accomplice here waiting for her, with a horse. The killer knew Adonis d'Ys, knew he was in Salisbury, and waited for the right opportunity to strike."

"Then escaped. At least they were seen by several villagers. This should free Alice from suspicion. We must send guards after them at once."

They returned to the villagers and gained the best description they could. No one had seen the woman's hair, but she was of medium height with the fair skin of a lady, not the sun-weathered complexion of a peasant woman. The man was tall and thin, with dark hair visible under a felt cap. Someone suggested that his appearance—perhaps the shape of his hat or the cut of his tunic—made him look like a foreigner, rather than an Englishman.

Armed with this knowledge, two of Ela's guards set out, in hot pursuit, in the direction of Southampton.

Ela and Haughton returned to the spot where they'd found the bloody clothes and searched the ground for any further hints of who these strangers were or where they came from. Depressions in the ground showed that their horses were both large beasts and shod with cleats for slippery winter conditions.

The wind was picking up and Ela's cheeks began to sting with the cold, so one of the guards gathered up the bloodied clothes and they returned to the castle.

ELA WAS MIGHTILY RELIEVED to release Alice from her solitary chamber, where—still in her blood-stained dress—it was obvious that she'd been weeping nonstop. She told Alice about the mysterious woman who'd been seen in the nearby villages and who had apparently swooped in to kill Adonis d'Ys, then vanished with her male accomplice.

Alice stared in astonishment. "How did she know he'd be under that tree?"

"I don't know. Especially since I banished him from the castle this morning. Had you met him under the tree before?"

Alice looked down at the floor. "Yes."

"Perhaps she hoped that you'd come find his body and be accused of the crime. Or perhaps you're lucky that she didn't find you there and kill you, too."

Alice shook her head as if it might disentangle her thoughts. "But why would a woman want to kill him?"

Ela could think of any number of reasons. And she saw no reason to spare Alice's feelings. "Perhaps he has a wife. A living one, I mean."

Alice blinked. "Surely not! If he did, then why would he —" Her lip quivered.

"Men are subject to carnal desires that lead them into adultery and sin. Even good-hearted men sometime fall victim to the sin of lust." At least that's what she told herself on the occasions that she'd learned her husband had strayed. Her mother had counseled her to endure it as she endured the pain of childbirth. "If he had a wife she might have followed him here and discovered that he was engaged in a romance with you."

"I would think that she'd rather kill me, then," said Alice, clearly confused. "To get him all to herself."

"You're assuming that she loved him. It's entirely possible that she imagined a life for herself without him in it where she might enjoy the privileges of the widowed state."

Alice stared. "He has no children, so she would inherit all his estates."

"I suspect his estates are imaginary, but I wouldn't be at all surprised if his wealth was quite real. He purchased his friendship with the mayor of London, after all."

Ela summoned Giles Haughton, to see if he'd learned anything further from his examination of the body. While she waited for him to arrive, she sat in the great hall, near the fire, sharing a wassail cup with her guests while her son Stephen regaled them with his morning's adventures chasing a fox on horseback with his brother Richard and Bill Talbot.

She struggled to stay focused on his account as her mind kept getting tugged away by worries for Alice, who might evade one charge of murder but would need more than luck to escape two.

Suddenly the great doors to the hall creaked open and a violent gust of cold wind guttered the fire at the far end of the hall. Everyone looked up in time to see Ela's two guards enter the hall, dragging a man dressed in a green tunic and matching hose.

They caught the killer! Relief rushed through her. Ela looked past him for the murderess that the villagers had seen leaving her stained clothing, but the two guards entered the hall, bringing only the strange man.

Ela rose from her place near the fire and strode the length of the hall. "Who is this man?"

"We caught him just outside Alderbury, my lady, on the Southampton Road," said one of the guards.

"He was with the lady that the villagers described, but she jumped from her horse and ran into the woods. I gave chase but couldn't find her. We brought both horses back with us."

"Without a horse she won't get far," mused Ela. She turned to a senior guard who'd hurried over to see what was going on. "Send more guards out to search the roads and the woods for her." She hesitated for a moment, half reluctant to drag the poor jurors away from their warm firesides for a second time on Christmas Day. "And call for a jury to attend us at once."

CHAPTER 19

It was full dark by the time the jurors arrived, and Ela had the servants greet them with wassail cups to soften the sting of doing their duty on a feast day. Alice's freedom depended on a productive deposition of the man in green and she didn't want to risk waiting a day and giving him time to make up a story. Instead she let him stew in the hall, chained to a chair, subject to the gaze of Ela, her guests, her children, her servants and all the garrison soldiers.

He hardly knew where to look and became increasingly agitated. A young man, probably not much over twenty, he had big brown eyes and a mop of shiny dark hair framing a pale face with delicate features. By the time the jurors assembled he looked ready to burst into tears.

Ela didn't bother ordering trestle tables but simply had the jurors crowd close around him, cups in hand, as if he were the main attraction at a bearbaiting.

"What is your name?" she demanded.

"Michel de Tours."

"And why did you gallop from my men when they called to you?"

He swallowed. He looked at the floor, then up at the wind and wine-reddened faces looming over him. "My mistress commanded me to."

"And why would she do that?"

He blinked rapidly. His lips fluttered but nothing came out.

"What is the name of your mistress?"

"I cannot say," he said quickly, and with surprising determination.

"Is she your lover?" asked Ela.

His face reddened, which answered her question. His lips remained pressed together.

"Perhaps you think yourself a man of honor, keeping your silence for your beloved," said Ela coolly. "Will you be so cool when the noose is slipped over your head for the murder she committed just outside my castle grounds early this morning?"

A shudder rocked his body and one of his eyes twitched. *He's weak. The woman, whoever she is, picked a poor accomplice in her crime.* "If you tell us what you know about her then you won't be charged with her crimes. If you don't, then you will surely hang for them." This was something of an exaggeration, since she didn't have the power to mete out death, but it wasn't an unlikely course of events, either.

The man's pale face blanched further.

"What is her name and why did she come here?"

Again, he remained silent, but this time he fidgeted slightly in the chair, looking at the floor and at the legs of the assembled jurors as if his resolve might be leaving him.

"Is she the wife of Adonis d'Ys?"

He looked up at her, shock written on his face. "Yes, she is," he rasped.

"And she came here to kill him because she knew he was

—" A sudden caution for Alice's reputation stopped her in her tracks.

"He was unfaithful and the very devil in human form," burst the man. "He used her most ill and left her at home with their children while he roamed the earth, fornicating like a wild rabbit."

Ela heard a small cry from behind her and turned to see Alice, who'd joined the company assembled around the prisoner.

I knew it. Of course he had a wife and children. She wouldn't be surprised if he had a wife and children in each of the great port cities of Europe. A pinch of pity for Alice's dashed romantic dreams salted her satisfaction at being right.

"And what are you to her?" asked Ela, peering into the man's big, liquid eyes.

"A friend," he said meekly, in a half whisper.

"Did you know she intended to kill her husband?"

He shook his head but said nothing. She wasn't sure she believed him. His green clothing, perhaps chosen for stealth, hinted that he was in on her plan. He didn't try to deny that she'd killed her husband.

"Do you love her?" she stared at him hard. Would he publicly deny his feelings for her if he had them? He seemed the type to have studied manhood in the old French romances like *Lancelot* and *Yvain*, where the valiant knight would lay down both his cloak and his heart for his beloved to step on, even though she was married to another and he was doomed to love her from afar.

"My love is a chaste and pure one," he stammered at last.

"I thought it might be," said Ela drily. "And I fear you'll hang for it."

The jurors asked him a number of questions about the escaped murderess and her likely whereabouts. Since it seemed most likely that she'd head for London, Ela penned a letter to Roger le Duc—who, having been sheriff before becoming mayor, would know just who to involve—informing him of Adonis d'Ys untimely death and the urgent need to apprehend his widow before she left the country.

Then she ordered for Michel de Tours to be put in the dungeon because he was at the very least an accomplice who had held the woman's horse while she stabbed her husband to death.

She invited the jurors to stay for the Christmas feast, apologized to her guests for the grisly interruptions of the day and proceeded to enjoy the splendid repast that Cook had prepared.

THE NEXT MORNING, Ela seized some quiet time in the chapel to meditate on the birth of Our Lord. She felt guilty at interrupting the celebration of his feast day with so much mayhem. Still, it was her duty as High Sheriff of Wiltshire to make sure that crimes were prosecuted, and her co-sheriff, John Dacus, was away visiting his ailing mother.

Once she'd said her prayers and her guests had taken their leave, she approached Bill Talbot.

"I'd like to ride to Mere to interview the servants there about the likelihood that Peveril poisoned his father."

"And perhaps the possibility that Alice did?" said Bill softly.

Slightly shocked, Ela inhaled. "I suppose we can inquire about that as well. Do you really think her capable of poisoning her husband?"

"I find myself constantly amazed by what people are capable of," said Bill brightly.

"I was intending to bring her with us, but perhaps I won't.

I have another purpose to my visit. A lawyer is working to secure her third of her late husband's estate, and I intend to get a better sense of the prize he's pursuing."

"Perhaps if Peveril is hanged for murder, she'll gain the whole estate."

"Apparently there are two young children, a son and daughter of Peveril, so that seems unlikely."

"Might they not be forced to forfeit their share of the estate to the crown if their father is found guilty of murder?"

Ela looked at his kind, handsome face in bemusement. "Sometimes the machinations of your mind take me quite by surprise."

THEY SET out shortly after breaking their fast, and the ride took a little over three hours. The winter sun, as high in the sky as it intended to get that day, cast a pale misty light over the frost-trimmed stone visage of the de Gilbert family castle.

The castle was of ancient vintage, likely built in the time of the Conqueror himself, a plain, square keep with only slits for windows. It sat high on a hill, with a view over the wooded valley below. A few squat outbuildings hunkered nearby, no doubt providing winter shelter for cows and sheep and pigs.

As they rode up the steep path, Ela reflected that Alice's newly refurbished manor would likely provide more comfortable habitation than this grim tower. While Salisbury castle was of equally ancient vintage, Ela's forbears had taken pains to install fireplaces and chimneys. She saw no such improvements evident in the de Gilbert family castle.

They waited a long time at the door, with Bill banging handily on the wood doors. Eventually an elderly servant managed, with much huffing and puffing, to open one of the doors and let them and their horses into the castle courtyard.

Bill announced Ela's purpose, and she asked for the servants to assemble for questioning. As the old man shuffled off, presumably toward the kitchens, a tall woman in a blue dress came striding toward them.

"Who are you and what do you want?" she asked in a shrill voice. "The master of this castle is not at home."

Ela felt Bill about to launch into a polite explanation of their purpose, but the woman's brusque tone raised her hackles.

"The master of this castle is imprisoned in my castle awaiting trial for murdering his father," she said quietly.

The woman's face dropped as she realized who Ela was. Then she composed herself. "When will the trial take place?"

"When the traveling justice arrives in Salisbury for the assizes. The dates have not yet been announced. Who are you?"

She lifted her impressive chin. "I am Bertrade de Gilbert, mistress of this house."

"Ah." Ela adopted a sympathetic expression. "I'm also a dear friend of Alice de Gilbert, widow of the late Humphrey de Gilbert, and my lawyer is currently seeking to secure her third share in this estate."

The woman's face hardened. "That woman doesn't deserve a bent half-penny. She has no issue—she's barren—and has no business here, let alone stealing away a third share of the estate! She has her own manor that she brought into the marriage, and she should be satisfied to leave with it."

"Happily, that is not for you to decide. The Magna Carta clearly states that widows receive a third of their husband's estate for their use during their lifetime."

Bertrade frowned. "And then it reverts to the heirs?"

"It does. Are you the mother of such heirs?"

"I am. Dear Wilibert is my oldest son. Naturally it's in my interest as his mother to preserve the estate whole and entire for him."

"As a mother myself, I quite understand," said Ela. "However, if your husband is hanged for murder, I'm afraid the estate might well be forfeit to the crown."

"What?" The words flew from her mouth in a half shriek.

The servants were starting to gather in the hall, all looking rather confused. They were a motley assortment of the very old and very young.

"It would be considered deodand," said Ela calmly. "The coroner would arrange the transaction in the wake of the execution." Bertrade stared at her, mind clearly galloping at a mile a minute. Ela worried whether she was more concerned about her husband being hanged, or her son—and by extension herself—being deprived of his inheritance. She strongly suspected the latter.

"A-and if the estate were to be forfeit, I would receive a third share as my husband's widow?"

"Oh, I don't think so." Ela tilted her chin up slightly. Bertrade de Gilbert was setting her teeth on edge. "In such a case I expect the crown would seize it all." She wasn't actually sure of this but wanted to see how Bertrade would react to the prospect of losing everything.

"Well, my husband isn't guilty so he won't be hanged," she said quickly. "Alice is the one who poisoned his father. She hated him. Ask her yourself!"

Ela found herself on the defensive. Alice had said that she wished herself rid of her tiresome husband. Perhaps she'd also—unwisely—expressed the idea, or at least made it apparent, here in the castle. But Alice had no opportunity to poison Humphrey de Gilbert's tonic.

"The poison that killed your father-in-law was given to

his manservant by Sir Peveril. Clovis then mixed it with a tonic that I made myself and which I'm absolutely certain was not poisoned."

"Alice could have easily slipped some ground leaves into the tonic when no one was looking. She's a cunning vixen!"

Alice was the least cunning person Ela had ever come across. But she wondered how much Bertrade knew about the method of poison. "Impossible, the poison is far too rare for her to have managed that."

"Foxglove is everywhere in the woods! Even at this time of year she could find some withered leaves—" She trailed off, perhaps realizing that she'd said too much.

Ela pinned her with a steely gaze. "How did you know that foxglove was the poison used?"

"I-I-I'm sure someone told me."

"Who? We hadn't yet identified the poison when Humphrey's manservant returned here from Salisbury. And both Peveril and his manservant have been secured in my castle since we revealed the manner of poison. In fact, there was much discussion of how the tonic was prepared and no one could entirely identify how it made its way from the kitchens to Sir Peveril. I now find myself wondering if you were the missing link in the chain."

Bertrade's face paled. "Why would I want to kill my father-in-law?"

"Because you were tired of waiting for Humphrey de Gilbert to die so you could take up residence in this castle."

"What nonsense! This castle is a frigid barrack without even a proper hearth."

"Yet still you moved here. And perhaps you even hoped that your husband might be swept up in the murder inquiry so that you could seize the castle and fortune yourself on the pretext of maintaining them for your son?"

Ela heard gasps from the servants. It was cruel of her to

accuse the woman in front of all her castle staff, but Bertrade de Gilbert seemed so unperturbed by her father-in-law's cruel death and her husband's imprisonment, that Ela was becoming increasingly certain she'd played a part in them.

At least the servants would serve as witnesses to this encounter if Bertrade found herself before the justice at the assizes.

"Is the cook here?"

A thin young woman with a pinched face stepped forward. "I'm the cook now, but I wasn't here when the old master was still alive."

"We were told the old cook was sent away before my guards returned to retrieve Sir Peveril. Is this true?"

"Yes." Bertrade had the decency to look flustered. "She was a terrible cook. She always overcooked the meat and stewed the vegetables down to a mush."

"Have you provided for her in her old age? It seems she'd been at the castle for many years."

Bertrade's mouth opened and then closed again. Silence thickened in the air for a moment. Ela heard the sound of church bells in the distance. "I'm sure she's found another position."

The church bells reminded Ela of the small amount of daylight remaining, and she ordered the guards to take Bertrade prisoner and escort her back to the castle. "What about my children?" protested Bertrade.

"Is there someone here who can take care of them? A nursemaid or tutor or your mother, perhaps?"

"Their nursemaid is a stripling girl!" She turned to the group of servants. One stepped forward. She couldn't have been more than eleven and she held the hands of a boy of about four and a girl of perhaps two. "My children are young and don't need a tutor yet."

Ela surveyed the group of servants and determined that she wouldn't leave her children in the care of any of them. "They shall return with us. Do you have a carriage to transport them?"

"I do, but you can't take me! I'm innocent. I'm sure my father-in-law's foolish wife poisoned him."

"You can tell your story to the jury in Salisbury." Ela gave the servants orders to ready the carriage for the journey to Salisbury. She also sent two of her guards to find the cook who'd been relieved of her duties, wherever she was, and bring her back to Salisbury forthwith.

With a carriage in tow they would not likely be back before nightfall, but she could hardly leave the woman's children there without adequate supervision, and the roads were easy enough to follow by night once they got back onto the main London road.

WHILE THE CARRIAGE and horses were readied, Ela, Bill and the remaining guards rode around the demesne of the castle and viewed the stock—mostly sheep and a few fine cows and bulls—to get some idea of the estate that Alice was laying her one-third claim to. She imagined the other manors were in no better shape than the one Alice had already inhabited, so she had little desire to see them, but the land might form a part of Alice's portion.

THEY RODE BACK to Salisbury as fast as they could with a carriage in tow and arrived well after dusk had fallen and the bells sounded for Compline. Bertrade was whisked away to the same room Alice had been lately imprisoned in, and Alice stood in the hall and stared at her as the guards took her away. "What's going on?"

Ela handed her cloak to Elsie. "Were you intimate with Peveril's wife?"

"Not at all. She didn't seem to like coming to the castle, and Humphrey wasn't enthusiastic about having the children underfoot either. We barely saw them."

"Do you think it's possible that she could have poisoned your late husband?"

"Why would she?"

"So her husband could inherit. Perhaps she grew tired of living in a dismal manor house and craved the high stone walls of the castle around her."

Alice frowned. "The castle is not a comfortable habitation."

"I noticed that. But I mentioned that you would be claiming your widow's right to a third of the estates and Bertrade almost had a fit. I could see she was very invested in her claim—or her son's claim—to the estates. She didn't even seem that worried about whether Peveril would hang or not."

"But how would she poison him? She doesn't even live at the castle."

"She and Peveril were there when Humphrey left to come here. Peveril—or perhaps it was she?—persuaded him to come here and chase you down.

"And you think they had a plot to poison Humphrey to get rid of him—and me?"

"I think it's a possibility. You and your husband weren't close with them?"

"No. There was no love lost between father and son. Peveril was always trying to persuade his father to spend money on the estates—repairing the roofs on buildings and the like—and Humphrey preferred to wait until something fell into disrepair before putting out money to fix it."

"I certainly saw that philosophy in action at your manor."

A shadow passed over Alice's face. She was probably remembering her tryst there. "I can't believe he's gone."

Ela wanted to ask which recently dead man she was referring to, but she knew the answer and held her tongue.

"Humphrey never spoke to me like that. He never once told me I'm beautiful or that my body delighted him." Alice's voice shook a little.

"Not all husbands have a way with words." Her own William had been one of the silver-tongued ones. It pained her that she'd never hear sweet nothings fall from a man's lips again. But she wasn't foolish enough to risk her fortune and estates—let alone her heart—on a new marriage. "A faithful man is better than one with a honeyed tongue."

"I can't believe he was married."

I can. Ela had smelled trouble from across the table that first night with the Mayor of London. "His wife has evaded capture so far. I've notified Roger le Duc to search the city and the ports for her."

"Is that man who was with her a lover of hers?"

"I suspect he was rather her fool. She used him to accomplish her foul deed and will now abandon him to endure the punishment that should have been hers."

"You don't think they'll catch her?"

"Not if she's wily. And I suspect she is."

"Without her to stand trial, the judge at the assizes might think I killed Adonis."

"I think that having her accomplice here will help. He may not admit anything in court, though. We must work out how she managed to lure Adonis to the tree outside the castle walls and kill him. And also how she managed to time it so that you would turn up at the right moment to look like the killer. It was quite ingenious of her."

"Perhaps she was listening at the door when we made our plans to meet there the night before."

"Which would mean that she hid in plain sight inside the castle—perhaps even inside the very room where you lay." Then, very early the next morning she somehow got word to her accomplice—perhaps she even walked in and out of the castle gates unnoticed at dawn since it was Christmas and there were a lot of people coming and going—and told him where to wait with the two horses."

"Why would the guards not question her when she entered the castle?"

"She could have claimed to be a farmer's daughter delivering smoked hams or even just tagged onto a group of carolers coming in to sing in the hall. A strange man would attract more suspicion than a woman. Likely no one even noticed her."

"If only I'd gone out to meet him sooner." Tears filled Alice's eyes. "I could have stopped her."

"She might have killed you, too. I suppose you're lucky she didn't do that anyway. If she'd been watching Adonis, she must have known that you were his lover."

"Do you think she was watching us at my manor?"

"I can't imagine she could have come too close, or he'd have recognized her when there weren't many people around. But perhaps she had that foolish man she used as her accomplice observe you. Have you seen him before?"

Alice frowned. "I'm not sure. There were so many people coming and going to repair the thatch and the woodwork and the plaster. He's not a remarkable-looking man. If he was dressed as a local peasant I doubt I'd have thought twice about him."

At that moment the peal of a child's cry tore through the air. They turned to see Bertrade and Peveril's little son, Wilibert, face red and crumpled, wailing into the air.

"Oh no, poor lamb!" cried Alice. She rushed over to the little boy and his sister and tried to remind them who she was. The cries of the inconsolable children tore at Ela's heart. It pained her beyond measure to separate a child from its mother—especially by death, which would happen if Bertrade was convicted of murder.

"We must get the children comfortably settled for the night." She summoned Elsie and Becca to settle them into beds alongside little Ellie and Nicky, so they'd have some company and distraction. She knew her own children would be kind to these younger ones, who were clearly overtired and overwrought and probably in need of food. Alice went with them, promising to tell them a story and telling them—quite falsely—that everything would be all right.

Tomorrow morning the jury would assemble to determine which of their parents—or perhaps both of them together—had poisoned Sir Humphrey de Gilbert.

CHAPTER 20

The next morning, Ela joined the jurors gathered in the hall to address the morning's urgent business.

Ela had briefed Giles Haughton on her reasons for bringing Bertrade back to the castle. He sat at her right hand, and Bill Talbot at her left, as Bertrade was brought into the great hall. Ela made sure to tell the servants to keep both Bertrade's children and her own younger ones away from the hall for the duration of their meeting.

Alice hung off to one side. She knew her own freedom and safety rested on someone else being convicted of the crime of poisoning her husband, but Ela counselled her not to draw attention to herself by intervening unless she was specifically asked to do so.

Bertrade looked relatively calm after her night under guard. She was a hard-faced but handsome woman, with a bold gaze. She'd been allowed to bring her lady's maid, and her hair was neatly arranged and her clothing smooth and unwrinkled as if she'd slept in her own home.

The guards escorted her to a chair set up between the tables, then Ela addressed the jurors. "Yesterday, I visited the estate of the late Humphrey de Gilbert. As you know, we are trying to determine who poisoned him here in my castle. His eldest son and heir, Peveril de Gilbert, has been under lock and key here at the castle for most of December. Since the de Gilbert estate, including the family castle at Mere, is still in the process of changing hands, I was somewhat surprised to find Peveril's widow in residence there."

Ela stood and walked around the tables until she stood directly in front of Bertrade de Gilbert. "When I arrived at the castle I asserted Alice de Gilbert's right, outlined in the Magna Carta of 1225 and witnessed by myself and my late husband, to retain a full third share of her late husband's estate for her use during her life."

Bertrade flinched and shifted in her chair.

"Bertrade de Gilbert seemed both shocked and appalled by that idea," continued Ela. "In fact, she protested against it with such force that I began to suspect she had an unusual interest in the disposition of the estate."

"The estate is my husband's to inherit," Bertrade burst out. "And my son's to inherit after him. What's unusual about a wife and mother seeking to protect her family's interests?"

Normally Ela would tell an unruly defendant not to speak out of turn on pain of being thrown in the dungeon. But Bertrade's arrogance and sharp tongue might yet drop the noose around her own neck—if she was guilty—and Ela wanted to give her the chance to make a mistake.

"Why nothing, in the ordinary course of things," said Ela. "But if she were to grow impatient for her husband to inherit, and to take matters into her own hands by hastening his father's demise, that would be a crime punishable by death."

"I would never do such a thing," protested Bertrade, pointed chin held high.

"Sir Humphrey de Gilbert was poisoned," said Ela. "The

coroner, Giles Haughton, tested the tonic he drank on the night of his death and demonstrated that it contained a deadly amount of digitalis. Someone put that foxglove in his tonic, with the intent of taking his life."

"It was her!" hissed Bertrade, pointing at Alice. She wasn't tied to the chair as a prisoner might normally be, because Ela had accorded her certain privileges as a member of the nobility.

"We've already determined that Alice, who had been staying in my castle for some weeks, had no opportunity to gather and prepare foxglove. Her husband's visit was unexpected, and he was here for just one night. It seems that the tonic his servant Clovis had brought with him to drink—as was his nightly custom—was the source of the poison."

"Perhaps Clovis had reason to poison his master?"

Ela thought this unlikely in the extreme, but it was another opportunity to reel out rope for Bertrade to wrap around her own neck. "Do you think Clovis was unhappy in your father-in-law's service?"

Bertrade drew herself up. "My father-in-law could be a difficult man. He was one to find fault with anyone who crossed his path. I suspect many of the servants would have preferred a different master."

"Did you find him difficult?" Ela moved closer to her.

"Me? Well, I-I barely saw the man. He seemed to find the presence of our children irksome, so my husband usually visited the castle by himself."

"So you would not say that you had a close family relationship with Humphrey de Gilbert?"

Bertrade shifted in her seat and tugged at her gown. "We maintained a cordial relationship. I had no reason to dislike him except for how he treated my husband."

Ela cocked her head. "He used your husband ill?"

"Yes. He suffered my husband to manage his estates, then

kept the purse strings tied shut so he couldn't actually do anything with them at all."

"Were you frustrated by this?"

Bertrade pressed her lips together. "Well, it's not really my business, is it?"

"I'd say it's your business that your husband is content. I would certainly be irked to find my husband frustrated at every turn by his own father as he tries to care for the legacy that he'll one day inherit and pass on to his children."

"Indeed! But the one time I raised the matter in Sir Humphrey's presence, he told me to mind my tongue and left the room."

Ela felt a tiny twinge of sympathy for Bertrade de Gilbert. She was fortunate that no one had ever dared speak to her thus. "And you never addressed the subject again?"

"No."

"But perhaps you harbored resentment in your heart that Sir Humphrey de Gilbert thought even less of your ideas than he did of your husband's."

"I...well...I wasn't happy about it, but I didn't plot his death, either."

"Yet you think that either his wife or his servant was motivated to kill him?"

"Perhaps they planned it together," said Bertrade, suddenly brightening. "That would explain why Clovis arrived with a fresh tonic to serve."

Ela felt a frisson of unease. "We established before a jury that Clovis was quite happy in his employ with Sir Humphrey and had no motive to kill his master."

"Where is he now? He's not in Mere," said Bertrade. "It seems he's slunk away like a fox that killed the chickens."

"He's here in my castle," said Ela calmly. "Tending to Sir Peveril in his confinement." She stared at Bertrade for a moment. "I find it perplexing that you haven't asked to visit your husband, now that you're under the same roof."

"I'm a prisoner. How would I ask to see anyone?"

"Did you not write to him since he's been here in Salisbury?"

Her face darkened. "My husband did write to me, but I can't read and write and there's no one else in the household who can."

Ela found that unlikely. Not that Bertrade couldn't read—which was hardly rare among women of her age and even her class—but that no one else could either. Then again, the children were too young for a proper tutor and her husband served as his own steward. And even if one of the servants could read, perhaps Bertrade hadn't wanted to share the confidence of her husband's letters with anyone who might read them for her. That was somewhat understandable under the circumstances, especially if she was guilty or if she and her husband had hatched the plot together.

"Your husband, Sir Peveril de Gilbert, appeared before the jury and said that he found the tonic sitting unattended in the hall of his father's castle and brought it to his father's room. He said that he normally had no role in handling his father's tonics, and he couldn't explain why he'd taken charge of the tonic that day."

Ela wondered if Bertrade would step into the snare she was laying.

"Perhaps he poisoned his father." The words seemed to float from her mouth like she was testing them.

"You think your husband capable of murder?"

She blinked, clearly not sure how to proceed. Ela suspected that having her husband hang was not part of her original plan. She preferred to be lady of the manor at his side. However, given the choice between pointing the figure of accusation at her husband or swinging from a gibbet...

Ela felt a breath—that she didn't realize she'd been holding—slip quietly from her chest. "But why would Peveril try to poison his father on a night when he wouldn't even be home?"

"So that suspicion would rest elsewhere." Bertrade now spoke with conviction. Perhaps she was already picturing herself a merry widow, free from her spineless husband and able to hire her own stewards and rent to her own tenants. "What better way to commit a murder than to have the victim fall ill far from the place where you are?"

Ela shivered slightly, remembering her husband's cruel and untimely death. It was a perfect crime, mostly because she couldn't risk accusing the most powerful man in the land of murder—even of a king's son and the current king's uncle. De Burgh could destroy her family and blight her children's futures if she dared to raise her voice against him.

It was this cruel injustice that drove her to pursue justice for others.

She looked up at the guards. "Please bring Sir Peveril de Gilbert to the hall at once."

CHAPTER 21

Sir Peveril de Gilbert was ushered to the room by several guards, with his manservant Clovis in attendance. Ela watched Bertrade's face as they entered the hall. To her surprise she saw emotion flicker across Bertrade's bold features.

"My dear," said Peveril softly, as his eyes met hers. Ela turned her eyes to his less striking features. He had the face of a man who was kind, perhaps, but not decisive. A weak chin and soft, droopy blue eyes. She could imagine that Bertrade ran their household and probably had better ideas about it, too.

Bertrade's lips twitched, but she remained silent.

Ela returned to her seat between Bill Talbot and Giles Haughton while the guards seated Peveril in a chair near his wife. "Sir Peveril, your wife states that you resented your father for refusing you access to funds required to improve the family estates. She even suggests that you gave your father poison so as to remove him as an impediment, so you could succeed him as heir."

Peveril's mouth fell open, and he turned to stare at his wife.

"It's not true! I said no such thing!" Bertrade's face paled. Peveril himself looked stunned beyond reckoning.

So they didn't plan it together.

"It never crossed my mind to poison my father," said Peveril in a half whisper. His gaze stayed fixed on his wife. "Or to do anything to hasten his death. I had my own manor that I could manage as I saw fit, and I had learned how to turn the modest profits from fleeces and lambs into greater ones. I had no need or desire to remove my father from his role as head of the family before his time."

"Did you ever share this knowledge about growing your profits with your father?" asked Ela.

"I did, with a view to growing the profits on the other estates. But that would have entailed additional expenditures that my father didn't want to make. I tried to convince him that the ultimate result would be more money, not less, but he was stubborn and set in his ways." Peveril blinked several times. "But at no time did I ever contemplate ending his life so I could pursue my plans for his manors!"

Bertrade's face had taken on a sour look, as if she'd have more respect for him if he *had* thought about murdering his father.

"Do your wife's suspicions shock you?"

"My wife knows that I'd never kill him or anyone else. She used to berate me for my difficulty in parting with livestock that was ready for market. In addition to a very reasonable fear for my immortal soul, I held a son's affection for my father. Even though he was a difficult man, he never beat me or berated me. At least not any more than is proper."

Ela thought that Humphrey de Gilbert was more likely the type to ignore his son. Continued rejection of a son's ideas and even his company might sting as sharp as a slap, but she couldn't picture this mild-mannered and rather feckless man as scheming to poison his father.

"Giles Haughton, do you have questions for either of the de Gilberts?"

"I do." Haughton leaned forward and tented his fingers. "How long have you been married?"

"Nearly eight years," said Bertrade, before her husband could open his mouth.

Haughton looked directly at Peveril. "Would you say it's a happy marriage?"

Peveril looked at his wife as if seeking her approval. She turned to meet his gaze with an encouraging look, but wisely held her tongue and waited for her husband to speak.

"Y-yes. Yes, I would," he said, looking like someone had knocked him over the head. "I think. Isn't it?" he looked imploringly at his wife.

"Indeed it is," she said as pleasantly as she could manage. "And we have been blessed with two wonderful children."

Haughton untented his pointer fingers and pressed them to his lips for a moment before continuing. "Who would you say—to use a popular expression—wears the breeches in your household?"

Peveril's mouth opened, and he looked at Bertrade again before he managed to say, "I do, of course!"

Bertrade nodded a silent assent. It was clear to all that they were both lying and that Bertrade was the one who decided who should jump and how high.

And no doubt it rankled that her husband had no power to improve their lives because of her miserly old father-in-law, who might live for another twenty or thirty years—especially given that he spent his days quietly reading in front of his fire, not galloping through the woods hunting boar.

Haughton cleared his throat. "Peveril de Gilbert, do you

think it's possible that your wife, growing resentful of your father's refusal to listen to your ideas or hers, took matters into her own hands and plotted to poison Sir Humphrey?"

"No!" His answer came out on a rush of breath. Once again, he turned to her as if for approval. Bertrade had the decency to look relieved, and pushed a prim smile to her lips. Ela suspected that Peveril's days revolved around such small mercies. "My wife is a good Christian woman who spends her days teaching our dear children the Ten Commandments, not scheming to break them."

Haughton let a tiny smile cross his lips, as if this was happy news. Then his expression hardened. "Did she perhaps see the bottle of tonic in your father's hall and suggest that you take it up to your father's room for Clovis to pack for his journey?"

Peveril froze. His whole body stiffened as if a terrible realization suddenly crept over him, under the gaze of the sheriff and all the jurors.

Yes.

Ela could hear it as if he'd said it aloud. No doubt he'd forgotten that detail in the flurry of excitement of his father departing to pursue Alice and leaving them alone in the castle.

"I-I-I don't think so," said Peveril, again turning to his wife for reassurance.

"Of course not," squealed Bertrade. "Why would I care a whit for his father's tonics?"

"You wouldn't," said Haughton. "Unless you saw them as a way to rid yourself and your husband of the nuisance that was his not-very-old father." He sighed heavily, his gaze focused tightly on Bertrade. "I don't believe you intended to implicate your husband in his father's death—" Bertrade flinched. "I suspect you were hoping that Sir Humphrey's wife or his servant or perhaps even the Countess of Salisbury herself would be suspected of dispatching him to meet his Maker here in Salisbury Castle."

Bertrade started shaking.

"But I believe that when the finger of accusation started to point at you, you were quite quick to try to push your husband from the battlements in an effort to save your own neck."

"I'm a loyal wife! I would never do such a thing." She avoided looking at Peveril.

At that moment one of the great doors at the far end of the hall creaked open and a gust of wind disturbed the parchments on the table.

"Mistress Mildred Parker!" announced Albert the porter. "Brought here by the guards."

"Bring her here at once," said Ela. Bertrade turned to stare at the door, looking increasingly nervous. "Perhaps your former cook can shed some light on which of you is more likely to have poisoned Humphrey de Gilbert."

Again, Peveril stared at his wife like he couldn't quite believe this was happening. She looked straight ahead, body rigid, as the cook made her way across the hall in the company of the guards.

A boy brought a chair for her and removed her cloak and hood and gloves, which were damp with snow, to hang near the fire.

"Good morning, Mistress Parker," said Ela, once the cook was seated. A woman of about sixty with wind-reddened cheeks and gray hairs peeking from beneath her kerchief, she looked around her in some astonishment. "Where have you been since leaving your old master's employ?" asked Peter Howard, the baker.

"I've had to go live in my daughter's house," said the cook. "Despite that there's no room for an old woman what with all her five children and the married couple in two small rooms."

"How long were you employed at the castle?"

"My whole life, sir. I grew up there, starting as a kitchen maid when old Sir Peveril, who's long dead now, was master of the castle."

"So it must have been a rude shock to you to be cast from your home and put out on the street."

"Indeed it was, sir." She looked again, with some censure, at Betrade and Peveril. "It's one thing to say I'm too old to cook but quite another to put me out on my ear after all these years of faithful service."

The jurors murmured their assent, and Ela agreed. It was customary to provide a comfortable retirement in a quiet part of the castle or its surrounds for someone who'd served the family long and faithfully.

"Which of them turned you out?" asked Howard.

"The mistress," said Mildred Parker, staring directly at Bertrade. "Said that with my tasteless cooking I wouldn't be needed any longer. And she put a serving girl in my place who barely knows how to toast a biscuit! I'm sure her food wouldn't be better than mine. I offered to use more spices if they were to buy them because there were none in the pantry. The old master didn't hold with them. But they didn't even give me the chance to try using pepper or nutmeg or what-have-you."

"Why do you think Bertrade de Gilbert sent you away without giving you a chance to prove yourself?" asked Peter Howard.

"I suspect it had something to do with the tonics," said Mildred slowly. "Since now they're saying it was my tonic that killed the old master. I'd been making his tonics for years, and he was so grateful for the relief they gave him. He suffered horribly with this toes."

"Did you make the tonic that killed him?" cut in Paul Dunstan.

"Oh, no, sir. Well, not the killing part, anyway. I made his tonic as usual with good ingredients from the pantry and the garden, then the mistress borrowed my pestle and mortar without even asking. She took them away and returned them not even clean."

All eyes turned to Bertrade, whose lips now pressed together so hard that they started to turn white.

CHAPTER 22

"What were you grinding, mistress?" asked Dunstan.

"Some herbs for a posset. My youngest son had a rash on his leg from stinging nettles."

"What herb did you grind to relieve the sting?" asked Ela curiously. She'd never heard of an effective antidote for nettles, which grew in profusion at the edge of the woods and could be most troublesome if their leaves touched bare flesh.

Bertrade shifted uneasily. "I don't remember the name of it. It has a pale green leaf."

"Sage?" said Ela, as if fascinated. "Lavender? There aren't so many herbs with a pale green leaf that are still growing at this time of year."

"Maybe one of those," said Bertrade, avoiding Ela's gaze.

"It wasn't neither of those," said cook. "It was a thinner leaf and dried out already. It wasn't something from the garden because the dead leaves are all removed from the herbs that die back at the end of the season. The gardener is most particular about it. Hates to have leaf litter blowing about the paths."

"Did Bertrade de Gilbert add her ground leaves to your tonic?" asked Dunstan.

"No, sir. They would need to be put in a linen bag and suspended in water to extract the goodness from them, then that fluid would be added to the tonic. Either that or the bag of leaves would be suspended in the tonic for some time and then removed. That's how we make them all. No one would drink a tonic with nasty bits of leaves floating in it."

"I see. And did Bertrade de Gilbert have the opportunity to suspend a bag of strange leaves in her husband's tonic?" asked Peter Howard.

"Indeed she did." The cook looked down her rather bulbous nose at Bertrade, who shuddered very slightly. "We kept the freshly made tonics on a shelf in the pantry. Sometimes I made a week's worth at once. She came into the kitchen and said that the master was packing and calling for his tonic, and I showed her which bottle he should take with him."

A muttering rose among the jury, who looked at each other and at Bertrade de Gilbert.

"Bertrade de Gilbert was not normally resident in the castle, was she?" asked Ela.

"No, my lady. In fact I rarely laid eyes on her."

"Do you have any idea why she was there that day?"

"I couldn't say for certain, but not long after she and her husband arrived, Sir Humphrey started packing for the journey to Salisbury."

"Could you say how long it was between when she asked for the tonic and when Sir Humphrey left on his journey?"

The cook frowned. "Well, they arrived at the castle well after the bells for Terce. I remember it because they wanted to break their fast even though it was already midmorning.

The master left in the early afternoon. I was busy in the kitchen since I had to pack them a good deal of food to take with them, due to the master's delicate stomach and not knowing if they might be waylaid by bad weather and would have to stop at an inn. The old master couldn't just tuck into a roast like a normal gentleman, you know. Not with his gout. He had to be very careful or he'd be in screaming agony."

Ela held up her hand to prevent anyone else from speaking. "So Bertrade had time to strain the new herb, which she could have collected on the way from her home manor to the castle, and add it to the tonic before Sir Humphrey left for Salisbury?"

"She did, my lady."

"Sir Peveril, did your lady wife stop along the way to collect any greenery on your trip to the castle?" asked Ela.

"No, my lady."

"Did she stop for any reason at all?"

Peveril hesitated. "Well..."

Bertrade's face darkened.

"I believe she stopped near a knot of woods to...you know."

"To relieve herself, perhaps?" asked Ela. She couldn't understand why people tied themselves in knots to avoid the mention of bodily functions.

"Yes, my lady." Peveril looked mortified by the discussion of his wife's private activities.

Bertrade's expression was as black as night.

"And could she, during that brief sojourn, have had time to gather a posy of foxglove leaves and secrete them under her cloak?"

Peveril glanced at his wife. Who avoided his gaze, then thought better of it and turned to glare at him.

"I...I'm not sure, my lady."

"No one was with her in the woods?"

"No, my lady. Her lady's maid offered to attend her but she told her to wait with her horse."

"I see." Ela looked triumphantly at Bertrade. "So she had ample opportunity to seek out and cut some withered foxglove leaves and bring them with her to Mere."

Peveril's lips twitched. "I didn't say that, my lady." He looked nervously at his wife.

"No, but I'm inferring it." She turned to Bertrade. "Do you admit to gathering leaves in the forest?"

"I do not," said Bertrade through tight lips. "I did nothing of the sort."

"So where did you get the leaves that you ground in the cook's pestle in Sir Humphrey's castle?"

"They were just herbs from the store in the kitchen. Intended to add some flavor to her tasteless food."

The cook let out a snort. "Stuff and nonsense! My herbs are hung up out of the way in the storeroom past the back kitchen to keep them dry and free from pests, and she couldn't have got near them without asking me for the key."

"Did anyone else ask for the key?"

"They did not. No one touches the key to my storeroom except me." Her face sagged. "Well, not back when I was mistress of my kitchen, they didn't. I was a good steward of my lord's provisions, herbs and all, and I made his food just the way he liked it."

"I'm sure you did. Thank you, Mistress Parker," said Ela. She was already wondering if this faithful and hardworking woman might find a new place in her own castle.

"So it appears that Bertrade de Gilbert saw an opportunity to rid herself of her miserly father-in-law by urging her husband to send him to retrieve his wife. On the way to the castle to engage in that errand, she gathered a known deadly poison that is readily available in the woods throughout our shire. She carried the leaves into Sir Humphrey's castle, hidden somewhere on her person, then secretly ground and bagged them and strained them into his to his tonic. Perhaps she did not expect to attract suspicion since she knew he would sicken and die far from home." She looked at Bertrade. "Do you dispute this version of events?"

"I do indeed! Why would I be foolish enough to prepare a deadly poison in the intended victim's own house, under the eyes of his staff?"

"You told me at the time that you were making posset for your own use," cut in the cook.

"As I was!" exclaimed Bertrade.

"You previously said it was for your son," said Ela. "Was he even with you on this journey?"

There was a short silence before Peveril spoke up quietly. "No, he stayed back at the manor with his nursemaid."

"Giles Haughton," said Ela, addressing him. "As coroner, do you have any further questions?"

Haughton leaned back in his chair. "Peveril de Gilbert, did your wife encourage you to send your father off to Salisbury after his wife, Alice?"

Peveril swallowed hard. "I suppose she might have."

Haughton tented his fingers again. "It seems clear as day to me that Bertrade de Gilbert planned to send her father-in-law away on a journey and poisoned the tonic he'd take with him. This explains why she came to Mere castle that day, when she would usually have stayed at home while her husband visited his father. Perhaps she thought that preparing the leaves there would attract less attention than preparing them in her own home where the staff knew her habits too well. The remaining question is whether she did it with her husband's knowledge and collusion."

Peveril blinked nervously. "I knew nothing about this. I

still can't believe it." Unless he was a mummer fit for a king's banquet hall, Ela was inclined to trust him.

Haughton looked at the cook. "Mistress Parker, do you have any reason to believe that Peveril de Gilbert was involved in poisoning his father's tonic?"

The cook, a self-possessed woman, took the measure of both Peveril and Bertrade with her steady gray gaze. "I've known young Sir Peveril since he was a suckling babe. His father was a harsh taskmaster and not one to shower a child with affection or even notice. Peveril has always been respectful and dutiful to his father and done his best to make his father pleased with him. I find it impossible to imagine that Peveril would harbor murderous thoughts or commit such a sinful act against his own father."

"And what about Bertrade de Gilbert?" asked Haughton. "Do you think her capable of such an act?"

"That I couldn't say, sir. I don't know her well enough. But I know for a fact that she ground leaves with my own mortar, and thus I do believe it entirely possible that she poisoned Sir Humphrey's tonic with them."

CHAPTER 23

Bertrade was taken away to await the assizes. Her guilt seemed so certain that Ela was very tempted to put her down in the dungeon, but due to her noble birth and her gender—as well as her family relationship to Alice, even if it was not a blood one—she locked her away in a remote castle chamber.

Peveril was released to care for his young children. Contrary to Ela's expectation, he didn't fume and stamp and demand restitution for the time he'd spent locked up in Salisbury Castle. Instead he seemed more consumed with the prospect of managing the children back at Mere without the help of a female companion beyond the nursemaid who was still a child herself.

"I could help you bring them back to Mere," offered Alice. "If I'm free to go, that is."

Ela blinked. This seemed like a terrible idea. Still... "I certainly have no reason to hold you here at the castle. You are free to move about as you please." And there was one good reason for her to go there. "You are still owed a full third of the estate of your late husband, so you have a claim to Mere yourself."

Alice looked annoyed that Ela had raised her property claim. "I have no wish to carve up my late husband's estates. I already have a manor."

Ela wanted to remind her that her marriage prospects would be improved by each additional virgate of land she brought into the marriage, but she held her tongue. They both looked at Peveril. White-faced and shaken by his imprisonment and trial, and by the chilling news that his wife was a cold-blooded killer, he seemed unable to utter words.

"Do you wish Alice to accompany you on the journey?" asked Ela.

He stared mutely at Alice.

"I've introduced myself to your sweet children, and I don't think they'll object to my presence," she said quietly. "I can help their nursemaid manage them and can entertain them with songs and stories in the carriage while you ride ahead, if you like." She looked almost eager to help. "I am their grandmother, after all. At least their step-grandmother."

"I suppose that is true," said Peveril at last, whey-faced and barely audible. "If you wish to keep them company and give them solace, I don't object."

"That's settled, then," said Alice with enthusiasm. "I shall have Minnie pack my chest, and I shall see to the children being readied for the journey with food and drink and warm enough clothes for the journey. Their nursemaid probably won't think of everything."

Peveril nodded, still looking like he was lost at sea.

"I shall call for the horses and the carriage to be made ready if you wish to leave today," said Ela. She was rather looking forward to seeing the back of Peveril de Gilbert.

Even Alice had worn out her welcome since she seemed to attract murders the way sweet fruit attracted flies.

Alice kissed her and thanked her and half skipped away in her excitement at spending several hours in a cold, bumpy carriage with two tiny children whose mother would probably hang before spring.

Ela took in a deep lungful of cool winter air and headed to the chapel to pray for peace.

BERTRADE DE GILBERT was tried at the first assizes held in Salisbury in the year 1228. The judge had requested for both Alice and Sir Peveril to attend the trial, so he could hear their evidence against Bertrade. Ela managed to convince him that the jury and the coroner were very well acquainted with the facts and that both Alice and Sir Peveril had suffered enough and should be left in peace.

The judge heard Giles Haughton and the jury describe what they'd learned about the last day of Sir Humphrey de Gilbert's life. Ela had found a new position for the de Gilbert's former cook, who now prepared plain and filling meals for the schoolboys at Bishop Poore's school in Salisbury. Mildred Parker appeared at the assizes and described how Bertrade had ground herbs in her own pestle and mortar and had hastened away with the bottle of tonic intended for Sir Humphrey to take that night.

The judge scolded her for not being a keener steward of her master's tonics, but she reasoned that since Bertrade was both a noblewoman and a member of the family, she could hardly have argued with her. The judge readily agreed, and Bertrade, after some hollow pleas on behalf of her soon-to-be-motherless children, was sentenced to hang.

Michel de Tours, the man they'd apprehended escaping

after the murder of Adonis, was sent to London to be imprisoned in the Tower. He'd refused to provide the judge or jury with any information that could lead to the capture of the woman who'd escaped. No one knew if she truly was the wife of Adonis d'Ys—or whoever he really was—but everyone, including the judge, believed her to be his killer, so Alice was out from under the shadow of suspicion.

Reports from the Continent revealed that the house of d'Ys did not exist outside of legend. The part of Brittany that Adonis had described as his ancestral homeland was in fact farmland reclaimed from the sea and cultivated with barley under the fief of the counts of Dreux.

Adonis d'Ys's estate in Burgundy seemed similarly illusory. Letters to officials throughout the province were met with perplexity and—Ela imagined—Gallic shrugging. The merry widow of Adonis d'Ys had vanished back into the Continent as if she'd never set foot in England, and no trace of her could be found.

JANUARY WAS ALWAYS A BUSY MONTH, what with preparations for a new year of administrative activities and estate management, so Ela didn't have much time to devote to worrying about Alice. So far gossip surrounding the second murder had been kept small and local by the victim's lack of connections. Adonis d'Ys was simply a stranger, and thus not of great interest to most people. Luckily rumors about Alice's dalliance with him failed to catch hold.

Even the murder of Sir Humphrey de Gilbert didn't attract much attention, perhaps because he led such a retired life that hardly anyone even knew he existed. By extension Alice was obscure and forgotten. While this didn't bode well for her remarriage prospects, at least her misfortune wasn't stirring the tongues of Wiltshire.

Ela had abandoned her interest in helping Alice pursue her portion of her husband's estate. If Alice wanted to throw away her legal rights and settle for less than she was owed, then so be it. Perhaps her lack of greed could be admired.

So it was with some trepidation that, one afternoon as she sat by the fire with her children, Ela broke the wax seal on a fresh letter in her friend's handwriting.

Dear Ela,

I'm writing to invite you to my wedding. I know that no one will be happier for my good fortune than you.

Ela stopped reading. She almost stopped breathing. How could Alice, flung from pillar to post by the events of last Christmas season, have managed to find herself a husband so fast? Was she delusional? Would this new swain be assailed by misfortune and find himself lying in a pool of his own blood before Lent? Her head spun.

"What's wrong, Mama?" asked Petronella, who looked up from reading her prayer book.

"Everything's fine." She picked up the letter and continued trying to decipher Alice's rather blowsy hand.

Dear Peveril proposed to me yesterday evening, as we shared a roasted hamhock by the firelight. I know this may seem precipitous to you, since each of us is barely widowed.

Again, Ela put down the letter. This time she blew out a breath. Peveril had been widowed less than a week! She felt sure that Alice herself must be pushing this marriage plan forward. She must have been soothing and comforting poor feckless Peveril for the last few weeks while scheming to marry him. All while his wife still sat—alive but doomed—in her private chamber.

"Something's definitely wrong, Mama. You can tell me. A trouble shared is a trouble halved." Petronella's calm expression tempted Ela. But she knew her daughter would be shocked beyond all reckoning by Alice's newest rash misadventure. Sir Peveril de Gilbert was Alice's own son-in-law!

"That's Alice's handwriting, isn't it?" asked Petronella, lowering her prayer book to her lap. "Has she seduced that poor fool Peveril de Gilbert into marrying her?"

Ela blinked. "How did you guess? I wouldn't have thought she'd be in the slightest bit interested in him. He's hardly handsome."

"I suspect her interest may lie in his children. They were a very sweet little boy and girl and took right to Alice. She had a way with them that made them smile and laugh even though they should have been weeping for their mother."

Ela crossed herself. "Is that good for them? Is it not better for them to mourn her loss?"

"I'm sure they will, but I suspect Alice will be a kind and caring mother for them. More so than that cold fish Bertrade, who seemed to care for nothing but getting her hands on the family castle, even if it meant her husband would swing for it."

"I thought Alice was desperate to escape the drafty old de Gilbert castle," mused Ela.

"She was tired of living there alone with her mean old husband," said Petronella. "But now she has a younger, kinder husband, two lively children and the prospect of more of her own. I can hardly blame her for seizing the opportunity she saw before her." Petronella turned her eyes back to her prayer book.

Ela stared at her, stunned. "I thought you believed that a

woman was only fortunate if she found herself safe inside the walls of a nunnery?"

Petronella looked up. "Some of us are born to pray for the souls of all mankind, and others are born to raise more souls to make mischief."

"I wonder where I fall on that continuum?" said Ela, with a lifted brow.

"Oh, you have your own place entirely," said Petronella, without expression. "Whoever heard of a woman being sheriff of all Wiltshire?"

Ela stared at her for another moment, then dropped her gaze back to the letter.

EPILOGUE

M*ere, Wiltshire, February 1228*

Alice's wedding took place in the great hall of the de Gilbert's grim, windowless fortress. Ela was very tempted to keep her distance from the whole affair. She'd had more than enough of Alice's madcap schemes and wasn't optimistic about her prospects for future happiness with Sir Peveril.

But…she mused that likely everyone in Wiltshire felt the same misgivings as she did. Alice desperately needed some sort of official seal of approval for her marriage so that she might not become a pariah among the nobles of Wiltshire and the surrounding counties.

So she gathered Petronella, who seemed warmly disposed to the proceedings, and set out to attend the wedding.

Like most castles, the de Gilbert castle had its own chapel. The dark, narrow interior had fallen into some disuse since Humphrey de Gilbert had preferred not to spend the required costs to keep a priest within his castle walls. Alice had since organized the staff into putting a new coat of whitewash on the walls and polishing the wood benches.

Since it wasn't a time of year that garlands of flowers could be found, green boughs of pine and holly decked the walls. A great illustrated Book of Hours from the family library stood open on a heavy wooden stand, and a cloth embroidered with threads of gold lay spread across the altar.

"Doesn't it look fine?" asked Alice. She was giving Ela a tour in the hours before her ceremony. Ela was glad to keep busy, as the thin trickle of guests did not provide much diversion.

"It is a sweet and peaceful space. I hope you'll continue to use it."

"Oh, yes, we intend to have a priest in residence here. He'll conduct all the Hours, and there will be choir boys to sing. I convinced Peveril that it was essential to restoring God's favor to the family after so much disaster."

The hall had been similarly hung with green boughs and colorful ribbons that greatly cheered its rather dour aspect. Alice herself was radiant as a summer's afternoon in the yellow dress that they'd bought that fateful day in the market in London.

Even Peveril de Gilbert looked different than Ela remembered. His shoulders seemed broader and his face had more of a jut to the chin and cheeks. Dressed in gray trimmed with red, and with his hair cut shorter than before, he looked almost like a handsome young nobleman that any young girl might be excited to marry.

Of course, there was the awkward matter of his freshly hanged wife and his newly bereaved children, which Ela could smell in the air almost like a dead mouse in the walls, but Alice kept events cheerfully trotting along so that no one had time to get distracted by tragedy.

The two young children seemed oddly cheerful about the prospect of their father marrying Alice, no doubt because they were too young to fully understand the circumstances, and perhaps because they knew her just well enough that it didn't seem too strange. She was already family, after all.

The ceremony took place in the great hall. About thirty people were assembled as the wedding party. Ela wasn't entirely sure how many of them were invited guests and how many were staff dressed in borrowed finery, but they presented a decent enough crowd for the ceremony.

Alice shed a tear as the priest pronounced them man and wife, then they all headed into the chapel for prayers to bless the marriage.

Afterward they filed out to sample the feast put together by the new cook, with all the spices that Peveril had procured for her to enliven her fare.

"Alice does look lovely," whispered Petronella. "You'd never guess she was so old."

"She's thirty-three, not sixty-three," rasped back Ela.

"I think she's a year or two older than her husband, but he seems delighted with her anyway." Petronella took a bite of a gingery biscuit.

"He does, doesn't he?" replied Ela. Peveril was very solicitous of his new wife, offering her cups of wine and complimenting her on every aspect of the decor and banquet, as if she'd made them herself. "I have a strange and rather uneasy feeling that they're going to be happy together."

"What a surprise. I was sure she'd run off with that pirate fellow. I suppose it's lucky he got murdered."

"Petronella!" Ela looked around to make sure no one was listening. Luckily two musicians stirred the air with a tune on their instruments, so they weren't overheard. "You shouldn't even think such things."

"I do hope she finally enjoys some happiness. She seems simple enough to survive marriage without entirely losing her wits."

"Marriage between two suitable partners is a joyous union," said Ela primly. "I was very happy with your father."

"Dear Papa was one in ten thousand," said Petronella with a sigh. He'd always indulged her pious nature, calling her his little sister of mercy. "If there was a man like him left in England, perhaps I'd even consider marrying."

Ela's heart leapt at this utterly unexpected statement. Perhaps Alice's longing for love and motherhood had lit a tiny flame in Petronella's flinty heart. "There are many wonderful men in England! Marriage and the joys of family are something you can experience before you take the veil."

"I'd rather be walled into my chamber alive." Petronella took another bite of her biscuit. "When exactly is the nunnery at Lacock supposed to be finished? I sometimes feel I shall be older than Alice before I finally get to take my vows and become a bride of Christ."

"Within five years," said Ela quietly. "You'll be twenty-three by then, not thirty-three like Alice."

"And you'll really let me go there?" Peering out from beneath her plain white veil, her daughter looked doubtful.

"Sometimes it's best to let people follow their heart, even when you question the wisdom of their decisions."

THE END

AUTHOR'S NOTE

Readers may recognize mayor of London, Roger le Duc, from book three—*The Lost Child*—in which he played an active role as sheriff of London. Roger le Duc was a real person who served as sheriff from 1225-6 and mayor from 1227-30. (The mayor of London was not called lord mayor of London until after 1354.) Le Duc was in fact the third member of his family to be sheriff of London.

Jury trials in the early 1200's were quite different from ours. Ela herself might well have pronounced the verdict for petty theft or a local dispute, but more serious crimes like murder were tried at the assizes. The traveling justice would move from one Hundred—an ancient name for each administrative area—to the next, overseeing these trials. The jury, composed of local men who likely knew both the victim and the accused, presented evidence rather than just deliberating. Their knowledge of the players involved was considered to be an asset, not a negative. They were called upon to bring their opinions about the accused and the circumstances of the crime to help inform the traveling justice, who was often unfamiliar with the area and its people. Our practice of seeking a consensus of twelve jurors to decide the verdict in a trial was still quite a new concept in Ela's time, replacing archaic practices like trial by ordeal and trial by combat. The last known trial by ordeal—in which the accused could prove their innocence by, say, retrieving a stone by hand from a pot of near-boiling water—was held in 1219, after which Henry III abolished the practice.

The mysterious Adonis attempts to pass himself off as a scion of the ancient domain of Ys. Well traveled and literate Ela instantly recognizes Ys as a place from a Brittany of legend, not somewhere found on a sailor's map. There are several versions of the legend, but all feature hapless King Gradlon giving or losing the key to the dykes that protect his lands to his wayward daughter, whose rash pursuit of passion with her lover leads to the kingdom being flooded and destroyed.

The deadly nightshade plant is a familiar poison, also known as belladonna (Italian for "pretty lady") since eating a small quantity dilates the pupils and gives the user a look of being sexually excited. It's still in use as the medicine Atropine, which I've used to treat an eye ulcer in one of my horses. It's amusing that one deadly poison is in fact the antidote for another deadly poison that is perhaps also better known for its medicinal effects. The foxglove, or digitalis, plant is still given to patients with congestive heart failure to strengthen contractions of the heart.

Mere Castle, the home of my imaginary de Gilbert family, is a real place. Only the castle mound remains, and it was in fact built a few years later than the period of this book. It was, however, a perfect location for the remote de Gilbert castle, deep in western Wiltshire, so I couldn't resist using it.

If you have questions or comments, please get in touch at jglewis@stoneheartpress.com.

AUTHOR BIOGRAPHY

J. G. Lewis grew up in a Regency-era officer's residence in London, England. She spent her childhood visiting nearby museums and riding ponies in Hyde Park. She came to the U.S. to study semiotics at Brown University and stayed for the sunshine and a career as a museum curator in New York City. Over the years she published quite a few novels, two of which hit the *USA Today* list. She didn't delve into historical fiction until she discovered genealogy and the impressive cast of potential characters in her family history. Once she realized how many fascinating historical figures are all but forgotten, she decided to breathe life into them again by creating stories for them to inhabit. J. G. Lewis currently lives in Florida with her dogs and horses.

For more information visit www.stoneheartpress.com.

Published 2022 by Stoneheart Press
2709 N Hayden Island Drive
Suite 853852
Portland, Oregon, 97217,
USA

Cover image includes: detail from Codex Manesse, ca. 1300, Heidelberg University Library; decorative detail from Beatus of Liébana, Fecundus Codex of 1047, Biblioteca Nacional de España; detail with Longespée coat of arms from Matthew Parris, *Historia Anglorum,* ca. 1250, British Museum.

Printed in Great Britain
by Amazon

83590191R00154